GATSBY'S VINEYARD

A. E. Maxwell

GATSBY'S VINEYARD

DOUBLEDAY & COMPANY, INC.
Garden City, New York
1987

MAX

Library of Congress Cataloging-in-Publication Data
Maxwell, A. E.
    Gatsby's vineyard

    I. Title.
PS3563.A899G3   1987   813'.54   86-29113
ISBN 0-385-23712-X

GATSBY'S VINEYARD

1

Jay Gatsby would have loved the Napa Valley—until someone found him face down between the vines. And they would have found him that way, make no mistake about it. There's more than wine, prestige and carefully nurtured romance in Napa. There's money. Real money. The kind people kill and die for.

Socially, Gatsby might have had an easier time in Napa than in East Egg. The vintage of the money in Napa is a lot less important than the vintage of the wines that are stored and poured there.

Some of the money in Napa is old, even older and more deeply rooted than the arm-thick vines in the vineyards that survived Prohibition. But much of Napa has been built in the last decade with money from semiconductors or sinsemilla or silver scams. As a result, there's a kind of rough-and-tumble economic democracy on Napa's flat and fertile floor. Growing grapes isn't a club tournament limited to members only. All you need to become part of Napa's economy is the admission fee. Joining the crowd of vintners is like signing on for a pro-am golf tournament in Pebble Beach or Palm Desert. Just ante up and play with the stars.

There is one condition, however: the money has to be real. None of this dollar-down-and-bet-on-the-come bullshit that works in the rest of California. Inherit your fortune, earn it, politely steal it or find yourself a wealthy silent partner. Whichever. Just make sure that your assets are as liquid as your Cabernet Sauvignon.

There's a very good reason for that kind of fiscal snobbery. You have to have money in order to lose it—and that's just what will happen. You'll lose money. A whole lot of it. When you strip grape growing and wine making of its romance, the process is called farming, and there are a thousand ways to go broke farming. Ask anybody who has ever tried to turn a profit with a pitchfork and a hoe.

Oh, sure, there's money to be made in the rich creases and on the flats between Spring Mountain and the Cedar Roughs, between the salt marshes of San Pablo Bay and the black rocks at the top of Mount St. Helena. Napa Valley grows wondrous grapes which become magnificent wines which fetch premium prices all over the world. A smart, trendy, innovative vintner can make a fortune in good years, break even in middling ones and hold losses below the threshold of bankruptcy in those years when the frosts come late in the spring and the rains come early in the fall, and when the mites and the leaf roll and the systemic viruses cripple the vines.

But all told, your odds of making a killing are probably a lot better in Las Vegas. Ask Coca-Cola or Nestlé or Seagram's or any of the other capital-rich conglomerates that fueled the vineyard boom of the middle 1970s. They poured cash into Napa as though it were a slot machine, and they kept on pulling the green handle. But they couldn't even turn up a double cherry. The guy who runs the casino had reset the drops while no one was looking. The payoffs were irregular, the return on investment minimal, the bottom line dismal.

One by one the conglomerates backed out of Napa Valley, leaving behind the only folks who could still afford to play the game: the old-time farmers who owned their land in fee simple, and the very wealthy boutique winery folks for whom the romance of the wine country was as bewitching as the sound of Daisy's voice was for Gatsby.

I can sympathize with Gatsby. I've been poor and I've been rich, and rich is indeed better. But as a group the recently arrived always have been and always will be the butt of well-bred disdain . . . and more dangerous forms of aggression as well. I know something about what the nouveaux riches are up against. My late and lamentable Uncle Jake, the last of the hippie outlaws, left me a steamer trunk full of untraceable currency that my ex-wife, Fiora, turned into a fortune. Granted, my asset sheet wouldn't intimidate J. P. Morgan or J. D. Rockefeller, but it gives me a freedom that is sometimes hard to describe.

You have heard, perhaps, of "fuck-you money"?

However much I enjoy the aspirations and excesses of the newly rich, my favorite folks in the Napa Valley are the old-timers, the farmers who are not necessarily rich but who have been there since before the boom, the people who rooted themselves and their vines in the land thirty or forty years ago, when the valley started to crawl out from under Prohibition.

Actually, some of these families go back more than a century. Barley farmers and dairymen and European grape growers gravitated to the valley not long after the gold rush. They were drawn not only by the soil but by the light and the clean air.

Unlike Iowa or Kansas, where farmland has the utilitarian aesthetics of a John Deere tractor, Napa has an enormous, fecund beauty. The hills are sexy, like black eyelet lace smoothed over tanned skin. There is a sensual fullness to the country that is palpable. The feeling comes from the contrasts of cool and heat, damp and dry, and from the visual impact of heavy, bushy vine heads along straight trellises in row on row of field on field of grapes. Even in the spring, when the vines are just past bud-break and the grapes are more potential than actual, there is a feeling of immense growth and fertility.

The nights are still crisp in the early summertime, when the gray evening fog spills over the crest of Spring and Diamond mountains along the west edge of the valley. Yet those same June days are warm and getting warmer; the sun is back and, like a young stud horse, just beginning to focus blinding, instinctive heat on the requirements of procreation. By July the days will bake. The south- and west-facing hills and canyons will become chimneys drawing up valley heat and pouring it over the small vineyards in the side canyons. All day long the vines will soak up sunlight, changing it into the complex sugars and tannins and acids that eventually will become fine wine.

The contrasts between the mountain and the valley vineyards are part of what has always fascinated me about Napa. The valley vines have an easy time of it, comparatively. Granted, the soil is rocky rather than Iowa-loamy. Each vineyard has its walls of red and brown and gray boulders, from hand-sized to head-sized, some grubbed from the ground by Chinese coolies a hundred years ago and some stacked last winter by Mexican field hands.

Up toward Calistoga, just off the Silverado Trail, I once ran across a rock pile that was ten feet high, a hundred feet wide and three quarters of a mile long. Every stone on it had been dragged from the soil by a pair of hands, tossed on a stoneboat and skidded to the pile. The huge rock pile was the proceeds of a few large vineyards, maybe a hundred and fifty acres. There are more than thirty thousand acres of vineyards on Napa's flat valley floor. Each of them had to be developed the same way. One stone at a time. That tells you a little bit about what farmers are up against on the flats.

But the mountains are even rougher. The mountains test a vintner's dreams, his wallet and his nerve.

Diamond Mountain was the first sizable mountain vineyard to be opened up in the recent boom. That was maybe ten years ago. A grape entrepreneur named William Hill took a real flier, brought in a couple of D-8 Caterpillar tractors and put them to work scraping the brush off one hundred and fifty acres of natural amphitheater on the shoulder of Diamond Mountain. The slopes were chillingly steep. The D-8s turned turtle a half dozen times, rolling over on their backs and waiting helplessly to be rescued. Nobody was killed, but it wasn't for lack of trying.

Then Hill brought in smaller, more agile Cats and cut stair-step terraces, gambling that the remaining soil was deep enough and special enough to justify development costs of ten thousand dollars an acre. St. George's rootstock went in first. That took two years to establish itself. Then the scion vines were grafted on—Cabernet Sauvignon, mostly.

The yield was low, maybe half of what the normally stingy Cabernet vines would produce on the flats. But what grapes those mountain vines grew. Good flatland Cabernets might return four to six hundred dollars a ton. The stressed vines of the Diamond Mountain Vineyard produced half as many grapes but the fruit was extraordinary, world class. Sterling Vineyards, the big Seagram's subsidiary down the road, was paying upward of two thousand dollars a ton when they finally got smart and bought Hill out.

There's a little one-lane dirt road that runs straight up Kortum Canyon from the edge of downtown Calistoga, such as downtown Calistoga is. The road, once the stage route over the mountain to Santa Rosa, cuts along one edge of the Diamond Mountain Vineyard. Just before the road drops over the ridge into the next valley, there's a spot where you can park and look down across the pepperwood and madrona and manzanita. In the foreground the vineyard is simmering in its natural punch-bowl microclimate, soaking up the hard summer sunlight. Beyond is the rest of the Napa Valley, all the way down toward Stag's Leap and a dozen other of the most special wineries in the United States. The view is so grand that you hate to tell the rest of the world about it.

That's the spot where Sandra Autry and I would go, back when we were seeing one another. Sometimes in the early evening, when the worst of the heat was over, we used to drive up there and park and admire the view and neck and get as hot and sweaty and passionate as a couple of teenagers.

After about an hour of that we'd both be lucky to get down the hill. Sometimes we didn't. Get down the hill, I mean. But other times we'd check into the little hotel on Lake Street. The place wasn't very genteel but it had its own rural California charm. With the windows wide open to catch the first evening breeze up from the bay, we'd sweat and love and drink cold white wine and have a hell of a good time.

Then we'd shower and go eat in the Mexican restaurant down the street, the one that was using mesquite charcoal a dozen years before the gringo importers discovered it. Broiled pollo and carne asada, carnitas and fresh corn tortillas. Mexican field hands tend to be beer drinkers, but as a nod to the lifeblood of the valley, the restaurant had a wine list of sorts. It extended from *blanco* through *rosé* to *tinto*. All of the wines, even the *tinto,* were kept in the cooler.

Sometimes Sandra would cook, which is what she had done every day since she was eleven and first discovered that canned tomatoes tasted better if you added something—almost anything—from the cupboard. Sandra was a natural cook. It came to her as easily as the violin had once come to me; but, unlike me, she learned early to value her gift from the gods. She didn't throw her talent away because it never came up to her expectations, the way I had. She just worked like hell to develop her gift.

And gift it was. She understood instinctively, almost intuitively, how foods and wines and herbs and spices work together, in the same way that I had once understood the immense possibilities of music. She dreamed of tastes in the same way that I dreamed of sounds.

There wasn't a pretentious bone in Sandra's lovely body. She seldom talked about what she was doing, what spices she used, what elements of Pinot Noir made it particularly suited to her veal dishes or her cheeses. But her sensory acuity was remarkable and her sensory memory was perfect. On a summer night in Calistoga, one of her three-egg omelets with herbs and a tomato vinaigrette was better than most four-star meals. She could look at a raw egg and know whether to use more or less basil, one or two grinds of pepper, a three-dollar Chablis or a twelve-dollar Grey Riesling.

I have eaten grand meals and known some world-class chefs, but Sandra was both the best at what she did and the least willing to dress it all with fancy words. So far as I'm concerned, that's the only reason she is less famous now than, say, Alice Waters, the trendy queen of Bay Area eating. Sandra could cook as well as anyone, but she didn't talk as well and her politics and aesthetics weren't as *avant*. So Sandra remained a quiet treasure.

Maybe it's simply that Sandra was too busy living and eating and loving and tasting to be bothered with the talking of it.

Sandra kind of put me together, I guess, after Fiora and I broke up the first time. Sandra was a wine-country girl. Her parents owned one of the most famous vineyards in the Napa Valley, a hundred and forty acres of fertile ground called Deep Purple. The Autrys were down-to-earth folks, in the original sense of the word, and that may have been where Sandra learned her natural reserve. She lacked the outgoing charm, the sense of showmanship, that professional cooks and hostesses often have. But her extraordinary talent had already taken her a long way when I met her at a fancy wine-tasting party in San Francisco three months after Fiora first moved out on me and went back to Harvard.

Sandra was tall and almost willowy. Almost, I said. She had a figure that most women would have killed for, but lots of men never noticed because she tended to dress in an understated way. She was not given to showing herself off, but she made quite an impression on me the first time I ever saw her.

The party was crowded, with people sliding this way and that to get through, and I was standing in the middle, watching it all with the detachment of the unattached. When I first saw Sandra making her way through the crowd, she was trying hard not to spill the tall glasses of champagne she was carrying in each hand. Most everybody else was having a good time impressing whoever they were talking to. I guess I had been a long time without a stirring, because I found myself watching Sandra—Venuslike with arms raised, seeming by her attitude to invite inspection—as though I had never seen a woman's body.

She had come about halfway across the room before I realized that I was staring. Then I realized that she realized I was staring. Then I realized that she didn't mind me staring, even if I wasn't looking at her eyes. I think I got a little flustered, turned a little red. But Sandra just kept coming toward me, smiling, calm and sexy as all hell.

It felt so good to want a woman again that I got over my embarrassment and just kept watching, albeit a bit less like a chained wolf watching a lamb gambol closer. Sandra drew abreast of me, quite literally, and then slid past without saying a word, a faint smile of pleasure or pride parting her lips. Three steps beyond me, she turned and looked back over her shoulder.

"You like them?" she asked.

"Yes," I said simply, because it was way too late to think up a polite lie.

Still smiling, she turned away and glided into the crowd.

Two hours later she was introduced to me as Sandra Autry. That's where I got lucky again, since it took me less than two minutes to remember that S. Autry was listed on the menu as the master chef for the evening. This was back in the relative Dark Ages, when a woman who wanted her cooking to be taken seriously might hide her gender behind a single initial. Sandra seemed genuinely pleased when I put that little puzzle together, and she allowed me—maybe even encouraged me—to hang around while she oversaw the cleanup. Then she took me home, all the way out to a Victorian at the north edge of Golden Gate Park.

Neither of us mentioned my previous lechery until sometime just before dawn, after she had given me a hickey on my neck. It was a reward, she said, for not being afraid to leer in public.

"If I ever get to feeling drab and little brown henlike," she said, laughing deep in her throat, "all I'll have to do is bring back the memory of the look on your face. Every woman needs that once in a while. When I got close and saw those gray eyes and that slow, sexy smile, I knew that if I never had another man I had to have you tonight."

That was Sandra's gentle way of defining our relationship from the very start. We never lived together, and often were not lovers when we did get together. She was independent in a deep and abiding way. There was too much of life she wanted to experience; she had too many things to do to allow herself to be tied to one man.

And I had too many ties and too many directions to go to be bound inextricably to her.

Yet we were very close when we were together. I told Sandra about my failed marriage, and she explained Fiora to me, without ever having met her, because they were quite alike. There is an independence in some modern women that ought not to be trifled with. This wine-country woman helped me to get over Fiora by eventually sending me back to her. Maybe Sandra and I never stuck permanently together because Fiora and I had already done so. But Sandra and I got pretty sticky, some of those hot nights in the little hotel in Calistoga.

Now I was headed north out through the Tejon Pass, leaving the smog of Los Angeles behind, with Fiora sitting beside me in the car, headed toward Napa's generous, fertile harvest because I had heard that Sandra was in danger of losing everything she had ever owned.

What I didn't know then, what I didn't discover until much later, too late, was that the trouble was bigger than Sandra, bigger than the hundred and forty acres of magnificent grape land called Deep Purple. The trouble was as complex as a good Chardonnay, as hidden as the roots of the silent vines, and as deadly as steel sliding between living ribs.

Yes, Gatsby would have loved the Napa Valley, but he wouldn't have survived it.

I nearly didn't.

2

My return to Napa Valley's fertile hazards began innocently enough. I was stretched out on my patio lounge, watching the koi watching me, listening to the hummingbirds complain that I was too close to their feeder, and thumbing through my junk mail all at the same time. Suddenly I turned up a flier hinting that Deep Purple Cabernet Sauvignon was to be had, cheap. Surprise hardly describes my reaction. Try shock. You know—the sound of square jaw hitting redwood deck. *Thock.* What was Deep Purple doing in the edible, upscale rummage sale known as Trader Joe's? Even Trader Joe doesn't usually use thirty-dollar Cabernets as loss leaders.

But there it was in the green print and cream paper that Trader Joe was using for this month's "newsletter." As always, Joe got right to the point. "Deep and Rich and Purple and So Cheap. Without question, this is the greatest of the great California Cabernets we have ever offered. We are allowed to sell it at the ridiculously low price of $6.99 a bottle on the condition that we not reveal its maker or the vineyard from which it came. But if you know your California wine history, you'll know that 1974 was a magic year for this piece of ground."

Yes, indeed. Magic. It was the year that wine made from Deep Purple grapes kicked ass and took names at a blind tasting in France. Deep Purple's Cabernet Sauvignon was declared *número uno, primo,* first, best, absolutely the king of world-class wines. It's rumored that a few aristocratic French vintners died of apoplexy when the results of the blind tasting were known. An exaggeration, of course, but not by much.

Deep Purple at $6.99 a bottle? Impossible. Was Joe lying, or had a whole year of Sandra's work gone from sugar to shit in some idiot vintner's vats?

If it had been anybody else's wine, I would have shrugged off the small mystery and gone back to watching the Pacific Ocean or the hummingbirds as they fought over the gloriously ugly feeder that Fiora had given me. I tried not to succumb to the mystery, and to the woman who was part of it. I sat and stared at the redheaded feathered warriors dogfighting through the clear California sunlight. All I saw was a pair of golden-brown eyes watching me from a gentle and healing part of my memories. I tried to listen to the waves breaking at the foot of my bluff. All I heard was my own voice muttering that if Sandra were selling Deep Purple wines at bulk rates she was in trouble.

And if I'm good at anything, it's getting people out of trouble. Not perfect, mind you, and I've got the scars to prove it. Just good. I've learned to settle for that.

After a few minutes of staring in front of me and seeing only the past, I got up, dressed, and headed inland. The closest Trader Joe's outlet was in El Toro, anchored securely in a dirty asphalt sea. It took me about fifteen seconds to find the floor display of the coyly advertised special. It took me less than a second to recognize the slightly tapered Bordeaux shape of the custom-made Deep Purple bottle, even with Trader Joe's own label slapped across its face. Just to make sure, I carefully slid the lead capsule up until I could see the name that was branded into the cork. Deep Purple.

That answered my first question. The wine was genuine. My second question could only be answered in one way. I bought a bottle and took it out to the huge parking lot. I settled into the Cobra, opened the glove compartment and pulled the cork with one of the many arms on my big Swiss Army knife. Figuring the brown paper bag was enough cover, I raised the bottle to my lips.

A familiar taste exploded in my mouth like a woman's hungry kiss. Memories poured through me, memories as rich and multiflavored as the wine itself. The savor of an extraordinary omelet. The smell of a woman hot in my arms. The smooth weight of her breasts as she slept against me. The feel of a silky midnight breeze over my naked back.

For an instant I just closed my eyes and let the memories claim me; then I tamped the cork back into place, knowing I had just sipped wine made from Deep Purple grapes. There was no doubt of it. My palate is what a serious drinker friend calls "Triple A utility infielder—good glove, no hit," but even I could pick Deep Purple

Cabernet Sauvignon out of a field of five. The depth of flavor was unmistakably there, along with the faintly tannic bite that would mellow and round with a few years of bottle age.

Three answers, all of them easy. The wine had the Deep Purple imprimatur, it was made from Deep Purple grapes, and it was good. Which only made the fourth question all the more urgent: why was it at Trader Joe's?

Don't get me wrong. Sandra is in the business to sell wine. It's just that finding Deep Purple in Trader Joe's is like finding chateaubriand at McDonald's. *Thock.*

Trader Joe's is a Southern California phenomenon—the good life at a discount, so long as you don't mind esoteric labels and odd lots. The chain is run by a guy who is a flat-out Libertarian, a political/philosophical party that is not to be confused with civil libertarianism. Joe is a free marketeer, one of those entrepreneurs willing to gamble on his own taste and his own ability to turn a profit on a thin margin and high volume. Most discounters hawk discontinued lines of Frigidaires or Sony Walkmans diverted from South American export. Trader Joe hustles wine, cheese, salted nuts and other upscale comestibles.

He comes up with the goddamnedest buys—delicious white cheddar from some unfashionable co-op creamery in Manitoba, manufacturers' discontinued lines of frozen gourmet dinners, unsalted macadamia nuts, imported French kiwi-fruit preserves, pretzels made from sunflower seeds. Trader Joe's is California's largest retailer of everything from pistachios to whole-bean mocha java, and each item goes on the block for about half what you would pay in the trendy delicatessens and wineshops of Beverly Hills, Newport or Malibu.

But Trader Joe's forte is wine, wine from France, Italy, Chile, Australia and particularly California. He has his own bonded winery and bottling operation in the Russian River Valley and buys up casks and vats of wine from boutique wineries all over the state. A big-time vintner might have twenty-five barrels of Pinot Noir that somehow caught too much sulfur dioxide in fermentation. The wine is still drinkable, just not so drinkable that the vintner wants to put his own label and ten-dollar price tag on it. So he peddles the lot to Joe, who bottles it himself and puts it out the door for $2.49.

But canny old Joe is not limited to second-tier wines. Often the wine he sells at $2.49 is exactly the same wine that the big-time boutique vintner sells at ten bucks and up. The problem usually involves not quality but that old, free-market rule of supply and demand. Growing wine grapes is like any other kind of farming; there are years when the crop is heavy, as well as years when the market for fifteen-dollar Cabernets and twenty-two-dollar Chardonnays is light. The market might be able to absorb fifteen thousand cases of some boutique winery's top-of-the-line wine. But what does the vintner do if the crush ends up yielding eighteen thousand cases?

Simple. Either he pumps three thousand cases of first-rate wine into the sewer or he peddles those cases to somebody like Trader Joe on the condition that Joe market the surplus in such a way that he doesn't cut the boutique's throat. Joe sticks his own label on the bottle, very quietly informs his clientele about the real origin of the wine inside, and sells out his consignment in two weeks.

Especially when the consignment he's selling is from Deep Purple.

Some of Trader Joe's customers are very canny about wines. They knew all about the Paris tasting in 1974. Comparative tastings have been a major tool in wine merchandising since the second vineyard was planted. Oenophiles can quote you tasting scores and gold-medal winners the way dedicated fans can quote Rod Carew's batting averages.

What many people don't know is that these tastings can be gimmicked a hell of a lot easier than baseball games can. The incentive is there—the first prize is worth millions of dollars in prestige and wine sales. That's not to say that somebody put a Deep Purple label on a Château Margaux bottle back in 1974. Not at all. It is to say, though, that a great deal of care went into what was a straight-forward effort to put Napa on the world wine map.

The Paris tasting was a publicity stunt from the beginning. It was the brainchild of a group of aggressive and inventive California grape growers and vintners who had become tired of being considered third-rate. They set out to win instant international recognition in the only possible way, by whipping the competition in the competition's home park.

These California comers were smart enough not to cheat. Deep Purple '74 was unquestionably made from Napa grapes, and the bottle contained one hundred percent pure squeezings from the

Cabernet Sauvignon grape. Still, it had been a ringer of sorts. The young growers and vintners, mostly graduates of the University of California oenology program, had virtually handpicked the grapes from what was widely regarded as Napa's best vineyard. They had crushed the grapes and fermented, aged, fined, bottled and prayed over the results with more care and skill than any batch of wine made before or since.

The result was, to say the least, superb, and it had quite properly blown some very fine French wines right out of contention.

The informal little cartel of men bent on making a name for Napa Valley managed to do exactly that, utilizing the same tactics that had been employed so successfully by the French and the Italians for a long, long time. Napa wine suddenly gained a worldwide respectability it had not enjoyed since before passage of the Volstead Act in 1919.

That special, award-winning batch of wine had been made with grapes from a Napa vineyard owned by Howard Autry, Sandra's father. As a result, wines from Deep Purple became the benchmark for California Cabernets. Deep Purple and a few other handmade prizewinners that flowed out of Napa also fueled an explosion in the California wine business that is still sending tremors through the land.

Deep Purple's hundred and forty acres on the west edge of the valley, between the Oakville Grade and St. Helena, became a mecca for wine connoisseurs, snobs and California chauvinists. They would come and stand on the dirt road beside the leafy green vines and sniff the air and taste the soil and say to themselves and to each other, "This is where it all began. This is holy ground."

Howard Autry used to say, "Bullshit."

He wasn't a wine maker himself and had not cultivated the social graces wine makers often find it profitable to acquire. He was just a farmer who respected and cared for his vines. He used to be driven crazy by the dust from pilgrims' cars which coated the leaves and choked the vines. Then there was the fact that every one of those pilgrims felt entitled to break off a cane or snatch a young bunch of grapes as a souvenir of the holy land. "Tourist blight," he called it, and he wasn't smiling when he said it. Tourists became such a problem that finally, just before he was killed in a tractor accident, How-

ard put a sign on the vineyard: PINOT NOIR GRAPES CONTRACT-
GROWN FOR GALLO.

But Deep Purple's reputation remained intact. It was a fearsome
reputation to live up to. It was also Howard's most valuable legacy
to Sandra. That was why I was so surprised to find Trader Joe pushing even Deep Purple's most ordinary Cabernet at twenty-five percent of its usual cost.

I went in, bought a case and stared at the orange plastic grocery
cart while I waited in line to pay. It didn't add up any better when I
got to the cash register. It still didn't add up at home as I stored the
wine in my cellar. My math and marketing savvy aren't in the same
league as Fiora's, but I've been known to balance a checkbook after a
lot of swearing. No matter how I played with these numbers, though,
the bottom line stayed the same. Sandra must have lost about a
dollar a bottle on my purchase, to say nothing of the winery costs.

The California wine business had been in trouble the last couple
of years, but that's ridiculous. Growers shouldn't have to be paying
people to drink the stuff. It didn't add up in any man's language,
particularly with a wine as fine as Deep Purple's.

One of my biggest weaknesses is the unanswered question. I
can't leave it alone. I knew there was an answer, and I knew how to
get it. At some level I even knew that the answer wouldn't be free.
I also knew I had to have it.

So finally I did what I had been trying to avoid doing since I
had picked up Trader Joe's ad in the first place. Despite my better
impulses, and despite the fact that Fiora and I had been living together peacefully for almost four months and she would be coming
home for dinner soon, I found myself reaching for the phone to call
an old lover and long-absent friend.

Sandra and I had not talked for a half dozen years, perhaps
more. We had begun to move amicably in different directions about
the time she started seeing Bob "Bulldog" Ramsey, the scion of
Sonoma grape growing and former prize quarterback of the local
junior college. I was invited to Sandra's wedding but didn't go,
though I'm still not sure whose sensibilities I was sparing—his, hers
or mine.

I did manage to run into Sandra and her husband several times
the first year they were married. The encounters were superficially
pleasant but always had the undercurrent of masculine tension that

usually leads nowhere except to trouble. I'm sure part of it was my fault. I had enough money of my own so that I probably wasn't properly impressed with Ramsey's inherited fortune. Besides, he adopted an overbearing, proprietary attitude toward Sandra that rubbed me the wrong way.

Ramsey is a big, lanky, muscular guy, about my size and build. He is the possessor of considerable charm, I'm told. The problem was, I never saw any of it. Every time we met he started a shouldering match. I can shoulder as hard as the next guy but I always stepped politely aside for Ramsey because I didn't want to embarrass Sandra. She was one of those warm and generous women who deserve to be happy and so rarely are. I hated to see unhappiness come to Sandra's golden-brown eyes as she silently tried to apologize for her husband's manners around me.

For her sake, I began to think of Sandra as a wonderful memory, a soft heat from the past that radiated through some of the colder, less kind memories I have acquired over the years. Sandra had given me a great deal at a time in my life when I'd had only money. I figured that the least I could do was make her life easier in return. She loved Ramsey despite his imperfections. I knew how that was. Fiora and I had loved each other—and still did—despite the fact that we often have hell's own time living together. The last thing I wanted to do was to tear the delicate fabric of Sandra's dreams of happily ever after with Ramsey.

So I stopped going to the Napa Valley. Unfortunately, there must have been more wrong with their marriage than six feet two of unwanted memories hulking in the background. A few years ago I heard that Sandra and Bob had finally split up. By then, the habit of thinking of her as a warm memory and a rare friend had become ingrained. But memories can have enormous power, particularly when they are rooted in the senses rather than the intellect.

I watched my finger punch in Sandra's number and hoped that Fiora would understand why I had to help Sandra if she needed it. Then I wondered whether I would have remembered the number of any other "business associate" after so many years. After a sharp struggle with my conscience, I decided that I would have. Phone numbers and addresses have a way of sticking in my brain.

At least, some of them do.

"Hello?"

More memories came, a flood of warmth. Sandra's voice, like her eyes, is golden brown, the color of harvest. I could see her standing in a shaft of sunlight coming through the beveled window of the old Victorian farmhouse.

"How are things at Deep Purple?"

"Fiddler?" she said. "I don't believe it. I was just thinking about you."

She hesitated, as though her reminiscences had been as ambivalent as mine, and as potent.

"No wonder my ears were burning," I said. "How are you?"

"Fine," she said, but the hesitation was just one beat too long. "What's wrong?"

The long-distance wire hummed for a moment. Then came the admission. "Oh, Fiddler—I'm afraid they're going to take Deep Purple away from me."

Softly, brokenly, Sandra Autry began to cry.

3

"Damn it," Sandra said after a moment. "That wasn't supposed to happen. You always had a way of taking me by surprise. I'll never forget watching you watching me carrying that champagne. . . ." She drew a deep breath and then one more. "Hi, Fiddler," she said, beginning all over. "How are you? You coming up for the crush this year?"

The voice was Sandra's again, rich with harvest possibilities. But I had heard the other voice, the one that knew all about winter.

"It isn't going to wash," I said as gently as I could. "I knew you were in some kind of trouble the minute I bought what the critics call 'a big, perhaps even an historic Cabernet' for the price of Ernest and Julio's Hearty Burgundy."

Sandra laughed, but there was irony rather than music in the sound. "You always were too good at looking behind the label and seeing what's really there, weren't you?"

Neither of us said the name Ramsey, but it was there between us just the same. I hadn't liked Ramsey from the first. But then he hadn't liked me either.

Sandra laughed again. "Most folks would just suck up their cheap wine and celebrate their good luck. I'm glad to know that someone out there is enjoying Deep Purple the way it was meant to be enjoyed."

"Deep Purple has lots of memories for me. Good ones." I hesitated, not knowing how to say it. I'm the direct sort, but I didn't want to steamroller Sandra. "Maybe I couldn't always be as good a friend as either one of us wanted," I said finally, "but I was never very far away, either." I hesitated again, biting back the words, *Why the hell didn't you call and tell me you were in trouble?* I sighed. "I want to help you, Sandra."

There was a long moment while Sandra struggled to keep her breathing even.

"Thanks," she said. "If there were anything anyone could do, I know you would do it. But no one can help, Fiddler. Not even you. I'm just a terrible farmer and worse at business, that's all."

"Lots of very clever growers have had their problems in the last few years."

"But not all of them have mortgaged their ground to take a flier in a business for which they were totally unsuited," Sandra said.

"Such as . . . ?"

"Such as a big, beautiful restaurant that served food nobody wanted to eat."

"Your food? Has Napa Valley gone crazy? I'd rather eat from your garbage can than from most of the restaurants in the world."

"You're the only one left who feels like that," she said wearily.

"What happened?"

There was a long silence and then a sigh. "Bob didn't want me to keep the catering business while we were married," she said slowly.

I made an encouraging sound.

"It was okay if I worked a few days a week preparing for his big bashes, but I couldn't be a 'paid servant' for the same people who would be guests in our home a week later," Sandra continued. "It just wasn't done."

The sound I made this time was more like a grunt. Inelegant, but that's how Ramsey affected me. He came first. Everyone else in the world came second. What other people saw as Ramsey's "bull-dog" determination in following a goal, I saw as blind selfishness.

"So when it all came apart," Sandra said, "I decided to open that restaurant I'd always wanted. I knew it wouldn't be easy, and it wasn't. Banks still don't like loaning money to unmarried women."

What Sandra didn't say—what she didn't have to say—was that she had been far too proud to take any of Ramsey's millions when she left him.

"Starting from scratch was kind of fun, actually. Like being young again. All hard work and high hopes." Sandra laughed. "You see, I still believed that everything would turn out all right in the end." This time her laugh sounded a little wobbly.

"Sandra—"

"No," she said quickly, interrupting me. "It's all right, Fiddler. Everybody has to grow up sometime. I was just a little late. And the restaurant wasn't a stupid idea. Really. Napa has become a cook's paradise. Wine is made to be drunk with food. Good food. I thought that, with my reputation as a cook, I would have a ready-made clientele. All I needed was a place to feed them."

I waited, knowing what was coming, not wanting to hear it. There is a difference between growing up and being stripped of your dreams. Not much difference, maybe, but it's all that makes life worth living.

"Do you have any idea how much it costs to put up a commercial building?" Sandra asked, echoes of old shock raising her voice. "Nothing fancy. I'm not the fancy type. But I wanted quality, the kind of quality you see in the old Victorians on Nob Hill, wood and glass and landscaping that makes people believe they're parking in a garden, not a shopping center."

"How much? A million?" I guessed, praying.

"Double it," she said, "and add some for good measure. I got by cheap, too. I already owned the land. I took out three acres of grapes, listening to my father's ghost complain the whole way, graded the ground for a building site and parking lot, and started to burn piles of dollar bills like they were last year's prunings."

"What about your partner?" I asked, praying from another direction.

"Are you kidding? Me? You know I like to work by myself. I didn't bring in outside capital. Not smart little me. I mortgaged the hell out of the other hundred and thirty-seven acres of Deep Purple to pay for my folly." She swore softly and very fluently before she sighed. "Well, I got my dream restaurant. I called it Vintage Harvest. I opened almost a year ago, just before the grape harvest began."

I didn't need to hear any more to know that what Sandra needed to solve her problems was an infusion of good old long green. There was no point in me reaching for my checkbook, either. I didn't have enough cash to pull an operation the size of Deep Purple out of the shit.

I felt anger and frustration rise like bile in my throat. Not enough money. I'd spent my childhood knowing that my parents didn't have enough money to pay their bills. I'd watched bad luck and lack of money kill my father and make an old woman of my mother before she was forty. Lack of money started Uncle Jake down the road to drug dealing and violent death. If there was anything noble about poverty, I never saw it.

A long time ago I had sworn that someday I'd have enough money. How much is that? Enough, that's all. Enough to buy a good car and a roof that didn't leak and something left over for other people who needed it. When Fiora turned Jake's illegal legacy into wealth, I thought I'd died and gone to heaven. Never again would I feel the raging impotence of a man with nothing but lint in his pockets and friends or family in need of money.

Never again. But here it was, staring at me. The woman who had helped me years ago needed money now—and I didn't have enough to give her.

"Vintage Harvest will close at the end of the month, unless there's some kind of miracle," Sandra continued, her voice toneless. "Nearly twelve months and two point four million bucks. I had a run of back luck you wouldn't believe."

"Try me."

Calmly, quietly, as though she were reading from a shopping list, Sandra told me about bartenders who tapped the till and highly recommended kitchen help who sold prime steaks and racks of lamb out the back door when she wasn't looking. In the end she was spending more time managing the help than she was cooking—and she was a much better cook than a manager.

In other words, Sandra had gotten a very expensive set of lessons in the business of restaurants. Did you ever wonder why fancy eating joints are often run by guys who look like thugs in tuxedos? Sandra can tell you. It's because you have to be a thug to stay alive.

But I heard another possibility in Sandra's list, something that I might be able to do for her to make up for my empty pockets. There were simply too many coincidences—the Immigration Service sweep that cleaned out Sandra's kitchen crew just before opening weekend, the replacement salad chef who showed up just when she needed him most and who turned out to be a hepatitis-B carrier, and the whispering campaign that spread that unhappy fact through the ranks of foodies and restaurant critics all over the state.

A run of bad luck? Maybe. And maybe not.

Sandra seemed no more than half aware of the pattern. I told myself that it was only my nasty nature, but the basement levels of my mind kept on trying to lift a ruff on the back of my neck. I've learned to listen to those primitive reflexes. Like everything else, I learned it the hard way, by getting my chops kicked until I paid attention.

I don't understand gravity, but I know it works.

It's the same for Fiora, my fey Scots ex-wife and present lover. When the lives of people she loves are in danger, sometimes she dreams with uncanny precision. Unhappy dreams. It's one of the things that has made it so hard for us to live together. Fiddling in other people's business can be hazardous to your health. Fiora woke up in the middle of the night and knew that Uncle Jake had died and that I had not. She knew I was alive before I did. She knew that her twin brother had died before the body was even found. And because she loves me she knows when I'm in danger of dying too.

I don't ask Fiora about her dreams anymore. She doesn't tell me about them, because she knows that I won't stop what I'm doing no matter how terrible her dreams are. But sometimes she kisses me with unusual intensity. Sometimes she makes love to me as though it were the last time.

And then I wonder if it is.

Not a comfortable way to live. For either of us. There are other ways in which Fiora and I mesh badly, as well. Fiora loves high finance. I don't mean money itself—for her, money is just a way of keeping score. She loves the fiscal manipulations themselves, the intricate paper castles that can be built. When she first discovered that world, it was like a drug. She couldn't enough of it. Eighty-hour workweeks were nothing.

I didn't understand her fascination with money shuffling when we didn't need any more bucks. She didn't understand why I'd take on jobs that were dangerous when we didn't need the money. In the end she left, pursued her paper castles and never stopped loving her ex-husband. And me? Well, I took more than my share of lumps from various kinds of thugs and never stopped loving my ex-wife.

We've learned to finesse our irreconcilable differences for weeks or months at a time, because on the whole we do better together than we do apart. It had been particularly good for us in the last few months, because I hadn't been working. A messy, sad run-in with an old man, the PLO and a renegade Mossad agent had left me . . .

tired. I'd felt the way Sandra sounded before she pulled herself together and put her harvest voice back in place.

Now I was listening to Sandra and hearing the past close in again. Not enough money. Bad luck. No money. And maybe, just maybe, the kind of human viciousness that I had discovered a flair for dealing with. If Sandra's problems were physical as well as fiscal, I could help.

"There were other things," Sandra continued. "Little things. Plugged toilets that stank up the dining area. Gas leaks. Bugs in the limestone lettuce."

"It sounds like more than bad luck."

"The restaurant critics called it bad luck when they wrote about my hepatitis carrier," she said dryly. "They all agreed. Just bad luck. Could have happened to any restaurant."

"Sure. Once. Your bad luck seems to be interlocked and timed for maximum impact."

There was a long pause.

"The food business, and the wine business for that matter, can be cutthroat, but not that cutthroat," Sandra finally said, but the hesitation had been telling.

"You know them better than I do. But you might ask yourself who would gain by sabotaging your operation."

There was another long, unhappy pause, but no denial of my words. Sandra didn't like the implications of my suggestion, but she had grown up. She knew that the world was full of things she didn't like. She could confront them as they came along or she could spend her life imitating the three monkeys that heard, saw and spoke no evil.

"I believe there's such a thing as bad luck," I said. "And I believe that sometimes what we label bad luck is malice, plain and simple. Labels don't change anything, Sandra."

"Damn you," Sandra breathed, but when she spoke her voice was resigned rather than angry. "You always were quicker to look into the shadows than the rest of us. I thought of sabotage, Fiddler. But I just can't . . ."

I waited, knowing that someone as spontaneous and generous as Sandra would have a tough time believing that some underhanded son of a bitch was bleeding her to death one sneaky "accident" at a time.

"What else has happened?" I asked. "Why were you thinking of me when I called?"

"I closed Vintage Harvest for a week so that I could concentrate on two huge catering jobs," she said in a strained voice. "There are a million things that could go wrong, especially with Vern Traven's pre-harvest party. And if just one thing goes wrong, I'm dead. Not literally," she said hastily, "not like what you run into. It's just that if something happens the bank won't think it worthwhile to refinance the restaurant loan and I won't be able to reopen Vintage Harvest and then I'll go under and Deep Purple will go with me unless the harvest comes off without a hitch."

The words came out in a rush, as though Sandra were afraid that if she stopped to listen to their meaning she would have lost her confidence.

"Is there anything especially tricky about the jobs you're doing right now, besides their size?" I asked.

"The party tomorrow night is no real problem. The new winery across the highway from me is having one of those 'y'all come' parties. All I'll need is food and lots of it." She took a deep breath. "Vern's pre-harvest party is different. It's a caterer's nightmare," she admitted. "Vern just pumped about ten million bucks into the old Villapando Wine Company property behind Deep Purple. He's invited a thousand people, not only wine folks but politicians, artists, famous foodies, newspaper types. God," she groaned. "Everyone. Just everyone. And I have to feed them all a sit-down dinner, outdoors, miles from the nearest real kitchen. That's why I closed the restaurant. I'll do the meat there and take it up in vans and . . ." Her voice trailed off.

"Christ, if the logistics are that bad, why did you take the job?"

"I thought it could salvage my reputation, and besides, Vern has been a good friend through all the bad luck. He's a Texan who made millions in the 'awl bidness' as he calls it, but he's a farmer at heart. He's fallen in love with the Napa Valley and with wine growing. He's turned his vineyard and winery into an incredible showplace."

"His party still sounds like more grief than you need right now," I said.

"I don't have any choice. I'm buying breathing space from the bank at ruinous interest for a few months at a time. Like every real farmer, I'm betting on the come. The harvest. If I can stay alive until then, I can save Deep Purple from bankruptcy and maybe even keep the restaurant open." Sandra's voice wavered, then firmed again. "I bought some of that time with the wine I sold to your liquidator down south. Now, if Vern's dinner works and nothing else goes wrong, Art said that he'll be able to roll the note over again. That will give me time to reorganize my assets."

I began to wish that Fiora were home and listening on the other phone. Something wasn't adding up again, but it was Fiora's field of expertise, not mine. Normally I'm the first to state Fiora's accomplishments, but it galled me that she was in a better position to help Sandra than I was.

"I don't understand," I said. "You're into the bank for just two million plus this year's farming costs, right?"

"Yes."

"Then why is the bank breathing hard on you? Your equity in Deep Purple has to be worth a lot more than a few million. Hell, I'd be delighted to secure that loan myself."

Sandra ignored the bait and stuck to the main subject.

"I thought my equity was golden, too, but when I went to the bank the other day to talk about refinancing I couldn't get a firm commitment, no matter how hard I tried," she said. "That's when I started getting paranoid, worrying about more bad luck or sabotage or whatever it is." She drew a ragged breath. "But it's such an awful idea, Fiddler. I don't like to think that somebody is really out to destroy me."

"Yeah," I agreed. "It requires you to reevaluate so many things you take for granted. There are plenty of folks in the world who would rather go under than change the way they think. Then there are the smart ones," I added.

"What do you mean?"

"The smart ones manage to hold onto a kinder view of the universe by turning their suspicions over to permanently warped guys like me, guys who've already lost most of their illusions about sweetness and life."

"I couldn't ask you to do something like that," she said quickly.

"I know," I retorted. "That's why I'm telling you that, ready or not, like it or not, I'm coming up to watch your back for a while, just to make sure that your friends are just what they seem."

"You'd do that, wouldn't you." It was an observation, not a

question. "After all these years, you would drop whatever you're doing to help me. Fiddler, you aren't permanently warped. You've still got some illusions."

"If you say so," I replied, looking at the faint scars on my hands where packing-crate nails had slashed through. There were other scars as well, other memories, some new and some not. I don't think that scars come under the category of illusions. "Actually, I'm just looking for an excuse to show Napa Valley to Fiora," I said, making up my mind. I was going to Napa, and Fiora was going with me.

Sandra is one incredible woman. Her voice actually brightened. "You mean I finally get a chance to meet her? When? Shall I pick you up at the airport or . . ." Sandra's voice faded. "Are you sure that would be such a good idea, though? I mean, I remember how Bob used to treat you."

"Relax," I said.

"Ummm," said Sandra.

"Fiora and I have had to get used to dealing with friends of various sexes."

Which was true. It was the unfriendlies that had pulled us apart.

"Fiddler?"

"I'm here."

"If you're really serious about—"

"I am. We're driving up Friday night."

Sandra took a deep breath. I would swear that when she started talking again she sounded relieved.

"If you get here before midnight, I won't be home. That's the party at the winery across the road."

"Can we crash it?"

She sighed again. This time I was sure it was relief.

"Please do," she murmured. "I'd love to see a friendly face. The winery is just across the highway from the Deep Purple turnoff. You can't miss it. Granite and glitz all over the place." She hesitated. "You're sure?"

"We'll see you Friday night."

"Thanks, Fiddler," she said softly, and hung up.

I stood for a long time and stared at the phone, hoping that

Sandra's problems could be solved by money rather than violence. For me, only time would tell. But for Fiora?

I wondered whether the dreams would change, and if she would tell me if they did.

4

"You go ahead," Fiora said. "I've got too much work to do."

Her tone was soft but the look in her wide hazel eyes suggested that she would cut my heart out if I did go to Napa without her. There was no need for that. Whether I went or stayed, my heart was not at issue and she should have known it. On the other hand, maybe my old frustrations in regard to not enough money were showing. Fiora always could read me too well. So I put my abraded pride on hold and reminded myself how often I'd wanted to share Napa Valley with the woman I loved.

"It's the end of summer," I said. "You told me last week that nothing's happening. Wall Street is recovering from Fire Island, the European markets are sluggish because all the traders are still in the country, and everybody in Century City wants to be somewhere else. If I recall, your exact words were 'The only people who are doing business are the Japanese' and there's no sweat there since they love blond American businesswomen without reservation. You can afford a couple of days away from the office."

"But that's just it," said Fiora. "This is the only time of year I can catch up on the analysts' reports and the rest of the research I've let slip."

"Papers! Great! Put them in a box and we'll take them along. Besides, Sandra says she's always wanted to meet you."

An odd expression flickered across Fiora's beautiful face before she turned away, as though she wanted to hide something from me. I know the woman pretty well. We were married for a while, after all, and we have never managed to live apart for more than a year at a time since. I know her moods and emotions. But this reaction was new to me. It was as though something had threatened her, yet I had done nothing except encourage her to bring her business with her to Napa. If anything, that should have made her happy. Frankly, I'm normally a hell of a lot less than thrilled when Fiora's business slops over into our life together.

I went over and put my arms around her. She stood unresponsively, her back to me as she looked out the wrinkled old glass of the cottage's picture window. Out over the ocean, the setting sun was doing what it had done a million years ago and would be doing a million years from now.

"Can't you even muster up a little injured jealousy?" I said lightly, brushing my lips over Fiora's fragrant hair. "If I were the nervous type, I'd think you were trying to get rid of me, sending me off alone to visit an old girl friend." I nuzzled beneath her honey-blond hair, searching for her ear.

"Is that why you're going? To make me jealous?"

There was a sharp edge to Fiora's voice that I hadn't heard for a long time. It matched the sudden tension I could feel in the smooth muscles at the base of her neck. I took her by the shoulders and turned her around.

"No," I said. "I'm going to help an old friend, and I think you might be more use to her than I am. It's no more complicated than that."

Fiora searched my face for a moment with those quick, intelligent eyes before she let out a long breath and softened beneath my touch.

"But it's no less complicated than that, either," she said, smoothing her fingertips over my mustache before she stood on tiptoe and kissed my lips.

Fiora's neck was still too tense, but I could feel all of her as she leaned against me. She has the kind of body that makes hugging a very worthwhile experience. I let my hands slide down her back and then up beneath the jacket of the pin-striped business suit she still wore. Her waist is taut and small, giving her a doll-like slenderness that is as deceptive as hell. Rapiers are slender too.

"It's complicated," I admitted. "But Sandra really does need some help, and she's too proud to ask."

Fiora tipped her head back, her body still flush against mine. She brought her arms up and slipped them around my neck, increasing the sensual contact. She swayed gently, smiling uncertainly.

"I'm sorry," she whispered. "I didn't mean to slash at you like that. Maybe I'm a little scared of Sandra. You make her sound like such an earth mother—a tall, wonderful, sensual paragon."

"It was a long time ago," I said. "The earth mother's probably gotten fat." I flexed my fingers into Fiora's narrow waist and satisfyingly round hips.

"Fat?" Fiora said. "Yeah. Sure. The way Sophia Loren got fat."

I couldn't help it. I laughed. Fiora speared her fingers through my hair and tugged hard enough to get my attention. Then she kissed me the same way. By the time the kiss was finished, I had lifted her until neither one of us had to stretch or bend.

"You've got to understand," Fiora said, biting my lower lip the same way she had kissed me. "A woman like Sandra puts one like me at several disadvantages. I'm nobody's mother and I sure as hell can't cook."

"No, but you make so goddamn much money that you can buy and sell a hundred cooks."

"That, dear man," she said, smoothing away tooth marks with the tip of her tongue, "is not a skill that ranks high on the womanhood scale. You should know. You've said often enough how much you hate my 'money shuffling.' "

"If you were any more of a woman we'd both have died in bed long ago."

I kissed Fiora hard enough and long enough to prove it to her. By the time that kiss ended and I set her back on her feet we were both breathing like middle-distance runners.

My hands moved along her ribs, tracing the delicate lines, brushing her breasts lightly through her silk shirt, undoing buttons as fast as I found them. I like her a lot better without the dress-for-power clothes, just as she likes me a lot better without my Detonics.

"Come with me," I said.

"Do you really want me to . . ." began Fiora, then forgot her questions as I finally got beneath all her business finery.

"You win, you bastard," she said, sighing and gasping in the same breath. "I'll go meet your earth mother. She can't be any sexier in the flesh than she is in your memory." Suddenly Fiora gathered my hands, pinning them between her bare breasts for a moment. "But there's one condition."

"Name it," I said, spreading my fingers. Sometimes having big hands is a distinct advantage.

Fiora arched against my hands, closing her eyes in pleasure. "You have to leave that goddamn Cobra home for once," she said.

At the moment I would have considered driving the Cobra off a cliff.

As I might have mentioned, Fiora is a complex woman. In addition to her occasional uncanny dreams, she has the shrewdest business mind I have ever encountered. You'll notice I didn't add a qualifier there. Not "male," not "female," just "shrewdest."

I'm not a fool financially. I can read a balance sheet and run the routine kinds of figures that anybody can. But when it comes to making money, I'll never be in Fiora's league. It's a bit like the situation that finally led me to throw my violin under the wheels of a passing Corvette when I was twenty-one. I was good, even very good, but Itzhak Perlman and Pinchas Zukerman and too many other guys in the world my age or younger were better and always would be. I couldn't stand knowing that and yet continue to devote my life to music.

But I still dream of music and wake up and stare at the big hands that never could be as perfect as the sounds I heard in my mind.

It was easier to give over control of Uncle Jake's legacy to Fiora than it was to trash my violin, but the principle was the same. When it came to turning cash into true wealth, Fiora just plain outclassed me and I knew it. Depositing that trunkful of ill-gotten gains in her trust account didn't end all of life's problems for either of us, but it put paid to the ones that were caused by lack of money.

Fiora took that pile of used tens, twenties and fifties and turned it into a respectable fortune. Respectable both in size and in the eyes of the law. Fiora did pretty well out of it too. She made her management fee and, more importantly, she made a reputation in Newport Beach and Century City. It wasn't long before a fancy venture-capital firm came along and offered her a junior partnership, which she parlayed into a senior partnership before she was thirty. And the rest, as they say, is history.

Unfortunately, by then, so was our formal marriage. We found we simply couldn't live together and do the things we had to do—

Fiora her eighty-hour-per-week career and me my restless wanderings and occasional brawls.

A big part of the problem was that, in my attempts to feel useful, I kept skirting too close to respectability. In reaction, I would jump back into the adrenaline-filled netherworld that was the only place I really felt alive, once I left music. I tried being a reporter but found it too constricting to slant reality to fit an editor's preconceptions. I tried being a cop and discovered that I wasn't cut out to spend my life thumping drunks and kissing political ass. Thanks to Uncle Jake and Fiora, I didn't really have to do anything, so I said to hell with formal job descriptions and did what so often happens here along the high-tech, high-speed Gold Coast. I started inventing my life and my career from day to day. I do what I think needs doing.

In other words, I fiddle around in other people's business.

Sometimes I'm described as a private investigator. That's what the plastic-laminated certificate of approval from the California Bureau of Consumer Affairs calls me. But it's been a long time since I accepted a fee from anybody. That leaves me absolutely free to mess around in other people's business as I see fit and on behalf of whomever I happen to care about. As a life style, it's as unstructured as hell, which drives Fiora crazy from time to time and satisfies something deep inside me all the time.

Our love for each other has survived this free-form existence, which is why we live together a lot of the time. Like I say, Fiora is a remarkable, flexible and complex woman.

And, like most complex human beings, she has very strong tastes and opinions. She loves order in her life. She demands to sleep on the right side of the bed. She wants the alarm set for six, no matter how late she goes to sleep. She loves being seduced, and seducing. She gets choked up over French and American Impressionist art and weeps over a nicely prepared balance sheet.

She does not, however, love my car, at least not the way I do. The vehicle we weren't driving to Napa is a 1966 Shelby Cobra roadster powered by a 427-cubic-inch Ford engine. It's a dinosaur by the standards of modern transportation, perhaps a *Tyrannosaurus rex*. A total of four hundred and one Cobras were made, but only three hundred and fifty-six were finished before somebody at FoMoCo decided that enough was enough and bought out old Carroll Shelby. Ford usurped the name and the power plant and began jamming it into Mustangs like the one Steve McQueen drove in *Bullitt*. But that transaction left one element out of the old Cobra equation—the AC Ace body. That voluptuously rounded carriage, which looks as if somebody crossed a young Elizabeth Taylor with an MGTD, defines auto styling for lots of people, including me.

Unfortunately, for some people, that body makes minimal concessions to the elements. In other words, when you're driving the Cobra you know exactly how heavy the rainfall is, exactly how hot or cold it is. You and the bugs on your teeth can sense a weather change the moment it happens because you are right out in it.

That, of course, is my idea of fun. And there are some days in the year when Fiora will not only put up with the Cobra but actually revel in it. The rest of the time she prefers wheels that are more practical.

"Classics," she mutters. "I'll drink one, hang one on my wall or listen to one. But I will never drive more than twenty miles a day in one!"

Which is why, when I picked her up in Century City the following day, I was behind the wheel of her BMW 635 CSI. Yes, yes, I know the Bimmer has become almost as trendy as a Volvo station wagon, but at least it ain't a Mercedes 300 TD.

In truth, I kind of like the Bimmer. If I didn't have the time and inclination to indulge my taste for the difficult and the exotic, I'd probably own one. Fiora's car is a lovely, lustrous vermilion called Cimarron Red. It has a muscular six-cylinder engine with some gray-market goodies normally unavailable in the United States. It also has a quick four-speed, a fine stereo and air conditioning. Even I will surrender a few horsepower for cool air on a long drive through the Great Dead Hot Heart of California, which is what we faced.

Fiora was on the phone cleaning up last-minute details when I walked into her Century City office. Her secretary, Jason of the thin ties and the slippery pastel shirts, showed me in, swiveled over to Fiora's desk and stood smiling, his index finger poised over the switch hook. Fiora removed his hand impatiently and tried to continue talking.

"Your orders were explicit, Ms. Flynn," Jason said, slipping his fingers beneath her hand and again threatening to cut off her conversation.

"Oh, all right," she muttered, her palm over the receiver. She lifted her hand. "Joel, look, I've got to go," she said into the phone. "Something serious has just come up. I'll call you next week and we'll finish this conversation." She hung up.

"Jason, she'd kill me if I tried that stunt," I said. "I owe you a night on the town."

Jason smiled sunnily. "Stag or drag, you should pardon the expression? I know some places where you'd be such a big hit."

I laughed and left the choice up to him. A long time ago Jason had thumbed a ride to LA from the small Nevada cow town where he had been born. He had spent his young life pretending to be a Marlboro Man, but he was really destined for bright lights and sequined tights. He's gay to the bone, and he works very hard at letting people know about it. Fiora has gotten used to his exaggerations, and so have I, because Jason is the kind of assistant that executives pray for and rarely get. Quick, intelligent and utterly loyal to the boss who had accepted the person beneath the deliberately outrageous exterior.

Jason took a ream of instructions in shorthand from Fiora, then bowed out. I tossed her the traveling bag she had packed that morning and then watched appreciatively while she changed from business dress to blue jeans, tube top and cotton shirt. She seemed oblivious to the fact that she was buck naked in front of the smoked glass windows of her eighteenth-floor corner office.

Thanks to Jason's efficiency, we were on the road by 5 P.M. and clear of the Los Angeles Basin rush hour by five-thirty. I gambled that most California Highway Patrol officers go Code Seven for dinner at the same time and cranked the Bimmer up to seventy-five. We cleared Fort Tejon before seven and made that long steep drop down the Grapevine into the lingering remnants of a 113-degree day in the San Joaquin Valley.

Interstate 5 is a great concrete garden path running up the west side of the San Joaquin Valley. We pushed north steadily through the richest agribusiness land in the world. Dozens of immense cultivated fields stretched on either side of the freeway, dry land turned productive by a man-made river that flows between concrete banks for four hundred miles. Cotton, alfalfa, onions, sugar beets, watermelons, tomatoes, cantaloupes, almonds. The list is staggering. There are even grapes—mostly Thompson Seedless for table use or for raisins.

This is the California that nobody ever sees. It isn't Disneyland or Hollywood or Fisherman's Wharf but it accounts for more than half the wealth of the wealthiest state in the union. The almost violently fertile land unrolls beside the freeway in mind-boggling, then mind-numbing vistas.

The air conditioning kept the heat and dust at bay, but even the filtered rays of sunlight had an oppressive weight through the windshield glass. I drove and let Fiora decompress while she stared at the rows of dark green cotton and light green table grapes, leaving the office behind her. I knew Fiora's rhythms well enough to understand that there was nothing personal in her silence. She was simply putting her mind in neutral, one layer at a time, so that she could gather it all together again and focus it on the pleasures of the moment.

There was also the winery party we had to face tonight. Not the kind of thing either one of us relished at the end of a long day.

I deliberately left the radio and the cassette player off for a while, knowing that Fiora valued the silence the same way that she valued a fine wine. But I love music when I drive, particularly when I'm driving the long Central Valley. I avoided the tape rack of symphonies—Mozart is hundred-mile-an-hour music and I didn't want to work that hard. Instead I played one of the tapes that Fiora had put together for herself. As evening claimed the land, we listened to Elton John and Phil Collins, Willie Nelson and Janis Joplin, U2 and Sting, and Bob Dylan doing "Billy the Kid."

I tried not to think as I drove, but I was less successful at that than Fiora. This morning, just before she left for Century City, she had turned to me and asked if I was sure that Sandra's problem was fiscal rather than physical. By physical, Fiora meant something that would end up with me bashed and bleeding, the kind of thing that would give her more bad dreams in the middle of the night. I told her that it was possible that someone was crowding Sandra but that, once Sandra's money problem were solved, whoever it was—if it was anyone at all—would go back under a rock. No problem. Fiscal rather than physical.

Fiora had given me a long look, bitten her lip against whatever else she wanted to say and left for work. I wondered again about her dreams, but I didn't ask. I had promised her before we went to sleep that I would keep everything on a fiscal basis. I didn't want to know if I was going to break my word.

We stopped to eat at Harris Ranch, which has all the necessary amenities for the I-5 traveler—four gas stations, a motel, a private airstrip and a restaurant that features the kind of feed-lot beef that is worth driving hours to get. Fiora deliberately avoided any conversation that didn't have to do with the moment. I didn't mind. Finding and losing each other more than once has taught us that some things are better left unsaid. So we talked about the tender beef and the diversity of crops, and she held my hand as we walked back to the car.

We drove with the windows open after dinner. It was still hot, but the air had a silky feeling to it and the agrarian smells were intriguing. Fiora napped, shaking off the last of what had been a grueling few weeks for her. It occurred to me that she had been working unusually hard, a fact that had begun to bug me before Sandra's call sent my thoughts in a new direction. In fact Fiora had been working like a woman who knew there was an unscheduled vacation just around the corner.

The thought disturbed me despite Fiora's past assurances that her Scots blood didn't stretch to outright prescience. She was always quick to point out the times that she was wrong, as though her fey dreams bothered her too.

Just before we turned off onto I-580, Fiora woke up, yawned and said, "I'll take it while you sleep. You're going to need it."

Suddenly she grimaced. "Don't look at me like that."

"Like what?"

"Like you're wondering if I've had any bad dreams lately." She closed her eyes and said quickly, "The only reason you're going to need some sleep is that I'm planning on tripping you and beating you to the floor just as soon as we get out of the party you got us into tonight."

Not an offer I'm likely to refuse. I pulled off the road, switched places with Fiora and fell asleep. I woke up as we passed the strange, humming windmills in the pass above Livermore and then again when Fiora braked to a stop and flipped coins into the toll basket on the Benicia-Martinez Bridge.

In Vallejo we both tried to shake off highway hypnosis over cups of epically bad coffee. The fresh, chill air rolling off the mud flats of San Pablo Bay was more effective, though, and a hell of a lot more palatable. We were bright-eyed as chipmunks when I turned onto

Highway 29 and headed north toward Napa, forty minutes from home.

As soon as I shifted into fourth Fiora began talking quietly, as thought commenting on a discussion that we had been having all along.

"Sandra isn't the only one in Napa who's having trouble getting refinancing on bank loans," Fiora said. "One of my partners has taken active positions in some agribusiness deals over the years, but he said he wouldn't touch a thing in Napa at the moment unless it were cosigned by the Swiss government. Is the wine surplus that bad?"

"It must be. She pulled out three acres of vines and put up a restaurant."

"She may be the cutting edge of a trend. When I started asking around I picked up hints about trouble with grapes in the Napa Valley."

"What kind of trouble?" I asked sharply.

"The people who are talking don't know, and the ones who do know aren't talking." Fiora shrugged again. "Someone will break, of course. The price will go high enough and the information will change hands. But right now the situation is what investors call 'very dynamic.' That means it could all go to hell in a handbasket real quick."

"Any way to force the issue?"

"You heard that list of names I left with Jason. Half of them make their living betting on agricultural futures. Three of them are wine brokers. They have wires out all over the world. If anybody knows, they will."

Fiora turned and put her hand on my leg. I tensed, knowing that she was going to tell me something that I didn't want to hear.

"Whether the rumors are true or false, someone is going to make a lot of money," she said. "That's how these things work, Fiddler. There's a lot of money coming out of Hong Kong and Mexico right now. Hungry money. So someone sends up a trial balloon. Even if it's just hot air, a whole lot of people end up being taken for a ride. I'm afraid your earth mother just had the bad luck to be caught in an exposed position when the balloon went up."

"Bottom line," I snapped, hating the whole thing, the paper

castles built on the corpses of people to whom money is a hell of a lot more than a way to keep score.

Fiora shrugged, silently telling me what she thought about international business rumors. She lived with them every day. They were both her life's blood and her bane. She had made fortunes and lost them. That was the lure of the game, and the thrill of it. Nothing was certain.

"If Sandra has to bail out," Fiora said, "she can always sell her land for development before the bank repossesses. I'll take it on myself. One of my clients is looking for—"

"No way," I interrupted.

"If your earth mother is really in the shit, she can't afford sentiment," Fiora said crisply. "If you won't tell her the facts of fiscal life, I will."

"It's not sentiment, it's zoning law. Nobody develops anything in Napa Valley but wine. Period."

"You're kidding."

"You can build a house in Napa Valley, but the minimum lot size is forty acres. Hotels and condos? Forget it. The zoning simply doesn't exist. And it won't."

Fiora frowned slightly and tapped her fingernail against the gold wedding band she wore on her right hand, factoring the new element into her fiscal equations. After a long silence she looked at me.

"Then I'm afraid Sandra's really in the shit."

5

I downshifted and drove hard for a while. The Bimmer wasn't the Cobra, but the engine had a satisfying howl and the suspension was made to stand up to hard use. Fiora didn't say anything about the sudden change in driving style. She knew that I think best at speed. She also knew how much I hated to deal with money in any way but to spend it.

Moonrise flooded over the familiar, jutting forms of Atlas Peak and Mount St. Helena. There was enough light to pick out the ragged shapes of mammoth eucalyptus trees beside the highway and the elegant thrust of evergreens on the first small hillsides off to the west. Although the air had cooled considerably, Fiora made no move to roll up the windows. She sat without moving, watching the vineyard rows flow by on both sides of the narrow highway.

Gradually I eased up on the gas. The Napa Valley is too beautiful to be taken at high speeds. To me, it's one of the most gorgeous places on earth, fertile and serene, changing beneath the weight of the seasons, transforming sunlight into flavors that set a man to dreaming.

Of course, I can afford to feel that way. I don't have to farm the land. Montana is beautiful enough to break your heart too. It sure broke enough hearts in my family.

Fiora reached over and rested her hand on my leg. This time I didn't tense. Her touch was simply a way of telling me that she was glad she was here, now, with me. Her expression grew dreamy as she watched the moonlit rows glide by. She called out the names of wineries as she discovered them—Trefethen, Vichon, Far Niente, Inglenook, Cakebread, Mondavi. Moonlight softened the Victorian houses and stone wineries, giving even the most functional farm outbuildings a shimmering aura of unearthly beauty.

At three minutes after eleven the headlights picked up an old familiar landmark beside the highway, a tall concrete standpipe at the head of a row of eucalyptus trees. I slowed, knowing the next road off to the left would lead to Deep Purple. But the road I was looking for right now was on the other side. I found it immediately.

Sandra had been right. There was no way to miss the Napa Valley Mountain Vineyards winery and tasting room across the road from Deep Purple. There was a handsome roadside sign announcing it to passersby, with a corporate footnote in small letters on the corner: Cable NaVaMoVi.

The NaVaMoVi folks didn't have carbon-arc searchlights out front to announce themselves to the world. Not quite. That would have been tacky and God knows you don't sell wine with tacky. But they had done quite a job on the rest of the presentation. The new building was built in the midst of a precisely laid out vineyard and set back from the highway a few hundred feet. The facade was washed with a rose-colored light that I suppose was intended to suggest the last rays of the setting sun. The result was a little theatrical for my taste, but then I'm not in the business of hawking the romance of wine.

The building itself was a masterpiece of misdirection, particularly in the roseate light. There was an air of solidity and permanence about the walls, as though they had stood there for at least a century. The effect sprang from the rough gray exterior of the building; fieldstone had been the building material of choice for nineteenth-century Napa Valley wineries. The problem was that when I had last traveled Highway 29 the winery site was occupied by a welding shop with corrugated metal siding and a Champion sparkplug ad painted on one wall.

As I got closer I saw how the transformation had been achieved. The welding shop was gone, of course, and in its place NaVaMoVi had erected a rather routine frame and stucco building. But they'd thrown a lot of work into the exterior, carefully sculpting the stucco to give the appearance of hand-set stone. Amazing what you can do with plaster and chicken wire. I wondered whether it might not have been cheaper to build the winery out of real stone in the first place.

There were some other flourishes, too. Real stone is not an affectation for winemakers. Stone walls help to moderate sudden temperature swings in the aging cellars. Stucco, on the other hand, doesn't control temperature worth a damn, certainly not in Napa with its forty-degree daily variations. Once again, the NaVaMoVi folks had attacked the problem with technology. Air conditioning. However, since they were into image, they had to hide their high-tech solutions the way Walt Disney had to hide Abe Lincoln's hydraulic heart. Cupolas were NaVaMoVi's discreet answer. As we parked at the edge of the lot, I heard the unmistakable sound of industrial-strength air-conditioning compressors roaring away inside their rustic little roof cupolas.

My first reaction was faint nostalgia for the welding shop. My expression must have given me away. Fiora threw me an amused look as she reached into the back seat for an exotically patterned pull-over dress.

"What did you expect them to do—let their wines swelter?" she asked.

"How about using the rock they're imitating and leaving the compressors in the warehouse?"

There was a muffled hoot of disbelief as Fiora pulled the loose, floaty dress over her head.

"Do you know how much that would cost?" she asked, emerging from the draped neckline in a cloud of crackling blond hair.

I forgot to answer as I watched her rustle around beneath the folds of the dress. A pair of shorts appeared in one of her hands. The tube top must have been harder to move. She squirmed around intriguingly.

"Need any help?"

She gave me a look that told me she was seriously considering the offer. Then she smiled slightly and shook her head. "If I remember correctly, you helped me get a bee out of my sundress on our first date."

"Yeah."

"We not only were late to the party, we never made it."

"Oh, we made it all right."

She threw the tube top at me.

While Fiora strapped on four-inch heels and ran a fast brush through her hair, I looked around the parking lot because if I kept looking at Fiora it would be our first date all over again. I had brought along a fresh shirt for the festivities but decided against it. If I'd started undressing right then it wouldn't have been for any damn party. NaVaMoVi would just have to take me in my baggy cotton beach slacks and lived-in shirt.

There were maybe fifty cars in front of the winery. Fiora's BMW fit right into a line that included a couple of Baby Benz sedans, a few more 500 SECs, a husky black Volvo 760, and a gentrified Jeep Wagoneer parked cheek by jowl with a burgundy Corniche. But there were some odd grace notes scattered through the lot: a ten-year-old Chevrolet pickup with a dusty windshield and a camper shell; a sedate, sun-struck Ford Granada that any farmer's wife would have been happy to own, and a 1963 Chevy low-rider with a chromed, chain-link steering wheel and a little doggy with lighted eyes staring blankly through the back window.

The mixture of vehicles was both exotic and pronounced. It was as though the valley were in transition and hadn't decided which way it was going to go—farming or high finance. If I had to bet, I'd go with the money. It has a way of winning over sentiment every time.

"Ready?" Fiora asked.

I gave her a look that made her smile.

"For the party," she added dryly.

Even in high heels, Fiora barely comes up to my shoulder. That's one of the things that has always fascinated me about her—all that steel and intelligence wrapped up in such a small package.

I drew a deep breath of the cool, damp night air, wondering if the day would come when too many people taking deep breaths turned the air sour. From inside the winery came faint sounds of music, a string trio playing something quiet and refined. The sound wasn't loud enough to drown out the gentle rustle of leaves as a breeze curled along the vineyard rows. If I hadn't promised Sandra to be a friendly face, I'd have turned around and walked out with Fiora among the vines.

"We'll put in an appearance," I said, "but we're not going to put the band to bed. I want to take you for a walk through Deep Purple in the moonlight. That's the real valley."

Fiora looked around. "Stucco and chicken wire are real, Fiddler. Moonlight is *not.*"

There's nothing as practical as a Scot with a Harvard MBA.

Behind the heavy, stained glass and oak doors, the evening was in full swing. A hundred people were crowded into the tasting room with its white walls and dark tile floors. A long line of wine sippers stood at the bar, glasses in hand. The rest of the crowd just mingled and chatted and noshed the food that was piled head high on two library-length tables. Fiora's expensively casual dress fit right in among the revelers. The string trio was an off-key touch in the informal ambience. They strolled by in tuxedos, playing two violins and a viola, as sweetly oblivious to the party as the party was to them. Playing Mozart does that to you sometimes.

The interior decor was ersatz Moorish, the sort of thing that was all the rage throughout California fifty years ago. We elbowed our way into the crowd. It felt altogether too familiar, like Century City or Newport Beach. Too many white shoes and too much cigarette smoke. I broke trail to the food tables, figuring Sandra would not be far away.

I snagged a plain, old-fashioned chicken sandwich off a tray and took a bite, despite the fact that I wasn't really hugry. Instantly I knew that was Sandra's work. The bread was yeasty and homemade, with a crust that resisted just enough to enhance the pleasure of chewing. The chicken had been boiled with herbs and chopped with homemade pickles and homemade mayonnaise. It was what a chicken sandwich is supposed to be.

I offered Fiora a bite. She took it more out of courtesy than hunger. As soon as the taste hit, she closed her eyes and made little humming noises.

"Sandra's?" Fiora asked, taking another bite. She barely missed my fingers with her neat little teeth.

"Sandra's," I said.

"I'm glad you're a fool." Fiora looked up at me with clear green eyes and a smile.

"What?"

"Only a fool would let a cook like that slip through his fingers."

I wasn't likely to respond to that line. Despite Fiora's statement, my mama didn't raise an entire idiot.

Fiora smiled at one of the waiters and was presented with two glasses of champagne. The waiter's eyes told her that, for a smile like that, he'd part with more than champagne.

"Trade you," Fiora said to me, holding out a glass.

"For what?"

"More sandwich."

I surrendered the rest of the sandwich and took a glass of champagne. It was an uneven swap. The wine was sweetish and neither terribly pleasant nor terribly unpleasant, kind of like the winery itself. More pretense than substance. After one sip I set the champagne aside. Bad wine is bad any time, but in the Napa Valley there's no excuse for drinking even mediocre wine. Life is entirely too short.

I muscled my way back to the food table. The roast beef sandwiches were on rye with thick slices of tomato and sweet onion. Fiora spotted the onions, pleaded self-defense and ate my sandwich before I could stop her. I was going back for more when I bumped into a stylish, pale-skinned blonde. She was standing with her hands on hips that were just straying into the ample range, surveying the bounty.

I was about to excuse my clumsiness when I realized that she had positioned herself so the collision was inevitable. I excused myself anyway because it seemed like the best way to strike up the conversation she obviously wanted.

The woman gave me a megawatt smile that she must have learned in stewardess school. "Oh, that's all right," she said. "Everybody's really friendly around the valley. But then you're not from the valley, are you?"

"Not really," I said. "I'm from down south."

"I could tell," she said with another glistening smile, "what with the tan and all." She told me what "and all" covered by giving me the kind of look that a breeder gives a potential stud.

I made the mistake of taking her personally for a moment, then realized that it was merely her style. Some women push their good looks at you, defining themselves by the most common of denominators. Not that this was a common woman. She had what I would have to call allure, the same kind of overripe appeal that marks the late-harvest grapes.

I rarely like late-harvest fruit. On the other hand, I was here to get to know people, to howdy and shake until some hints about Sandra's bad luck popped out of the ersatz bonhomie.

"You aren't drinking," the woman said, noticing my empty hands. "Can I get you something or are you that rare bird in this valley, the teetotaler?"

"I didn't care much for the champagne," I said. "And you sure don't look like a waitress."

She smiled sleekly. "Sweet of you to notice," she said, smoothing the fit of her dress over her hips. "I guess it's just my first instinct to make sure everyone is eating and drinking and enjoying themselves. I have a few little restaurants here in the valley. My name is Cynthia Forbes."

A few little restaurants? Like Deep Purple produces a few little grapes. Cynthia Forbes was one of the most familiar names in the Napa Valley. She was featured in *Gourmet* and every other upscale wine and food magazine to elbow its way into the yuppie market in the last five years. The consensus was that Cynthia was chiefly responsible for putting Napa on the culinary leader board with her innovative foods and theatrical presentations. Her biggest restaurant —a high-ticket place with four-star aspirations—had become the foodie mecca of the valley.

"I don't blame you for passing up the champagne," Cynthia added. "It really is rather modest, isn't it? But then so much of what this valley produces is modest. I mean, just look at this table. Extremely, er, modest. A field hand would be right at home. Chicken and beef sandwiches, as though Sandra were cleaning out her refrigerator."

Ah, yes. This must be one of the unfriendly faces Sandra had alluded to. I wondered how deep dear Cynthia's animosity toward Sandra went. One restaurateur would certainly know the best ways to sabotage another.

"What would you have served?" I asked.

She shrugged, making the black silk of her dress tighten across her full breasts. "I would never create food for a party like this without first making a thorough study of a number of factors," she said. "I would have to understand the wines that were to be showcased, the sophistication of the guests, the sensual effect the host was seeking to attain. So many elements have to be aesthetically balanced or the experience simply won't be harmonious."

I knew that I wasn't going to be able to pull off a civilized discussion of food-as-art or food-as-religious-experience with a woman who disdained Sandra's cuisine simply because it wasn't precious or pretentious. So I changed the subject.

"By the way, who is the host?" I asked, picking a neutral topic. "I haven't paid my respects yet."

Cynthia blinked, surprised by the question. "Napa Valley

Mountain Vineyards winery is owned by General Food and Beverage Corporation. I'm not sure who the official host is tonight, perhaps one of the board of directors."

"General Food and Beverage?" I asked, snagging a fresh peach tart off the dessert table. "They're the folks who are working on a permanent cure for hunger, aren't they?"

Cynthia blinked again. Then her eyes focused on a spot beside me. Fiora's hand closed over my fingers as she leaned into me with the familiarity only longtime lovers have.

"Bite?" she murmured, giving me an up-from-under look.

I held out the sweet. She nibbled on equal parts of it and my finger.

"Wonderful," Fiora said huskily, licking up a stray crumb that was wedged between my fingertips and her lips.

From the corner of my eye I watched Cynthia fading into the crowd at flank speed.

"Tacky, love, really tacky," I said. "You made her leave."

"Only because I know you don't like showy blondes," Fiora murmured.

"Really?" I asked, nuzzling her lovely blond hair. "Since when?"

I barely snatched back my hand in time to avoid the same fate as the peach tart.

Fiora and I decided to circulate in hope of spotting Sandra. The tasting room was an old-fashioned showplace—leaded glass windows, Spanish tile floors and glossy dark wood. When it got to making wine rather than selling it, the decor rapidly gave way to stainless steel, concrete and high-impact plastic. The working area was exactly what you would expect from a winery owned by a conglomerate that also marketed decaf freeze-dried coffee, six brands of presweetened breakfast cereal, a popular no-cal cola and a leading contender in the deodorant tampon sweepstakes.

Not that there's anything wrong with those products. It's just that they're not exactly shot through with romance, and I'm as sentimental as Fiora is fiscal.

It took me a minute to orient myself in NaVaMoVi's sterile expanse. Floor-to-ceiling stainless steel fermenting tanks dominated the center of the building. Once I spotted them, I could trace the wine-manufacturing process.

There were no crushing facilities on the premises, which meant that grapes had been harvested mechanically and crushed in the field in a single process. Then the must—juice and skins—had been brought in tanker trucks and pumped into these twelve-thousand-gallon fermenters, seeded with yeast and left to ferment.

From there, the new wine could be transferred around the building through a series of stainless steel and glass pipes with in-line filters and centrifuges. Ultimately, the wine was aged in redwood or oak tanks that were the size of the water tower back in my Montana hometown. Classy wineries usually do their final finishing in oak barrels or, if they are economizing, in thousand-gallon casks. NaVaMoVi had opted for efficiency and the bottom line. The smallest receptacle in the joint was five thousand gallons. So much for finesse. They probably got the barrel-aged flavor into their Chardonnays and Cabernets with a high-speed pump.

"It looks like an Amoco cracking plant," Fiora said. "Whatever happened to those crusty old wine makers you used to rhapsodize about?"

"Damned if I know."

"Let me give you a hint. If they had to compete with this refinery they went bankrupt."

I grunted. Money being used as a weapon irritates me. The more I thought about Sandra and the new high-tech, high-finance Napa Valley, the shorter my temper got.

Fiora looked at a huge vat. "How bad is this stuff?"

"It contains alcohol and you can tell that it was made from grapes, which is a damn sight more than I say for some of the European wines recently."

Fiora nodded. "One of my clients really took a bath in the Italian scandal."

That was the problem with treating wine, or any other food, like an ordinary commodity in the futures game. Some cheapjack Italian vintner had tried to pump up the alcohol content of his bulk table wines with ethylene glycol and had sent the lethal result out on the export market. As soon as the adulteration was discovered, Italian wine sales crashed. You can't give away the stuff.

Frankly, that type of thing sounds more like sabotage than greed to me. Nobody, but nobody, kills off paying customers by adding poison to his own menu. Hell of a way to close down the competition, though.

When American bulk wine makers want to jazz up the mix they add pear slurry and yeast rather than antifreeze. But that doesn't polish the romantic image very well, so you don't hear about it on the wine commercials that feature weddings and harvest celebrations. The backgrounds are shot in vineyards, not orchards, even though the ratio of pear to grape in some bulk wines can damn near reach parity.

After seeing NaVaMoVi's entry into wine making, I understand why the really big boys like Gallo don't offer tours. Bulk wine making is a bit too much like bulk sausage making to be appetizing.

As I put my arm around Fiora's waist and prepared to urge her out of the factory, I finally spotted Sandra. Even at thirty feet I recognized the lustrous brown of her hair and the curving lines of her body. She stood behind the glass window of the automated bottling room, talking to a big man whose back was to me. I walked closer, wondering why Sandra was standing so defensively, her arms crossed over her breasts and her back straight. It was obvious that the only thing keeping her from leaving was her companion's bulk blocking her path.

Sandra had changed very little. Her long, thick hair was still straight, glossy and shoulder length. She still dressed simply and wore little in the way of extras, instinctively knowing that the subtle browns and golds and bronzes of her natural coloring wouldn't marry well with flashy jewelry. The California sun isn't kind to some people but it had been to her, turning her skin the warm color of toast.

Suddenly Sandra's chin came up. She took a step to the side as though to go around the man blocking the doorway. He turned as his hand shot out to hold her in place. As he turned, I recognized him.

Ramsey.

His face wore an impatient, belligerent expression. He was a big man, and he was using his bulk to tower over the woman who had shared his home and his bed. He wasn't being very subtle about the intimidation, either. I could see the white beneath Sandra's tan where his hand was clamped on her arm.

"I'll be right back," I said to Fiora.

I yanked opened the door to the bottling room. "Hello, Ramsey. Seems like old times."

I held out my right hand, giving him a choice. He could take his right hand off Sandra's arm and complete the handshake, or he could be a surly bastard and take the consequences. The look in his eyes told me that he was thinking it over. I smiled. Sandra flinched. Reluctantly, Ramsey let go of her but made no move toward me. Before I could feel hurt that he didn't want to shake my hand, Sandra took two steps and filled my arms with a welcoming hug.

"Fiddler! What a wonderful surprise! I wasn't looking for you until after midnight."

"We made good time."

There was nothing extra in Sandra's hug, just the spontaneous gesture of someone who was glad to see me. Ramsey didn't take it that way, though, so I smiled at him while I hugged Sandra back.

Like I said, Ramsey and I never did get along real well.

When I introduced Fiora to Sandra, there was a lot of speculative feminine interest between them, and a fair amount of frank examination, but also surprising warmth. Surprising because they shared little in common except me. The Earth Mother and the Businesswoman, each confident and self-possessed.

"The woman who made him wealthy," Sandra said, smiling warmly and holding out her arms as though to a sister.

"And the woman who taught him everything he knows about wine and food," replied Fiora, returning the hug. "It's a shame neither of us could housebreak him."

Ouch.

Ramsey made an impatient noise designed to draw attention back to himself. It wasn't an introduction he wanted, though. He stood frowning, his hands on his hips, looking at me as though I were on the opposite side of an unfriendly scrimmage.

"I hope we weren't interrupting anything," I said, lying through my smile.

"You've got it in one, buddy. You're interrupting." Ramsey turned away, giving me a view of his razor-cut hair and chiseled profile. "I'm not going to let you go hide in your kitchen until you give me an answer."

The laughter left Sandra's face as she turned toward her ex-husband. "Nothing has changed," she said.

"Don't be an emotional little fool," he said impatiently. "You know you can't make it by yourself. Your father would have wanted you to—"

"Leave Dad out of this," Sandra said tightly. "He's dead and Deep Purple is mine."

"It should have been *mine,*" retorted Ramsey. "He never got around to changing his will after we were married. You know it and I know it."

Sandra's expression changed from patience to irritation, and I got the distinct feeling of old arguments being rehashed for the umpteenth time. "Leave it alone, Bob. It's done and it can't be changed. For once in your stubborn life, just give up!"

Ramsey simply lowered his head slightly, set his shoulders and kept on coming. "You can't pass up an offer like mine," he said. "It's damned generous, considering. I'm giving you cash and enough stock in Ramsey Wines to make you very wealthy. With a merchandising gimmick like Deep Purple as part of the package, that stock will triple in value overnight, once we go public. Only a silly, vindictive bitch would turn down an offer like that."

I clenched my jaw as I saw the familiar unhappiness cloud Sandra's golden-brown eyes. She looked away from Fiora and me, not wanting to see how we were reacting to the unhappy scene.

"I won't sell," Sandra said quietly.

"Don't be so quick," he retorted. "A few days from now I won't be so generous."

"What does that mean?" asked Sandra, staring at him.

Ramsey gave me a hard look, then focused on Sandra again. "You know just what I mean, baby. You can't keep the lid on unless you get money to refinance. And when that lid comes off, you won't be able to give your land away!"

"This isn't the time to discuss—"

"If they don't like it, they can leave," Ramsey interrupted brusquely. "You've been hiding your head in the sand for months. I want an answer."

Sandra glanced at Fiora and me. "I'm sorry," she said quietly. "Bob's timing never was very good. That's why he's so stubborn."

It was like dropping a match in a fuel dump. Formerly married couples know just where the incendiary spots are.

"God damn it, Sandra, who don't you listen to reason for once instead of being so goddamned bitchy!"

As Ramsey clenched his fists and began to tower over Sandra again, I looked at Fiora and jerked my head toward the door. She took Sandra with her as I turned toward Ramsey.

"Other than that, how have things been?" I asked.

I could see him thinking about how good it would feel to knock me on my ass. I was hoping he'd try. I might not shuffle money worth a damn, but no one ever accused me of not holding up my end of a brawl.

Ramsey disappointed both of us. He set his jaw and his shoulders and stalked out the door. He passed the women without a glance. Sandra watched him go, a sad, angry expression on her face. Then she turned toward us.

"I'm really sorry," she said. "But thanks. He's had me cornered in here for twenty minutes and I was beginning to think he wouldn't let me out before the pastries burned." For a moment a hunted look came to her eyes. "Oh, God, I hope nothing's gone wrong with the food while I was here."

"Everything looked fine and tasted better," I said. "You're still the best cook on seven continents."

She smiled suddenly. "You mean I haven't lost my touch?"

"Better than ever," I said honestly, ignoring Fiora's rather fixed smile.

"Thanks," Sandra said, her voice soft. "You're good for my ego, Fiddler. You always were."

"I've already met Cynthia Forbes and Ramsey," I said, immediately thinking of two people who definitely weren't good for Sandra's ego. "Any other friendly faces here tonight that I should vet?"

Sandra shook her head. "The rest are just drunks, or rapidly becoming so. They don't even know my name." She put her hand on my arm and looked at me earnestly. "Really, Fiddler. The more I think about it, the more I believe I've just had a run of really rotten luck. But it's good to see you just the same. Sometimes it gets a little lonely in the valley."

Before I could say anything, Sandra rushed on.

"I've set up the guesthouse for you two. If you're still awake when I'm finished here, we'll talk. Okay? But I've got to run now or those pastries will be ashes."

She brushed a kiss on my cheek, smiled at Fiora and hurried away.

As I watched Sandra's long-legged retreat, I wondered what had happened to all her friends. She had changed from the warm, laughing Sandra I remembered. Now she looked hunted, like a doe that had been singled out of the herd and was being brought to bay by hungry wolves.

And then I wondered if she knew the secret of Napa Valley that Fiora had alluded to, the one that had brought all the smart, money-shuffling predators to quivering alert.

6

Fiora and I worked the crowd until after midnight and then gave up. Anybody who knew anything interesting wasn't talking. The rest of the people were shouting.

"Come on," I said finally, pulling Fiora after me into the darkness outside. "We've earned a little clean air and silence."

Most of the cars were still in the parking lot, testimony to the lure of free food and wine. The Bimmer started as though it was as eager to be away as we were. I crossed the highway and started down the side road toward Deep Purple. The road's surface was asphalt where once it had been dirt, and I could see a new building rising where once there had been only vineyard rows. The rest was the same, though, the land and the moonlight and the delicate whispering of the vines.

I pulled over and parked the car on the shoulder of the road. Fiora paused only long enough to trade her high heels for canvas scuffs. Hand in hand, we walked between some legendary vines, drinking air as fine as anything ever poured from a bottle.

"I can see why she doesn't want to sell it," Fiora said quietly. "You only get one chance at Eden." Her hair shimmered in the moonlight as she turned toward the unexpected angles of the building that grew among the Cabernet vines. "And one snake. Frankly, from here that doesn't look like two million dollars. It must be gold-plated inside."

The same thought had occurred to me. We walked along the road toward the dark windows of the Vintage Harvest restaurant. Despite Fiora's comment, it was a handsome building. Part of the two million had gone to pay a high-class architect. There was a Victorian flavor to the resultant restaurant, a reminder of the historical continuum that is California. The building recalled some of the fine old grove houses from turn-of-the-century Pasadena. Big bay windows opened into a dining room that had unbounded views of the vineyards and the shaggy hillsides leading up to Sugarloaf Ridge and Spring Mountain.

The restaurant was dark, but at one end, close to where I judged the kitchen to be, I could see a low wall and the orderly rows of a large garden wrapping around the corner of the building. Knowing Sandra, the plants were probably a mix of flowers, vegetables and herbs. Along the front of the restaurant, ghostly white lines showed on random patches of asphalt that comprised a pleasing, free-form parking lot.

"Very nice," Fiora said, calculating the layout with a few trained glances. "But I see why Sandra was upset about two million bucks. I doubt it could seat more than fifty people."

"She once told me that a quality restaurant should never try to feed more than fifty at once."

"Then she must have charged an arm and a leg for her meals," Fiora said. "If she did that, she would have run into customer resistance. No matter how fine the food, people want more than a meal at a hundred bucks a plate. They want to feel part of a select, very elite group of tastemakers. That's why the waiters wear tuxes and the patrons dress to kill. But that isn't a glitter palace," she said, gesturing toward the building. "It isn't even Rodeo Drive casual. It's like Sandra. Honest, open, warm, genuine."

"I'd pay a hundred bucks a plate for that. Hell, I'd pay three times as much."

"But you're notoriously retrograde," Fiora said, smiling up at me. "Downright primitive, in fact."

She reached for me even as I bent down to her, and she gave me a kiss that said this was one of those times when primitive wasn't a dirty word.

Suddenly she stiffened and pulled away. "Fire. There's a fire somewhere."

I opened my mouth to make a smart remark and then saw the lines of fear tightening Fiora's face. I spun toward the restaurant. Where before there had been only darkness and reflected moonlight in the windows, now there was a tiny red glow deep within the building. Before I could take a breath the glow expanded wildly. Streamers of fiery light licked out from beneath what must have been the inner kitchen door.

I dug out the car keys, slapped them into Fiora's hand and started talking fast. "Go back to the winery. Call the Napa County fire department. Use the words 'full structure response.' Tell them there are flames showing inside the kitchen area of the Vintage Harvest restaurant."

Fiora grabbed my arm as I turned toward the restaurant. There was steel in her fingers, the kind of strength that only comes from fear.

"Don't go in there."

It was so unlike Fiora that I stopped dead. "There's bound to be a hose for the garden along the back of the building," I explained. "I've got to try to—"

"No!" she said sharply. Then she closed her eyes. Her face was strained. "Last week I saw you running into a fire. *I didn't see you running out.*"

Fiora opened her eyes and I saw the residue of her fey nightmare. But I had no choice. A garden hose now could make the difference between saving and losing the building. I knew it. So did she.

Fiora turned and ran toward the car.

Before I found the hose at the side of the building, the BMW's engine revved hard and the tires barked as they bit into the asphalt. Fiora acclerated fast, hit second like a professional rally driver and was gone. As I turned on the water, I heard her hit the horn all the way up the winery's drive. In the silky night the sound was alien, shattering.

I spun the handle of the faucet wide open, turned the hose nozzle shut to hold in water, grabbed up the neat coils and began paying them out behind me as I rounded the corner of the building, heading for where the back door ought to be.

The smell of petroleum distillates hit me in a choking curtain that seemed almost visible in the mild Napa midnight. A shadow was crouched in the back doorway, outlined by a guttering, sullen glow. There was just enough light for me to see that the man wore a ski mask.

He must have thought he would have the place to himself again once the BMW had pulled away, because he was hunkered down with a highway flare in one hand and a striker cap in the other. I realized that what I had seen through the front windows was the cherry glow of the first flare he tossed. Its incandescent red light now glared back through the doorway, outlining him.

There was no cover except for the knee-high garden wall. If I took the time to eel up on him behind that, he would have the second flare lit, tossed, and Sandra's restaurant would be history. So I dropped the hose and headed for him at a run.

As I ran, I bellered like a kung fu amateur. Surprise was the only weapon I had.

The bastard in the ski mask had good peripheral vision, better reactions and the balls of a burglar. Instead of bolting, he spun around toward me, reaching for his belt with his right hand. I've seen the motion often enough that my reaction is pure reflex. I ducked and rolled into the kitchen garden, cursing the pistol that was hidden in my duffel bag in the trunk of the car.

The torch artist had a sizable weapon, maybe a .45. It went off like a howitzer and the muzzle flash was as long as my forearm. I kept rolling until I fetched up against the side of a trash dumpster. It offered a hell of a lot more cover than the two rows of sweet basil I'd just rolled through.

The guy had guts. When I didn't return his second shot, he quickly figured out that I was unarmed. I chanced a low look around the corner of the dumpster in time to see him shove the pistol back in his belt. Free to concentrate on his primary business again, he scraped the striker cap once more across the open end of the highway flare. There was a sharp little "pop." The flare blossomed into fierce red light, giving me a good look at the ski mask before he tossed the flare through the door and into the restaurant.

Then the torch artist calmly pulled out his gun again, flicked two more shots in my direction to make sure I stayed put, and took off. He sprinted across a piece of the parking lot and ran down between two rows of Deep Purple Cabernet vines. I could see his head, but all features were blurred by the ski mask. He must have realized that he was still in sight, because he suddenly crouched as he ran.

That was the last I saw of him. I could have chased him but, unarmed as I was, it would have been rather like hunting rattlesnakes with your eyes closed; success would be a mixed blessing, at best.

Three seconds after the arsonist disappeared I was at the back door. There was a steady red glow, but nothing overwhelming. I could still make a difference, even with a garden hose. I grabbed the hose and dragged it to the back door of the restaurant.

Once I was inside, the raw smell of kerosene almost floored me. Not surprising. The torch artist had splashed at least two gallons of kerosene around the interior. In the flare's red light, one of the gallon cans was upright but the other was on its side, a pool of liquid spreading from its open mouth toward the flare that had been tossed inside. The throw had been short by a few feet because I had distracted the bastard, but the kerosene was moving to correct his error even as I watched.

Off to the left there was a flicker of genuine flames in what looked like a kitchen storeroom. He had set that fire first, and it was burning hard. Had Fiora and I been thirty seconds later, he would have had the second fire launched and unstoppable. As it was, in a few seconds it was going to be unstoppable anyway.

The storeroom fire would have to wait. If the second flare touched the puddle of kerosene in the main room, the whole place would go up within seconds. Water was useless against the flare. I dropped the hose, ducked out for three quick, hard breaths of relatively fresh air and stepped back inside, thanking God that the arsonist had been a professional. Kerosene was the pro's choice for a fire accelerant. An amateur would have used gasoline. Gas fumes would have exploded by now in the enclosed restaurant, blowing everything to hell, and likely the amateur firebug with it.

A few steps inside the kitchen, the kerosene fumes became mixed with the sulfurous fumes of the burning highway flare. It was enough to gag a skunk. I did a short broken-field run across the room, leaping some puddles of kerosene and sidestepping others until I could grab the flare. I made the return trip in record time and launched the flare into the night with a hard sideways throw.

As I bent over and took in great gulps of air, I heard the sudden shrill revving of a small two-cycle engine in the distance. The sound came from across the vineyard in the direction the arsonist had fled. I listened to the engine for a few more seconds, trying to get a fix on its location. The sound accelerated, slowed, then accelerated again through three forward gears. Probably a light motorcycle running blind, no head- or taillight, because no light showed anywhere in that direction.

As I turned back toward the restaurant the faint keening of a siren began somewhere up the valley. Too faint, too far. They wouldn't get here in time to keep the storeroom fire from reaching the puddles of kerosene on the kitchen floor. I'd have to make a run at holding down the storeroom fire before it spread too far.

I ducked back into the resturant, picked up the hose and started for the storeroom. The fire had only been burning a few minutes, but heat was already leaping out through the open door. Flames licked at the door casement and generated oily clouds of black smoke poisoned with burning paint and insulation. I twisted the hose's brass nozzle and was rewarded with a hard stream of water. It hit the burning wood and killed one tongue of flame, but the moment I shifted the stream to a new spot the original flames leaped back to life.

Smoke came down from the ceiling like a Bay Area fog, only this fog was choking, nauseating, potentially lethal. I dropped to one knee, seeking cleaner air. The hose wasn't getting the job done. My only chance was to choke the fire the same way it was choking me, by cutting off its oxygen supply.

As I crawled toward the crackling, hissing flames, I twisted the little brass nozzle on the hose. The stream of water changed from a hard flow to a wide, cool circle, like a silver flower blooming on the end of a hollow rubber stem. Using the fragile blossom as a shield, I crept closer to the open storeroom door. The water helped, but I could feel the vicious heat on my face before I got close enough to touch the door. The cotton shirt on my chest was no protection. It caught the heat, held it and sucked moisture out of my skin. Too damned hot.

I backed off and turned the hose on myself. The siren was closer now, but not close enough by miles to do me or the restaurant any good. As I soaked my clothes I looked around for a way to get the door closed without cooking myself in the process. The only reason I persisted was that the storeroom door opened toward me rather than back into the storeroom itself. It would be so damned easy to slow down the fire by kicking the door shut—if I could just get close enough.

It took me a couple of seconds to spot the industrial mop leaning against the wall. I grabbed the long-handled mop, tore off my dripping shirt and threw it over my head to cover my all too flammable hair. Seeing through the thin cloth was no problem. The fire was burning with frightening brilliance.

Breathing through the wet shirt helped. This time I got to within five feet of the storeroom door behind the tenuous, cool curtain of water from the hose. It was almost close enough. I dropped all the way to the floor, bellied in and shoved the mop toward the open storeroom door.

As though in a dream I heard Fiora's voice behind me. She was screaming my name. I hollered that I was all right. At least I think I did. I know I wanted to. Things were getting a little furry around the edges. Lack of oxygen will do that to you.

I slid another body's length forward. By now the heat was so intense that the water was turning into steam. My face wasn't blistered beneath the shirt yet, but I couldn't stand the heat much longer. It seemed like an eternity before the mop handle connected with the door. Thank God the hinges still worked. One good stab and the door swung inward through three quarters of its arc, cutting into the flames.

Suddenly it was darker, cooler. Water stopped turning to steam. I threw the mop like a lance, slamming the door shut. The kitchen was still full of smoke, but the flames were reduced by half. The door wouldn't last more than a few minutes. While it held, though, it would throttle the fire behind it.

I knew how the fire felt. Not breathing was getting to me, too, but breathing seemed even worse. And I was tired. It took a lot of willpower not to just lie full length on the kerosene-soaked floor and celebrate my victory over the door with a little nap. The primitive part of my mind jumped up and down and shouted at me that resting right now was a really dumb idea, so I turned around and began crawling out. I couldn't see the back door, but I could hear it. It was screaming my name.

About the time I figured out that doors didn't talk, I felt two narrow steel bands clamp around my left bicep and yank upward. It was all the leverage I needed to stagger to my feet. Within seconds, cool, rich air hit me like a freight train. As my head cleared I realized that Fiora was holding onto me, aiming me away from the restaurant.

"Your dream was wrong," I rasped. "I got out of the fire."

Then I went down on my hands and knees and tried to cough

up the fiery little animal that was clawing my throat. I didn't get him, but I did get everything I'd eaten for the last week.

A fire truck came down the restaurant road, lights flashing and engine howling. I was too sandbagged to do more than watch as the truck pulled up ten feet away and men began pouring out, dragging a big hose behind. The firemen were all husky young fullback types in yellow Nomex turnout gear, helmets and breathing apparatus. As I watched, the hose came to life in their hands, writhing and bucking like a hungry python.

One of the firemen came over with a medical kit and gave me a quick exam. Once he saw that I was still breathing on my own, he gave me a few hits from a breathing mask that put the world back into focus. Pure oxygen. Nothing beats it when you're suffocating.

"You see what the problem was?" he asked, removing the mask when I nodded.

"Kerosene. Flares," I said.

I'd heard more musical sounds out of an steel file than out of my throat, but the fireman got the drift. He said something that sounded like "Son of a bitch," shoved the mask against my face again and shouted a warning to the men going inside.

The big hose had a fogger nozzle. It blossomed suddenly, filling the night with a shining mist. The two firemen wrestling the hose charged into the restaurant, fighting the hose every inch of the way. I didn't envy them a bit.

"Storeroom's burning like hell," I said. "I got the door shut, but—" I started coughing and he slapped the mask over my face again.

My mouth tasted like I'd been sucking on a kerosene-soaked sock. There was an odd, underlying sweetness to the aftertaste, like a late-harvest Riesling.

"Finished with him?" asked a cool, feminine voice.

The fireman glanced up at Fiora. "For now. We'll have more questions after the fire is under control."

Without a word Fiora took over feeding me the oxygen. I was quite capable of holding the mask in place myself. I was also quite capable of enjoying the feel of her small hand bracing the back of my head.

The fireman adjusted the oxygen mix before he jogged off to join his comrades. Over the mask I watched black, dense smoke boil out the back door of the restaurant. Black smoke meant the fire was still vital, still alive, still dangerous. The good news was that the volume of smoke hadn't increased. The heavy diesel fire engine was running at high idle, pushing water through the pump and hoses.

A second rig pulled in beside the first, laying hose from a hydrant at the corner of the parking lot. Two firemen patched together a hose network that assured a steady supply of water for the two hose lines that were now inside.

One of the firemen trotted over, flashed a light in my eyes and fiddled with the regulator on the oxygen unit. "How ya feeling now?" he asked.

"Like I've been drinking kerosene."

His teeth flashed whitely. "Officially, you're a bad boy for taking on hell with a garden hose. Unofficially, you're a hero."

I smiled. Fiora muttered something unflattering about all males in general and me in particular.

"Need anything?" asked the fireman, ignoring Fiora after a sidelong, admiring glance. He had a name, Dunston, stenciled above the pocket of his turnout coat.

"I'm okay," I said. "But someone better call the cops."

"Jim Jacoby's on the way," Dunston said. "He's our fire marshal. Cap'n called him right after he spotted the kerosene cans. Jim'll want to talk to you."

I nodded. I didn't want to mention anything else with Fiora right next to me, but there was no choice. "Better tell somebody to look for shell casings around the back door of the restaurant."

"Say again?"

"Shell casings. Brass. Probably from a .45 auto. Some guy in a ski mask took a couple of shots at me."

The fireman gave me a startled look. Fiora's hand tightened almost painfully on the back of my head.

"Shit, this was really your lucky night, wasn't it?" he asked.

The fireman stood up just as I heard Sandra's voice say, "Oh, my God, Fiora. I thought you were mistaken about the shots."

Fiora said nothing. She gave the mask back to me, stood, and walked away a few steps before she stopped with her back toward me. I knew she was both frightened and furious. I wanted to get up and go to her but my legs wouldn't cooperate. Sandra dropped down and put her hands on my shoulders.

"Stay put," she ordered as she bent over and gave me a hug. "I would have stopped you if I could have, but thanks for saving my restaurant. Even though it might have been better if the damned thing had burned to the ground," she added, glaring over my shoulder at the big, handsome building with disgust.

Sweet, uncomplicated Sandra. Never an unspoken thought. I swore silently when I caught the sideways, assessing look Dunston suddenly gave her.

"You own this place?" he asked.

"For better or for worse," she said, sighing.

Then she realized that she was the one person in the world with something to gain from the destruction of the building. Insurance fraud is the number one cause of fires in the United States.

"I didn't mean that," she said quickly. "I was just kidding about wanting the place to burn." She turned to me. "Tell him, Fiddler."

I took her arm. "It's okay, Sandra. Nobody's accusing you of anything. I sure as hell know it wasn't you who took the shots at me. So does Fiora."

Immediately Sandra looked relieved. Uncomplicated, transparent, one of the last innocents God made before He gave up innocence as a bad risk. It didn't occur to Sandra that there were restaurant owners in the world who would have hired some Louie the Torch out of San Francisco or Fresno and then arranged an alibi party for two hundred witnesses.

It didn't occur to Sandra, but it sure as hell would occur to the arson investigator.

The chance of catching the arsonist and squeezing the truth out of him was about as good as putting out the fire by pissing on it. The man hadn't been an amateur. He had just been unlucky that Fiora and I happened along when we did. He'd pinned me down with gunfire, calmly lit the second flare and tossed it into the fire. Only then had he run. A pro all the way.

I tried breathing without the mask, coughed, and went back to sucking up a richer mix. The gawkers circled closer like great, thick, earthbound moths. In the reflected fire glow Sandra's face looked both worried and resigned. A smudge of dark soot marked her forehead. I reached out and rubbed it away. She turned back toward me and smiled that warm, generous, comfortable smile of hers.

There was a brush of warmth at my side, then Fiora's slim hand took the mask again. As she knelt beside me, I could see her eyes. They were saying, *Fiscal rather than physical, huh?*

It wasn't the first time I had broken that particular promise to Fiora, but the fear and sadness beneath her anger made it one of the worst.

7

After a few moments of silence Fiora took a deep breath and let it sigh out. Her nose wrinkled at the odor of kerosene and sweat.

"You stink," she said.

"Yeah. I smell bad, too."

Fiora almost smiled and she almost cried. I snaked an arm around her and pulled her into my lap before she could get away. For a moment she was rigid in my arms. I could feel the fine trembling of her body and knew that it was the aftermath of both anger and fear. Finally she reached out with one arm, hooked it around my neck and drew herself closer to me. She may be small, but she's a fierce, strong woman.

She replaced the mask on my face and sat quietly, leaning against me, stroking my hair slowly with her free hand.

"It's just that you're always the one who's around when things go wrong," she said after a long silence. "The one who will risk it all for strangers or friends or the sheer hell of it, or even for your foolish ex-wife. . . ."

Fiora hesitated, then touched the back of my hands. There are circular scars there. I got them one night in the mountains between Palo Alto and Santa Cruz. A Russian spy called Volker had tried to kill both Fiora and me. He was her lover at the time and one of the most charming men I've ever met. One of the coldest, too. I came as close to dying that night as I ever have. Fiora knew it too. She had told me later that she realized that night how much she loved me—and how much she was afraid of loving me and losing me.

Her fear was an old one, probably the oldest we humans have. Pain. We have an intricate network of nerves whose sole function is to deliver pain in sufficient quantities that, as long as the memory lasts, we avoid similar situations. The more pain, the more deeply entrenched the memory. If a dog bites you, you're afraid of dogs.

The bigger the bite, the greater the fear. It's called learning. Without it, survival wouldn't be possible.

My learning scars are on the surface. Fiora's aren't. I hadn't been good enough to save Fiora's twin brother from dying of his own blithe stupidity. His death had torn her apart in ways that I still don't understand, because she had been connected to her twin in ways I can't comprehend. She knew when he was unhappy, when he was afraid, and ultimately she felt him die. She had loved him and she had lost him irrevocably to death.

The night I almost died Fiora realized that she was connected to me in the same way; and that I, too, could die.

At some irrational level, she sometimes seems convinced that I get myself into trouble just to make her life hell. I don't. It's just that there is something primal and satisfying about the kind of experience I had just gone through with the fire. The simple, savage truth is that, the closer you dance to death, the more alive you feel if you survive. Adrenaline is the world's oldest addiction.

There's another side of it, too, a more civilized side. Most men have jobs or families or the sheer necessity of earning a living to make them feel useful. I have none of those things. I threw the violin away before I was old enough to understand the difference between satisfaction and perfection. Even if I wanted to go back to music, it was too late now. When Volker slammed down the lid of the packing crate, the nails broke bones and ripped tendons. I can fight or shoot a pistol or make love to a woman, but the truly fine control that I once had of my fingers is gone.

So I work with what remains, and what remains is a talent and a taste for helping people out of some of the deep holes life can drop you into without warning. Unfortunately, there's always the risk that I'll be buried in the same hole as the poor soul I'm trying to help. Fiora has none of the satisfactions of my job and all of the fears.

I turned aside from the oxygen mask and took a deep breath. This time I didn't feel as though I were trying to breathe vacuum. I took another breath and got a whiff of the smoke that clung to Fiora's hair. Suddenly I remembered the small, surprisingly strong hands that had helped me to my feet and steered me out of the smoke.

"Fiora?"

She made a small sound of contentment.

"What the hell are you jumping on me for? I didn't notice you standing around waiting for the proper authorities to drag me out of the fire."

There was a long pause. Finally she leaned even closer to me. I could feel the soft, intimate weight of her breasts against my arm. They seemed alive, inviting, and her breath whispered warmly on my ear.

"Fuck you, Fiddler."

"Think we have time?"

This time Fiora laughed, but her eyes still shone with unshed tears. We held each other for a few more minutes and then it was time for me to try out my legs. She walked close to me without getting in the way. It's another talent that she has, a rare talent in women or men.

Sandra was talking to someone whose back was to me. In the shadows of one of the parking-lot trees he looked slight, like a teen-ager, only a few inches taller than Sandra, slender, attentive. When we approached he turned quickly, instinctively. He looked at us and I realized that he was no youth. Perhaps thirty-five, the man was a Mexican with a deceptively lean build. I say deceptive because his bones were long, hefty and covered with unobtrusive muscle. He was one hell of a lot stronger than he looked. He had a striking face that was Aztec rather than Spanish, handsome as sin and every bit as hard. He wore the rough clothes of a field hand. They looked better on his work-toughened body than Bulldog Ramsey's hundred-dollar silk shirt had looked on him.

The man continued to talk to Sandra, but he kept watching us. He had a strong, hawklike nose and startlingly clear, dark eyes that were intelligent and watchful. Very watchful. He kept turning slightly as we approached, as though he were a man who had made a lifetime habit of not letting people approach him from behind.

Sandra looked past the man's shoulder, saw me and touched his sleeve as though to silence him or to apologize for cutting him off in mid-word. She started toward us, only to be enveloped by Cynthia Forbes.

"Oh, I'm so sorry!" Cynthia said, hugging Sandra without actually touching her. It's a technique learned in Hollywood; bend at the waist and touch cheeks. "After all the terrible luck you've had, and now this! It's just too awful!" She straightened and smiled. "Oh well,

I'm sure the insurance money will come in handy, but what are you ever going to do about Vern's party? It's only two days away. You'll simply have to use my Nouveau Printemps kitchens, but it's such a long drive down the mountain that all your food will be cold by the time you get to Vern's, won't it? Or are you serving leftovers—er, sandwiches—again?"

I felt Fiora tense beside me. If Cynthia had been shoveling that kind of "sympathy" in Fiora's direction it would have come right back at the speed of sound.

Sandra disentangled herself and stepped back. "I wouldn't know about leftovers," she said coolly. "You're the expert on them. Beltrán was just suggesting a barbecue."

Cynthia's smile slipped, telling me she understood Sandra's remark about "leftovers" in a very personal light. "A barbecue," she said in a carrying voice. "How like you. The common touch. But, dear, I don't think there's enough blue corn in the whole state for that many tortillas, and anything else is just Mexican food. I suppose you could dye your dough," she added thoughtfully. Suddenly she slapped her hand over her mouth, only to remove it an instant later. "Don't worry, dear, I won't tell a soul."

Someone on the far side of the crowd started calling for Sandra Autry, so I didn't hear what she said to Cynthia in return. All I saw was the thousand-watt smile that Cynthia flashed in our direction before she swung her hips in a beautifully timed exit from stage center.

"Now I understand why animals eat their young," Fiora said distinctly.

There were other mutterings around us, but the glances that followed Sandra were more speculative than sympathetic. Cynthia may or may not have been the best cook in the Western tier, but she was surely the best known. She was the reigning queen of presentation.

She wasn't bad in the back-stabbing department, either.

From the corner of my eye I caught a pale flash of movement. I turned and saw Beltrán, the watchful Mexican. He had stepped out of the shadows as though to go after Sandra and then must have changed his mind. He sensed me watching him, turned his head just enough to see who I was and nodded once to me before he turned and walked back into the vineyard rows. Within seconds he had disappeared.

It occurred to me that Beltrán wasn't the first man tonight to use the vineyard pathways. If anyone had asked, I would have said the arsonist striking flares was taller than Beltrán's five feet nine, but I wouldn't have sworn to it in court. Depth perception requires color vision. Moonlight is black and white only. I had never seen the man standing against anything that would have allowed me to nail his height within a five percent error either way. When he wasn't squatting in the doorway or shooting at me, he was crouched and running.

If you're talking six feet, a five percent error is plus or minus almost four inches on either side. Most of the men gathered around the fire were comfortably within that margin of error. Put another way, the arsonist hadn't been a dwarf or a giant, and he was neither potbellied nor skeletal.

On the other hand, there's nothing to lose in taking a good look and comparing what I saw with my memories. Fiora and I stood on the fringes of the crowd, watching as the county firemen began their cleanup. One fireman used a huge squeegee to push the inch-deep water from the Vintage Harvest's kitchen door. Several big fans were sucking the rank air from the dining room. Sandra's restaurant was still standing, but it was a shambles.

There's no surgical way to fight a fire. The smoke and water damage would be in the thousands, perhaps hundreds of thousands, of dollars. At the very least, Sandra was going to have a hell of a time convincing her insurance company that she hadn't hired some lowlife to cremate the remains of her dead restaurant.

I wondered when the fire marshal would be through with her and when he would start in on me. It was going to be a long night.

The crowd was slowly thinning as people realized that the fire was out, the fun was over, and more free wine awaited down the road. The flashing red lights and powerful white work lights of the firemen picked out faces at random. I spotted Ramsey talking to Cynthia. She was gesturing gracefully and speaking quickly, but it was a wasted effort. Ramsey never got his eyes above her collarbone. When he put his hand on her hip as though to test the finish of the silk dress, Cynthia smiled. They were very comfortable with each other physically. Lovers, no doubt, if the word "love" can be applied to someone as calculating as Cynthia Forbes.

"Bon appétit," I muttered.

"What?" Fiora asked. She followed my glance. "Makes you believe in God's wondrous plan, doesn't it?"

"It does?"

"Yeah. A bitch for every son of a bitch."

There was a stir as the crowd parted to let through a fireman dragging a hose from the restaurant. When the spectators shifted around again, one man stood slightly apart from the others. He was short, five feet eight, and slender but without a hint of Beltrán's lean power. This man was light-haired. He looked perhaps twenty-seven, was dressed casually in a soft-shouldered linen sport jacket and stylishly pleated slacks. As he shifted slightly, his face was flooded by harsh light. He watched the wrecked restaurant with an expression of pure pleasure.

It made me wonder if maybe I had been wrong about the arsonist's professionalism. Maybe Sandra's restaurant had been burned down by a psycho. Firebugs are the one class of crooks that nearly always return to the scene of the crime. They get off watching the fire and the spurting hoses.

"Someone's calling you," Fiora said.

"Wait."

I turned back in time to see the light-haired man step into the darkness beyond the fire truck. He was gone. No one followed him into the parking lot. He got into a white Volkswagen cabriolet, started up and drove away, jacklighting various gawkers as he turned and headed down the road.

What had Sandra done to him that he enjoyed her misfortune so much?

"Your name Fiddler?"

The voice was roughened by too many cigarettes or too many fires. Probably both. A lot of firemen smoke.

I nodded.

"Fire marshal wants you. You too, ma'am, if you're the one that turned in the alarm."

Silently I led Fiora over to do her civic duty. Silently she gave me a look that told me it was all my fault. I didn't argue. I knew that the fun had just begun.

8

Someone's knuckles whacked the front door with the kind of authority that's taught at the police academy. I knew before I pried my eyelids open that this would not be the way I wanted to start my day. I let the knuckles bruise the wood again before I hauled myself out of bed. On the way to the front, I grabbed the towel I had used after my shower last night. By the time I opened the door I was no longer at risk of being arrested for indecent exposure.

There were two of them standing in the brilliant sunshine. Only one of them mattered. He was the cop in the neatly pressed blue jeans. He was six-three and had the build of an aging linebacker. No gut, just a general impression that gravity was winning the tug-of-war between youth and age. He sucked on a mentholated, low-tar cigarette that was fighting on gravity's side. His eyes were the color and warmth of blue marbles.

The other man was very medium. Medium dark, medium age, medium everything including weight, height and intelligence. I had met him last night. Jim Jacoby, the fire marshal. I had known instantly that he wasn't a cop. His eyes were compassionate.

"Sorry to wake you, sir," Jacoby said, "but Deptuty Fleming and I would like to talk to you for a few minutes, if you don't mind. I'd like to go over what you told us last night."

I looked at the cop. Fleming's eyes said that he wasn't sorry to wake me. They also said that I had to speak to him whether I minded or not. I squinted into the bright sunshine and guessed it was about nine. I shrugged.

"I'll be out as soon as I change," I said, and closed the door.

Deputy Fleming gave me the distinct impression that he wanted to come in and watch, just to make sure I didn't split out the back window and start setting more fires. I didn't take his attitude personally. Hostility is reflexive in a certain kind of cop—any kind that survives the first ten years.

I pulled on a jockstrap, a pair of running shorts and a T-shirt. I'm a surly bastard in the morning. When Fiora's around I try to brighten my act, but she was already up and had been since seven. That was when she had kissed me and slid out of bed, ready to climb Mount Everest or slay dragons, whichever fate offered first. Not me. At seven o'clock I couldn't move.

I rooted a pair of running shoes and some socks out of my duffel bag, opened the front door and stepped out into the hard white sunshine. The two investigators were holding up their car, a black and white Bronco with with four-wheel drive and the county's seal of approval painted on the side. As I shambled across the sun-struck yard, Sandra and Fiora came out the kitchen door of the main house.

Sandra called the three of us over to the flagstone patio, where the shade from a couple of mammoth old oaks took the curse off the valley's summer sun. She laid out plates, pots of jam and a loaf of fresh bread. My salivary glands stirred. Sandra's homemade bread is special.

Fiora carried a pitcher of orange juice and a pot of coffee I could smell from fifteen feet away. The temptation to eat was nearly overwhelming but I had a lot of smoke to clear out of my system and only a run would do it. I drank a small glass of orange juice and ate the heel from the loaf of bread. It was still warm from the oven and smelled as yeasty as a good champagne.

Jacoby was both delighted and very polite in his thanks for the food. He took some of everything including the homemade peanut butter. Fleming took coffee, black, and said nothing.

"That was quite an experience you had last night," Jacoby said, swallowing bread. "Tell us about it again, will you?"

Fleming looked bored. He hadn't been on the scene last night, but his whole attitude said that he'd heard it all before. He probably had. I knew I had. I took a deep breath and began to tell Jacoby exactly what I'd told him last night, when Fleming cut me off.

"If the ladies will excuse us," Fleming said to Fiora and Sandra. Then, as an afterthought, he added, "Please."

The words were polite enough, but Fleming's tone was as cold and suspicious as his eyes. Sandra looked confused for a moment. Fiora didn't. She disliked overbearing men, because in the world of high finance she had to deal with so many of them. She opened her mouth to take a strip off Fleming's thick hide, but she glanced at me first. I gave her a small shake of the head. She didn't like it, but she took it. Cops were my field of expertise, not hers, and she was more than pragmatic enough to take my advice in the matter. Without a word or a backward look, she took Sandra by the arm and returned to the house.

I looked at Fleming. "Feeling better?"

Jacoby stepped in hastily. "It's policy to—"

"—question witnesses one at a time and not in the presence of the major suspect," I finished, bending over in my chair to pull on a sock. "So you really think Sandra torched her own place?"

"Well," Jacoby said delicately, "I don't know if I'd put it that way."

"How would you put it, then? Maybe you'd better read me the Miranda warning," I said. "Sandra and I have been good friends for a long time."

Fleming blew smoke at me. "Yeah. We know."

He was beginning to irritate me. If he knew all that much about Sandra, then he knew he was being a prick for no better reason than to exercise his tough-guy image. Sandra is the kind who takes her losses, licks her wounds and gets on with life. She isn't the type to burn down her mistakes for the insurance money. Fleming should know that, if he knew anything at all about her. But he wasn't thinking. He was reacting. Napa County has about a hundred thousand residents; not too many by big-city standards but more than enough to sour a man on the prospects of perfecting the human race.

I turned to Jacoby. "This is what happened last night."

I went over it slow and thorough, giving him plenty of time to take notes or scratch his ear or any other little thing that appealed to him. I didn't hold anything back. Jacoby made a few notes along the way and asked a few questions. Fleming drank his coffee and watched a red-tailed hawk circling a few hundred feet above the vineyard.

Don't get the impression that Fleming wasn't listening. He was. When I finished, he took a sip of his coffee.

"You a cop?" he asked.

"Why?"

"You're pretty thorough and you know the right words," he said. "Or else you're making it all up," he added as an afterthought.

"I was a cop for a while," I said, "as well as a reporter."

"That's no big recommendation," he said, crushing the cigarette butt beneath his big heel.

"If you don't believe me, go check the physical evidence," I suggested.

He didn't like my attitude. No surprise. It was mutual. He studied me with his blue marbles, then fished around behind the pack of cigarettes in the pocket of his plain, pearl-button cowboy shirt. He came out with a little plastic bag that contained two spent brass cartridge cases. In his big hands they looked like .22s but I had been right. They were .45s.

"Gas cans and what was left of the flares are at the lab now. Know something, Slick? We ain't exactly stupid, even if we do live in the country," Fleming said.

"Doubt we'll get anything from them, though," Jacoby said quickly, trying to head off a confrontation. "Whoever set the fire was pretty careful."

"Why do you say that? Because of the kerosene?" I asked, ignoring Fleming.

Before Jacoby could answer, Fleming shook his head once, emphatically. "Every farmer in the valley uses kerosene to burn his prunings," he said scornfully. "That doesn't tell us shit."

"What about the motorcycle I heard? You find any sign of it?" I asked, still concentrating on Jacoby.

Jacoby looked at Fleming, taking his cue. Jacoby was a nice enough guy, but Fleming was the man with the pistol on his belt and the handcuffs in the back pocket of his jeans.

Fleming shrugged and said nothing. He wasn't going to discuss an investigation with somebody who was at best a witness and at worst a suspect.

Jacoby cleared his throat. "That would be a real long shot. There are a lot of motorcycles in Napa Valley. They go up and down these vineyard roads all the time. No way of telling one track from another, much less when the track was made. Besides, that part of Deep Purple is mostly sand. It won't take tracks."

I shrugged and let it pass, even though I thought it bad form to ignore any kind of investigative lead, no matter how long a shot.

Fleming wasn't interested in my advice and Jacoby wouldn't buck Fleming.

There was a long pause while Jacoby reviewed his notes. In the silence I could hear the hawk that Fleming was watching. The bird's call was a faint, sharp *scree,* lonely and remote in the still morning air. I watched the bird turn and soar in a rising thermal. Sunlight brought out the russet fire of the hawk's tail feathers. Off farther to the east I saw a brightly colored hot-air balloon lifting on the same thermals. The three passengers in the balloon were clearly visible, taking their $125-an-hour flight above the dusty green vineyards. The thought of floating with the hawk intrigued me.

Jacoby snapped his notebook shut and glanced at Fleming, who set down his coffee cup and shrugged. It was Fleming's way of announcing that the interview was over. Jacoby stuck out his hand and apologized again for waking me. Fleming gave me a long look, as though memorizing my face so he could compare it with the "Wanted" posters back at the office. He nodded slightly and strode off toward the Bronco. Jacoby followed, working hard to keep up with Fleming's long legs.

With rising impatience I watched the Bronco leave. Despite the heat of the sun, I was looking forward to running this morning. I needed it. The long drive, the fire and the rude cop had left me with too much pent energy and no civilized way to let it out. I began stretching the long muscles of my legs, trying to loosen them before I ran.

While I stretched, Fiora came out of the house and walked toward me in pink shorts and a white cotton top. She looked surprisingly rested after only a few hours of sleep.

"What did Country Joe and the Cold Fish have to say?" she asked.

"About what you'd expect."

"They think Sandra hired somebody to burn her place, don't they?"

I switched legs on the table and began slowly stretching again. "The primary suspect in the restaurant fire is always the owner," I said. "Tell Sandra not to take it too personally. They're just doing a job."

"I got the impression the cowboy really likes playing sheriff," Fiora said, snagging a slice of the fresh bread and smearing it with ruby-colored jelly. "You're going to have to put a lock on the breadbox or I'll end up doing commercials for Goodyear."

"They'll have to paint you gold. Silver isn't your color."

It was a good thing I had finished stretching. I only avoided a jelly facial by outrunning her. When I looked back she was standing in the hot sun, laughing.

The first half mile of the run was on blacktop that absorbed sunlight like a huge sponge and squeezed it back into the air, distorting everything behind a shimmering veil of heat. There was just enough breeze to stir the leaves on the grapevines. They rustled softly, like children whispering among themselves.

Off across the flat valley floor, men and machines were at work. The Chardonnay and Pinot Noir harvest was under way. Crews had been at work picking since dawn. Tractors towed gondolas full of the frosted yellow-gold Chardonnay clusters and the darker red-black Pinots. The harvesting was a reminder of Sandra's vulnerability. Now, with the restaurant out of commission, the fragile, ripening grapes in her vineyard were all that stood between her and ruin.

The blacktop ended at a windbreak of mixed evergreens and sycamores whose roots were buried in the bank of a small stream. I turned and ran along the windbreak for a half mile, my shoes raising small puffs of dust in the dirt path. The shade from the trees was cool and the sweat streaking my body felt good as it evaporated. A pair of ebony crows dropped out of the trees beside the road, then veered wildly aside and screamed at me as I approached.

I was running the perimeter of Deep Purple. The vines beside me were Cabernet Sauvignon, their grapes already starting to acquire the blackness of ripe fruit. The berries were small, nothing like that fat Thompsons or Red Flames you see in the supermarket. These were wine grapes, bred and grown for flavor rather than size or texture.

A cloud of starlings had been feasting on the early fruit. They rose up as I approached, crying their anger at being run off from the dark bounty. I jogged beside the vines the birds had been savaging and snatched a single small bunch of grapes as I ran. Juice trickled down my arm as I lifted the bunch to my mouth. The liquid was warm and astringent. The fruit was just beginning to acquire its ultimate sweetness. I crunched a few more grapes in my mouth to cleanse my palate, then spat out skin and seeds. There was a sense of

expectancy in the still air, as though the valley were alive and swelling with anticipation of the harvest to come.

After a half mile on the dirt road I decided that I was about as
far away as the arsonist had been when he revved up his motorcycle
and took off into the night. I turned north, back toward the highway,
trying to cut his trail. I spotted a narrow little tractor road and took
it, heading back through a vineyard toward the Autry ranch house.
The tall oaks and single Washington palm that grew around the old
Victorian were my markers.

The tractor trail took a sharp dogleg to the right. As I turned, I
spotted a man kneeling in the sand fifty yards ahead of me. He was
bent over the ground, motionless, intent on something just beyond
his knees. I stopped in mid-stride, recognizing Beltrán, the field hand
who had been watching the crowd and the fire with such intensity
last night. And Sandra. He had watched her as well.

Now he was watching the ground I had come to check for signs
of the arsonist's motorcycle.

Before I had time to think about it my reflexes had me off the
trail and out of sight, crouched among the vines. Beltrán had been
too caught up in his study of the ground to notice me. I wanted to
keep it that way. As quietly as I could, I moved forward between the
vineyard rows, hunching down to stay hidden and trying to keep my
breathing soft. A desultory breeze stirred the currents of heat among
the vines. The whispering sound of the big green leaves masked my
approach.

When I got within ten yards of the end of the row I stopped
again and cautiously looked up over the vines. Beltrán was still
kneeling. There was a canteen and a coffee can beside him on the
ground. In one hand he held a short, flat implement of some sort. He
was using it to work the ground in front of him.

It looked like he was wiping out tire tracks.

The only way to find out was to get closer. The idea was not
inviting. I remembered the long fiery tongue and loud report of the
arsonist's .45 last night. Moonlight shooting is tricky. Sunlight
shooting isn't. I didn't want to give him another chance at an unarmed target in broad daylight. On the other hand, any evidence a
crook thinks is worth obliterating might be damned useful to Sandra.

I slid under the arbor again, stepped into the road and rushed

Beltrán. I was still ten feet away when he heard me and began to rise, trying to turn at the same time.

I was already launched into a flying tackle when I saw that the implement he held in his hand was a locking knife with a four-inch blade.

9

My shoulder slammed into Beltrán's back while he was still trying to straighten up. Despite the impact he managed to hold onto the knife. It didn't do him much good, because by then he was face down in the dirt with me on top of him. He was as strong as I'd guessed and determined as hell not to be taken. I grabbed his knife hand, barred his arm and dragged it up between his shoulder blades. Then I put enough pressure on the wrist to get his attention.

"Drop it," I said, and then repeated the command in Spanish.

Beltrán tested my strength and my leverage for a few seconds longer before he opened his hand. The knife slid over his thick black hair and dropped into the dust by his face.

"¿Habla inglés?" I asked.

"I speak English."

His accent was pronounced but didn't interfere with communications one bit. He had been in the country long enough to become fluent. Even more interesting, he had taken the time to learn English. Not many of the migrant workers did. Even if they decided to stay here, they could live and die without ever speaking a word of English.

"Lie still or I'll break your arm. *¿Comprende?"*

Without moving, Beltrán flexed his body, testing me again. I cranked a few more pounds of pressure against his wrist. He lay still while I checked to make sure that he didn't have a gun in his waistband or his boots or his armpits. When I finished I picked up the knife and stepped back, releasing him.

My heel sank into something mushy, like fresh cow shit or mud. I didn't take the time to check which it was, because Beltrán had rolled over fast and was up on his feet like a feral cat, moving his arm to test the damage. I doubted that there was any. He had the flexibility of a whip.

Silently I inspected his knife. It was a Buck, expensive and well made. The rosewood handle was scarred and the blade showed heavy use. I tested the edge by shaving a sweaty patch of forearm. Gillette would have been satisfied. Scarred, honed, well oiled and well used, the knife looked more like a vineyard man's tool than an assassin's weapon.

Beltrán stood with his weight balanced on the balls of his feet and his eyes on me. His expression was calm and watchful. He was a tough man who made very few mistakes. The knife suited him. As I stared to fold the knife I realized that the backspring had been altered. I shut the knife completely, then held it in one hand and snapped my wrist. The blade locked in open position with a satisfying metallic click.

" 'Gravity knife' in English, *flic* in Spanish," I said. "Illegal in either country."

Beltrán said nothing. He simply stood waiting, watching. I had the feeling that he had spent a lot of his life like that. Waiting and watching. I wondered if he was here illegally and if that was the only reason he was so wary.

"If *la Migra* catches you with this, they'll ship your ass back to Mexico no matter what your green card says. If you have a green card," I added.

His eyelids flickered, telling me that I had hit a sore spot. Beltrán didn't have a green card. He was one of the hundreds of thousands of Mexicans who lived and worked in California without benefit of official sanction.

"It is a very old tool," Beltrán pointed out calmly. "The spring, it is very weak. Too many hours. Too many hard vines."

I closed the knife, snapped my wrist again and listened to the blade lock open. Scarred, honed steel glittered in the harsh sunlight.

"Tool, huh?" I shrugged, keeping an open mind. Somehow Beltrán reminded me of myself as I had faced Fleming—no uneasiness, simply the realization that there were questions to be asked and answers to be given. "Well, let's see what you were using it for."

I stepped to the side until I could keep an eye on Beltrán and at the same time look at the ground where he had been kneeling before I tackled him. What I saw almost made me laugh, for he had been doing exactly what I had suggested Fleming might do—make a plaster cast of a set of tire tracks from a two-wheeled vehicle. I looked at the heel of my running shoe. About half of the white plaster of paris had ended up on me.

I still didn't know what Beltrán was, but I knew what he wasn't: he wasn't the arsonist. "Sorry I knocked you down. I wasn't sure whether I was going to get shot at again."

Beltrán's smile was genuine and amused. *"Seguro que sí.* That puts a man off his stride, no?"

"It sure puts this man off." I looked at the plaster of paris that I had mangled.

"No matter," Beltrán said, following my glance. "The sand, it is too soft for tracks, but I had to try."

I scuffed the plaster of paris off my shoe, then turned my back on Beltrán as a demonstration of trust and looked off between the rows. Patches of plaster showed in several places, but the ground was too soft there as well.

I turned around. Beltrán hadn't moved. I folded the knife, balanced it in my hand and flipped it to him. He put it in his back pocket with the easy motion of someone who has done it thousands of times before.

"How do you know these are the right tracks?" I asked. "The ground is too soft to show tread marks."

Beltrán motioned me to follow and walked over to a spot of earth that looked damp. He dropped to one knee and read the marks the way other people read print.

"He parked his machine here," Beltrán said. "You can see his footprints here and here and here. There, I think, is where the kickstand dug into the dirt. This is where he spilled some of the kerosene he carried to start the fire."

I scooped up a pinch of the wet-looking ground. The dirt felt oily. I held it to my nose. The sharp stink of kerosene made me want to sneeze.

"You saw him park here?"

"No," Beltrán said, shaking his head. "I followed his tracks in the hour after dawn. That kind of light, the light from the edge, is the best for tracking."

"Sidelight," I said, standing up, remembering how Uncle Jake had hated sidelight because every little bump on the desert stood out. Trackers loved that light. Smugglers hated it, and Jake had been a smuggler.

"*Sí.* That is it," Beltrán said, nodding emphatically. "Sidelight."

"That explains everything but why you're here," I said. "Who the hell are you—the Lone Ranger?"

For a moment Beltrán looked puzzled. Then he smiled widely. "Was he the one on the golden horse?"

"Nope. The white one."

Beltrán laughed. "My name is Ramón Beltrán-Aplamado," he said. "Mostly I am called Beltrán. I work for Miss Autry."

"Doing what?" I asked, still not able to make Ramón Beltrán-Aplamado add up without a whole lot of things left over. He was too damn sure of himself to be just an illegal farmhand.

"I am her majordomo, her foreman. I work in the vines," Beltrán said. "I cultivate in the spring and summer, pick in the fall and prune in the winter."

That explained some of it, but not all.

"What does this come under?" I asked, hooking a thumb at the useless plaster of paris. "Fertilizing?"

Beltrán gave me the peculiarly graceful shrug that only Mexican males have mastered. I could tell from the set of his jaw that he had no more to say on the subject.

"I'm Fiddler," I said, offering my hand. He shook it with less force than an American would have, and more force than Mexican custom required. "Sandra is a good friend of mine."

That news didn't loosen his tongue either. He bent down to pick up the canteen and coffee can before he turned back to face me.

"I ask that you say nothing to Miss Autry about this. She would think it a foolish waste of time."

Beltrán turned and walked away, leaving me sure of nothing except that my list of suspected arsonists had just shrunk by one entry.

I checked the motorcycle tracks. Beltrán was right about the quality of the impressions they would yield. Vines like a nice, sandy soil. Great for grapes and lousy for tracks. There was nothing for me to do now but finish the run and get back to Deep Purple. I headed east, toward Highway 29.

The closer I got to the two-lane road, the more clearly I could see the radical changes that had taken place in Napa Valley in the past few years. It wasn't even eleven o'clock yet, and the highway was stop-and-go. Cars headed both north and south in uninterrupted streams. There were agricultural vehicles—tractors towing gondola trailers heaped with grapes and heavy trucks loaded with everything from fertilizer to empty wine bottles. But the bulk of the vehicles had the look of Disneyland about them, recreational vehicles and motor homes and station wagons with out-of-state plates and stickers all over the rear windows.

At the highway I turned north, heading back toward Deep Purple's driveway. The heavy traffic disturbed me. It was an unmistakable reminder that memory is much more seductive than reality. I didn't do well breathing concentrated exhaust fumes and I was used to smog. I wondered what effect heavy pollution had on gravevines.

The ersatz stone of NaVaMoVi's contribution to the valley's congestion humped up out of the green sea of vines. The tasting room was dragging cars off the highway like a powerful magnet. The parking lot overflowed with baking metal. People in shorts and sweaty faces streamed toward the tall oak doors that promised cool air and free wine.

A half mile farther north I could see another tasting room rising out of the vines, flanked by another big parking lot where parked cars simmered in the sun. And farther on, another tasting room, another full parking lot. It was like the main street of a boom town lined with saloons. I had no doubt that some of the tourists would consider it a challenge to suck up every drop of free alcohol they could get. By midafternoon some of those motor-home jockeys wouldn't be able to stand up long enough to piss.

With a feeling of relief I turned down Sandra's driveway, jogged past the restaurant with its burned-out kitchen and waterlogged dining room. I understood now why Sandra had such ambivalent feelings toward the restaurant she had built. Restaurants and tasting rooms and other tourist attractions would be the death of the Napa Valley life style that the Autrys had enjoyed for more than fifty years.

Maybe I should have let the damned restaurant burn down.

A few minutes later I came jogging up to the quiet green yard of Deep Purple. It was like stepping back twenty years from the traffic jam on Highway 29. I was covered with sweat and dust from the vineyards, and all around me rainbird sprinklers were irrigating the lush grass, leaving a wake of diamond drops glittering in the sun. I went to the center of the lawn and let the cool, man-made rain pour over me, washing me as clean as the blades of grass.

The idea of wearing slacks in the genteel furnace of Napa didn't appeal to me. I settled for shorts the color of the dust I'd run through. Knowing Sandra, I didn't bother to try the front of the main house. The kitchen was in back. The sounds of utensils and voices came through the screen door. I stopped and listened for a moment, recognizing Fiora's voice and Sandra's. I couldn't hear their words, but their laughter was as clear and refreshing as the water drifting down over the lawn. It occurred to me that jealousy was overrated as a feminine attribute.

The screen door rapped shut lightly behind me. The kitchen was hot but not oppressively so. It was a living kind of heat filled with bread baking and women working and food smells so rich they were almost nourishing. Fiora was perched on a stool next to a long table. Over her shorts she wore a full-length apron. The mixture of covered lap and uncovered thigh was frankly sexy. As I watched, she flicked a spoonful of something from a large mixing bowl into the tiny pastry shells arrayed in front of her on trays.

For a moment I stood without saying anything, just watching Fiora. She is more at home in the boardroom or the bedroom than the kitchen. She can fry an egg and program a microwave oven, but she'd rather operate a Dow Jones ticker. I, on the other hand, love to cook. I'm just not very good at it.

Sandra was better than good. She was extraordinary. She stood in front of the large six-burner stove, stirring a huge copper skillet full of frying sausages. The complex aromas of fat and meat and seasonings made my salivary glands contract painfully.

"Looks good enough to eat," I said, hovering hungrily over Fiora's shoulder.

"So far so good," Fiora said. "I haven't ruined more than half of them."

"Don't listen to her," Sandra said. "She's doing better than I would in Century City."

"In a pig's third eye," muttered Fiora, too low for Sandra to hear.

I looked over at Sandra in time to see her attempt at a cheerful smile fade into weariness and worry as she turned back to the sausages. I knew then how much the visit from Jacoby and Fleming had unsettled her. She was doing what she had always done when events closed in on her—cooking up a new, savory, far more pleasant world.

I hated to corner her in this safe, cozy place and start asking questions that she didn't want to hear, much less answer. But it had to be done. Arson is a quantum leap in malevolence over "bad luck." No matter what Sandra wanted to believe, someone in the valley wanted to hurt her. The thought that she could have been the one to encounter the arsonist with the loaded .45 had kept me awake for quite a while last night.

Fiora looked up at me. "Don't just stand there with your teeth in your mouth. Grab a spoon and be useful. Sandra's got a thousand of these bloody little quiches to make for the Traven party, and her kitchen help stiffed her this morning. I'm not much good, but it doesn't take a cordon bleu grad to fill pastries."

"Bloody little quiches?" I repeated. "You've been hanging out with the Ice Cream King too long."

That brought a slight smile to Fiora's mouth. Benny Speidel, a.k.a. the Ice Cream King of Saigon, was a transplanted New Zealander whose command of international slang was transcended only by his genius for inventing and using high-tech electronics.

I reached past Fiora to snag an empty pastry shell off the tray. I popped the shell into my mouth. The pastry came apart in a shower of flakes that dissolved into a rich buttery taste.

"I think the lord and master wants his breakfast," Fiora said.

"Two minutes," Sandra said.

I dragged a high stool over to an empty worktable and sat down. The questions could wait for a little while.

Sandra was a joy to watch. She was so completely at ease in her kitchen. She moved with an economy and certainty that were fascinating. Within ninety seconds she put a plate in front of me that featured a Sonoma Valley veal sausage still hot from the pan. To one side of the sausage, a trail of vinaigrette glistened over big, ripe, perfect slices of a tomato that had been decorating the garden that morning. There was a mound of German potato salad with a tart-sweet dressing that had been marinating for a day or two in the refrigerator.

Without ceremony Sandra pulled a gallon jug of dark red wine off a shelf and poured me a glass. The rich, mouth-filling flavor was

soft, comforting and very familiar. Sensory memory brought back
simple, quiet meals, lazy hot days and cool fall nights long ago.

My reaction to the wine brought Fiora over to taste from my
glass. She sipped and made a small sound of pleasure.

"Is this the famous Deep Purple that swept Paris?" she asked.

Sandra shook her head. "Not by a jugful," she said, smiling.
"It's just plain old country wine. It's actually a blend—Cabernet and
Merlot and, if I recall correctly, just a touch of zinfandel in this
batch. We made it two years ago. Crushed out in the field, fermented
in the garage and aged in barrels in the basement. This wine wasn't
meant to blow your socks off at some highly structured Four Seasons
tasting, or to make a bold statement in gold-medal competitions at
the Institut de Vin. This is what we call 'family wine.' "

Her smile widened as she added, "It may turn your teeth a little
purple, though. Unfiltered wine sometimes does that."

I was hungry, but I ate slowly. The food was worth savoring.
Despite the simplicity of the meal, there was a marriage of flavors
that was unique and very satisfying.

Which led to the first of the many unhappy questions that were
crying to be asked.

"What happened with Vintage Harvest?" I asked. "I know guys
in Beverly Hills who'd pay twenty bucks for a lunch like this and
think they got a deal."

Fiora glanced over. "Thirty-five with the wine," she observed.

After a moment's hesitation, Sandra began to talk. "I guess I
didn't make enough 'culinary statements' for the critics," she said,
shaking her head. "Too many of them go crazy for things like kiwi-
fruit quiche and I didn't want to play the game. I mean, kiwi fruit in
season is okay, but kiwi-fruit quiches are culinary bullshit—invention for the sake of invention."

"That's the problem with putting out a magazine every month,"
I said as I chased an elusive bit of tomato. "You have to say something new and cute whether or not there's anything worth saying.
People who eat because they're hungry never seem to get tired of
cherry pie. Critics make their living eating. Two different things."

"Very different," Sandra said, sighing. "I was trying to serve
simple food that was in season and prepared sensibly. It's what I
believe in, but it didn't work. Call it country pâté and serve it on
little plates with tiny sour pickles and you can charge twelve bucks a

shot, even if it's mediocre. Call it meat loaf and you're in trouble, no matter how good it tastes and how much care went into making it."

I couldn't help smiling. "Meat loaf, huh?"

"Boy, was I dumb. I thought people wanted to eat." She stopped slicing and looked disapprovingly at her knife. The edge didn't meet her standards so she found a chef's steel and expertly honed the blade. "People don't want to eat," she said, testing the knife again and then returning to her slicing. "They want a fancy stage show, with themselves as the star attraction."

She let out her breath with a rush. "Oh, hell, talk about sour grapes . . . It's not anyone's fault but my own. A lot of people loved Vintage Harvest's food and comfortable atmosphere. But restaurants run on a thin margin for the first few years. My margin was eaten up by bad management. My fault, not anyone else's."

"What about Cynthia Forbes?" Fiora asked, frowning at one of the tiny pastries. "Is she really the Eighth Wonder of the Culinary World?"

Sandra's body stiffened. She turned toward the stove to get another sausage. Using a handful of her own apron as a hot pad, she moved the sizzling skillet to the worktable, speared a sausage and returned the pan to the low fire. While she was busy, I picked up the knife she had just used. It was even sharper than the one Beltrán carried. She took the knife from me and went to work on the sausage. It was something to watch. Pieces seemed to leap off and keel over in a neat row. I had seen her bone a chicken with the same ease. She had handled knives all her life, and it showed.

She finally answered Fiora's question. "Cynthia was a good cook at one time. Some would even say great. More French that the French, if you know what I mean. But I don't think Cynthia has had a pan in her hand for five years. When she wasn't chasing my husband she was promoting herself in other ways. She's very good at it."

It was the first I'd heard of what had gone wrong with Sandra's marriage. After seeing Cynthia and Ramsey at the fire, I wasn't surprised. I was, however, amazed that Ramsey had had enough taste to marry Sandra in the first place.

"Other than your ex-husband and the fact that you're a better cook, what does Cynthia have against you?" I asked.

"Deep Purple," Sandra said succinctly.

That surprised me. "Why? Does she want a reputation in wines, too?"

Sandra drew in a deep breath and let it out slowly. The flat line of her mouth told me how much she hated talking about this.

"Cynthia is relatively new to the valley," Sandra said finally. "Some of the more established families find her . . . difficult."

I could see how they might. The backbone of Napa Valley society wasn't impressed by dyed blondes, no matter how internationally famous. Particularly dyed blond home wreckers. Sandra, on the other hand, was native born and Napa grown.

"Does Cynthia find you 'difficult'?" I asked.

"She'd as soon slit my throat as look at me," Sandra said calmly.

"Do you mean that figuratively or literally?"

Her mouth flattened. She said nothing more.

"Look, Sandra," I said gently, "the two men who were here this morning have a crime to solve. Jacoby is nice enough, but Fleming isn't out to do anybody any favors except himself. He's not going to shake the grapevines for arson suspects when he's got you handy."

Sandra said nothing except, "I'm innocent and you know it."

"So what? By the time Fleming admits that he can't make the case against you, your reputation will be ruined by innuendo and insinuation. To avoid that, we have to give him better game to chase."

She put down the knife and looked at me, so I asked the question she didn't want to answer.

"Who in this valley hates you besides Cynthia Forbes?"

10

Sandra still wasn't having any of it.

"What about your foreman?" I asked.

"Beltrán?" she asked, startled. She looked at me with wide, golden-brown eyes. "Why would you suspect him?"

"Because he's not your run-of-the-mill *mojado* from Guanajuato," I retorted.

She smiled. "No, he isn't, is he?"

"Beltrán had the means and the opportunity to start the fire," I said impatiently, baiting her, hoping to get her talking despite her reluctance. "Did he have a motive?"

"Beltrán is an unusual man," she said. "He's very intense, very intelligent. And he loves the land as much as I do. He's absolutely trustworthy, Fiddler. He began working here a year before Dad died. Without him, I would have packed it in a long time ago."

"Okay," I said agreeably. "Beltrán's a good guy. What about Ramsey? Was the divorce nasty?"

Sandra grimaced and laid aside her knife. After a moment she began talking in a low voice. "It was pretty ugly," she admitted. "Bob wanted half of Deep Purple. There are times when I don't think he ever wanted me, not really. He just wanted Deep Purple."

I wished I'd never brought up the subject. The admission had cost Sandra too much—more than Ramsey was worth. I took her hand and squeezed it in silent apology. But there were more questions to ask and more painful memories to talk about.

"I thought the Ramsey family owned half of northern California," I said.

"Oh, the Ramseys have a lot of land," Sandra said. "But it's all in Sonoma County. That's like owning Avis in a market dominated by Hertz. Sonoma grape land doesn't have the same international cachet that Napa has. In wine circles Sonoma wines are considered second class. It's bullshit, of course," she said flatly, "but it's the kind of bullshit that makes the wine world go round."

"Why didn't Ramsey buy some Napa land?" Fiora asked. "Or isn't any for sale?"

"Oh, it's for sale. All it takes is money. Lots and lots and lots of money." Sandra's mouth turned down as she let go of my hand and poured me some more wine. "Bob doesn't have the cash. Owning a lot of land isn't the same as being cash rich. Not if it's farmland. He's a proud, determined man. He wants Ramsey Vineyards to be a real power in the wine world. He's convinced that won't happen until he can put the 'Napa Valley' appellation on his flagship wine varietals. It's almost an obsession with him." She shrugged. "A lot of Sonoma growers feel the same way."

"Why don't he and the other Sonoma growers hire a public relations firm to hype their own product?" Fiora asked, looking up from her quiches. "Napa does."

"Oh, they're trying, but Napa has a long lead. That Paris tasting is the cornerstone of Napa's reputation."

"And Deep Purple is the cornerstone of that victory," I said.

"Yes." Sandra's mouth turned down in an ironic smile. "Funny, huh? I don't give a damn about international wine prestige, and I own the most prestigious vineyard of all. That's what Bob wanted. So after I found out that he had been seeing Cynthia, I—" Suddenly Sandra interrupted herself with an impatient sound. " 'Seeing.' What a crock of shit. He was screwing her and had been since the day we were married."

Sandra let out her breath in a long, tired sigh. She stared through me, seeing the past. I watched her face, remembering a time when she had been a woman who knew how to laugh and love, a woman who made each minute both exciting and oddly peaceful. A bad marriage and worse luck had taken much of the laughter from her. I would have given a great deal to be able to put it back.

"Anyway," she continued, "when I demanded a divorce Bob said fine, so long as he got Deep Purple in exchange. You see, before we were married Dad had told me that my husband would get half of Deep Purple. But when Dad died his will stated that the land belonged only to me. I think he knew about Bob and Cynthia a long time before I did."

"What made Ramsey change his mind and not fight the divorce?" I asked.

Sandra looked away from me. "After a while I guess he realized that it was hopeless."

There was more to it than that, but the set of Sandra's shoulders told me that I wasn't going to hear it from her. It didn't matter. I had heard all I needed to; Ramsey was not one to forgive and forget.

"All right," I said. "We have Cynthia and Bob. Anybody else who would enjoy your bad luck? Angry wives or unhappy former lovers? Wine competitors? Disappointed suitors?"

Sandra smiled and shook her head.

"You sure? What about this Traven guy I keep hearing about? Did you ever go out with him?"

"For a time. No sparks, though, at least not for me. Vern wouldn't have minded an affair," she said frankly, "but he wasn't upset when it didn't happen. He has more women than he has time to worry about them. You see, he's land *and* cash rich. The land is in Napa Valley and the cash is everywhere in the world."

"What does he do?" Fiora asked, intrigued by the thought of worldwide cash.

"Invests."

"In what?"

"He made his first money in oil," Sandra said. "He told me once that he made his first million by the time he was twenty-five, and once he found out how easy it was he got down to work. When he stopped to take a deep breath, he was forty and he was worth four hundred million in everything from real estate to electronics. That's when he decided there was more to life and moved to the Napa Valley."

Fiora wasn't the least bit boggled by all the zeros. "You make it sound like he's retired."

"Not exactly, although he's not as active in business as he once was," Sandra said. "You should see his home. It's a replica of a French château. It doesn't stop there, either. Everything he has is the best that money can buy." Sandra smiled as she turned toward me. "He's been a good friend to me, Fiddler. He has no reason to hate me."

I made a neutral sound and asked, "What about a youngish,

slender man with a continental look about him? He drives a white VW convertible."

"Guy Rocheford drives one of those."

"Is he a friend too?"

"His family owns one of the finest first-growth estates in France. They're one of the biggest names in wine in the world, right up with the Rothschilds and the Mondavis. Guy's family bought some property here in the valley. Most of the European vintners are doing that. Covering all the bases."

"Wonder where they're getting the money?" I asked. "The wine market hasn't been that great lately."

Fiora looked interested again as the subject veered back to assets. She was in full money-shuffling mode. Even as the thought came to me, I tried to stifle the reflexive flash of irritation that was left over from older, unhappier times. Fiora was doing what I had brought her here to do—exercising her fiscal expertise on behalf of Sandra Autry.

"One of my partners brokered a deal with someone called Rocheford a few years ago," Fiora said. "A fair amount of family money, a long pedigree and a competitive business sense that went right to the bone. I seem to remember a rumor that the Rochefords were fronting for a French consortium."

Sandra blinked several times and then looked toward me. "She's wasted in the kitchen."

"I know," I said. "So does she, most of the time."

Fiora slanted me a green-eyed look and kept on dabbing at the pastries.

"Anything else about Guy?" I asked Sandra.

"He's been here for years, on and off. He has a wife and kids in France but spends most of the year here, managing the Rochefords' U.S. operation."

"Wife and kids?" I asked, remembering the slender young man. He hadn't looked like the father of this or any other year.

"He brought his family over last Christmas. They went to Disneyland for a week."

"Does Guy have any reason to dislike you?" I asked.

"I barely know him. Why?"

"He really enjoyed watching your restaurant burn."

Sandra picked up a spoon and began filling pastries. After a moment she nodded. "I suppose you may as well hear the whole mess," she said without looking at me. "I guess the wine business is as bitchy as the food business after all. Guy is an arrogant Frenchman who figures that the rest of the world—California particularly —is in the Stone Age as far as wine, culture, cuisine and sex are concerned, and he doesn't mind saying so."

"Show me a Frenchman who doesn't feel that way," Fiora said dryly, "and I'll show you an impostor."

"Yes, well, with Guy it's a bit more personal," Sandra said, sighing. "The Rochefords' most prized wine was one of the first growths that lost to Deep Purple in 1974. Guy has no reason to cry at my funeral."

I winced at Sandra's choice of words. "What about—" I began, only to be cut off by someone knocking at the front door. Sandra's hands were full so I motioned for her to stay put.

The front door was unlatched, but the man stood patiently on the porch waiting to be let in. He was about six feet tall, well tanned, in his early forties and still in shape. He wore blue jeans, a white linen shirt and work boots that were beautifully tooled leather. There was a carefully rolled and creased white straw stockman's hat in one big hand. The clothes seemed casual until you looked closely. The shirt and the boots were handmade and the jeans were tailored.

"Hi. I'm Vern Traven. Is Sandra around?"

There was the faintest trace of the Southern plains in Traven's voice. Beneath that soft accent there lay urgency. He was trying to hide it, but Vern Traven was a man under pressure.

"I'm right here," Sandra said from behind me. "Come in, Vern. Can I get you something to drink?"

"Hello, Sandra," he said. He turned the hat in his hands a few times, then cleared his throat. "Sorry to bother you like this, particularly after last night, but I need to talk with you. Privately." He smiled apologetically at me.

"It's okay, Vern," said Sandra. "I just finished laying out all my secrets to Fiddler and Fiora." She introduced us.

Traven was discreet about it but he summed me up in a single glance—shorts, no shirt, no shoes, and too much at home to be run off of Sandra's troubles by a few words from one of Napa Valley's multimillionaires. He was like Fiora in full fiscal mode. I could practically hear his mind adding up assets and filing them away for future deals.

Underneath that soft voice and gentle manner Vern Traven was one shrewd son of a bitch. That didn't surprise me. People who make a lot of money tend to be shrewd.

"It would be better not to involve your friends," Traven said to Sandra after shaking my hand. "But if you're sure—"

"She's sure," I said, interrupting. "If it's urgent, we're wasting time."

"You'll probably want shoes," Traven said.

With that he turned and went out to the dusty maroon Jeep that was parked along Deep Purple's drive. I remembered the maroon balloon I had seen that morning. Same color exactly. I wondered if Traven color-coordinated his bath towels and underwear too.

When I looked over my shoulder Fiora was standing in the kitchen door untying the apron that came below her knees. "I'll meet you out front with some shoes," she said, dumping the apron and running out the back door.

The Jeep was turned on and impatient to go by the time Fiora jumped in back with my sandals. As I kicked into them she braced herself on the seat with a resigned look. She likes open Jeeps even less than she likes the Cobra. Traven drove the same way he dressed —carefully, with the understated flair of a genteel showman.

"All right, Vern. What's wrong?" Sandra asked.

Traven glanced at me in the rear-view mirror, hesitated, then went ahead. "Remember I told you I was having some production loss in the southeast corner next to you?" he asked, pitching his voice to carry over the noisy Jeep.

Tension fell over Sandra's face like a veil, dimming her vitality.

"I remember," she said uncertainly. "Those are the older vines, aren't they?"

"I hired Eric Karger to check into the problem."

Sandra flinched.

"He thinks it's phylloxera."

She went white. "What kind of rootstock do you have in that block?"

"AxR-1," he said heavily. "Just like your daddy put in Deep Purple."

"Oh, God, no," she whispered.

Whatever Traven's words meant, it was worse than the restaurant burning down. I touched Sandra's shoulder. At first I thought that she hadn't noticed. Then her hand came up and she gripped my fingers with enough force to hurt.

In the rear-view mirror Traven's eyes pinned mine. "This must be kept absolutely confidential," he said flatly. "If word gets out before harvest I'll lose millions and Sandra will be ruined."

I could sense Fiora's sudden interest and remembered what she had said about a megabucks rumor being loose in the Napa Valley.

I had a nasty feeling that the rumor was true.

"What is phylloxera?" I asked.

"A parasitic insect," Sandra said dully. "A root louse. It's kind of like an aphid and it lives on the rootstock of grapevines. A century ago it destroyed the wine industry in France. It also did a hell of a lot of damage here in California."

"How did they get rid of it?" I asked.

"They started using a rootstock called AxR-1. It was resistant to the lice," she said. Her voice thinned. "At least, it was supposed to be resistant. Oh, God, Karger has to be wrong. We can't have phylloxera here."

Traven looked at me in the rear-view mirror for a moment, saw I still didn't understand, and looked away.

"AxR-1 has become the standard rootstock," Traven said. "Probably two thirds of Napa Valley is planted with it. And now it looks like the phylloxera has mutated enough to live off of our most resistant rootstock."

"It just can't be," Sandra said in a dazed voice.

Traven gave her a sympathetic look and shook his head. "Karger told me that pathologists have been expecting this kind of change for years. I just had the bad luck to own the land where the phylloxera are making a comeback."

Bad luck. I'd heard those words too much, lately.

Traven made a helpless gesture. On him it looked odd. I had the feeling that Traven hadn't spent much of his life being helpless.

"I'm sorry," he said, glancing over at Sandra. "If something I've done—some cultivation practice or anything—has caused this, I'll never forgive myself. Traven Winery is nothing. I can pull out every vine on the place and take it all as tax credits. But Deep Purple is different. It's an irreplaceable international treasure."

Traven's voice was fervent, reminding me of the faithful who worshiped at the borders of Deep Purple's vineyards, driving Sandra's father crazy. Traven may have come late to the valley, but its mythos had gotten under his skin all the way to the bone.

"Don't be silly, Vern," Sandra said wanly. "Nothing's your fault and Deep Purple is simply one of a hundred vineyards. Farming is a risk. It's always one thing or another—mold or Pierce's disease or hail or frost. We don't blame one another for bad luck."

"Yes, but I can afford bad luck. You can't." Traven looked over at Sandra. "Whatever happens, you won't go broke," he promised. "If necessary, I'll buy every acre of infested ground you have. No matter what you say, I blame myself."

"You're reacting like a new parent with a sick kid," Sandra said. "Don't assume it's acute pneumonia. Maybe it's just colic."

Traven smiled faintly. "I hope you're right," he said. "I do love Napa. For the first time in my life I feel at home. That's worth getting worried about."

Fiora looked at me. I could guess what she was thinking. Once men have made enough money they look around for some other focus, some higher purpose. Like me. Some start making movies or giving money to charities. Some dabble in politics. Then there are the collectors; some go for old masters and some for acres of vines that are a gentleman farmer's pride. Traven had discovered the wine-country life style, like a hundred other Napa Valley boutique vintners. Wine and fine food and the land, a tradition that went back a lot further in history than any recent zillionaire's pedigree or cash.

Traven turned south to the dry creek bed and then turned east. We quickly reached the edge of Deep Purple. Immediately across the next section road a John Deere had been backed a few yards down a vineyard row. The big tractor's engine was idling, a shimmering heat ghost dancing above its rusty exhaust pipe. Directly behind the tractor a man was bent over a bushy green vine that had been jerked out of the sandy soil and left to wilt beneath the merciless sun. The vine dangled helplessly from the cable of the tractor's power winch. Gingerly, the man was wrapping an opaque plastic bag around the roots.

The man stepped back from the upended vine and hurried over to meet us. He was thin, long-haired, in his early thirties and dusty enough to look at home in the vineyard. Behind old-style wire-rim glasses, his eyes had an adrenaline shine. He was like a reporter covering a plane crash: excited but trying to hide it.

Traven introduced him as Dr. Eric Karger from Stanford. We exchanged handshakes and then Karger stood and shifted his weight uneasily, as though unsure what to say.

"It's all right, Eric," Traven said. "These are Sandra's friends. They won't reveal anything that would hurt her."

Karger gave us a last, intense look and turned back to his boss. "It's no good, Mr. Traven. I haven't had time to check the extent of the infestation, but there's no doubt that it exists."

A small, stifled sound came from Sandra. I leaned forward to look at the plastic packet Karger was holding out. Inside the envelope were a number of bright yellow insects about the size of Culiacán bedbugs.

"I got these from just below the surface before I pulled out that vine," Karger continued in his light, dry voice. "That indicates a heavy infestation, which means it is virtually certain that this particular strain of phylloxera can live on AxR-1."

Motionless, Sandra stared at the plastic bag as though it were a loaded gun. I put my hand on Sandra's shoulder. She didn't respond.

Karger put the plastic envelope into his shirt pocket and retrieved another envelope from the cargo pocket of his khaki pants. "And here are a few of the parasites that I found across the road in Deep Purple." He slanted a hesitant look at Sandra. "I hope you don't mind my technical trespass, ma'am, but I considered it vital to check as soon as possible. I won't make broad generalizations without more careful analysis, but I'm afraid your problem may turn out to be as great as Mr. Traven's. Perhaps greater."

"Why?" I demanded.

"Well, Miss Autry's vines are the same AxR-1 rootstock as Mr. Traven's," Karger said, "but Deep Purple's vines are older and therefore probably more vulnerable." He hesitated, took a deep breath and got on with the bitter academic truth. "If I had to choose a likely location for the origin of this strain of phylloxera, I'd choose Deep Purple. That's why I suspect that Miss Autry's infestation may turn out to be worse than Mr. Traven's."

Karger must not have liked what he saw in my face, because he started speaking very quickly.

"Of course I don't mean that Miss Autry is to blame. No one is to blame for the random mutations of nature. It's simply that, the older the vine, the more likely it is to lose its edge. It's like people. A parasite that's unnoticed in a young man may be debilitating to an old man."

"Okay. Great. Sandra's vineyard has bugs. So treat it before the bugs kill off the vines," I said.

Karger looked at me as though I had just crawled up from the roots of an infested vine. He opened his mouth to respond but Sandra was already talking.

"There is no treatment for phylloxera."

I looked at Karger. He nodded.

"If I find more phylloxera I'll be forced to recommend that both vineyards be sterilized," he added.

"Sterilized," I said flatly. "How?"

Again it was Sandra who answered. "You pull out the vines, burn them to ash, deep-treat the soil with fumigant and then replant. If you can afford it by then. I won't be able to."

Traven took Sandra's hand. "Please, don't worry about money," he said in a low voice. "I said I would buy the infested land and I will."

Sandra simply shook her head. "I can't sell Deep Purple," she said bleakly. "It's all I have left of my life."

Traven looked at her for a long moment, patted her hand and said softly, "Don't worry about it, honey. We'll talk later, when you've had a chance to think."

"Excuse me," Fiora said, her tone both feminine and very distinct. It's her business voice, the one she uses when she runs the numbers on a deal four times and gets four different answers. "Both Deep Purple and Mr. Traven's land take in a hundred of acres. That vine"—she pointed to the plant wilting in the steel cable's embrace— "is just one of literally thousands, yet you're talking as though you're going to destroy everything in sight just because a few vines are infested. That doesn't make business sense, Dr. Karger. You don't fold an entire franchise just because a few outlets are badly managed."

"You do, however, cut out and destroy cancerous cells before they destroy the human being who is their host," Karger said. His voice was dry, light, relentless. "As long as these phylloxera live and flourish uncontrolled, the entire Napa Valley wine industry is in danger. And that would be just the beginning. Sonoma would be next, and then Lake County and Alexander Valley and Mendocino and even Fresno. It would be like France at the turn of the century, when a whole industry died out."

I looked at Sandra. She closed her eyes, silently telling me that Karger wasn't overselling his case.

"Wait a minute," I said through clenched teeth. "Let me get this straight. You uproot one vine, stick a few bugs in a plastic show-and-tell envelope and then recommend that Sandra destroy one of the most famous vineyards in the world."

Karger bridled. "No. Of course not. I'll need to study the situation very carefully. I won't recommend sterilization until I'm certain there is no other course." Karger turned and addressed Sandra and Traven equally. "However, in the interim, I'll send you a list of suggested cultural practices that may help to prevent the spread of the infestation."

He paused, took a deep breath and delivered the rest of his bleak diagnosis.

"I must, of course, go to the state Department of Agriculture."

"Quarantine," Traven said flatly.

Karger looked away. "I can't say, Mr. Traven. That's up to them."

"There must be another way," Traven said. "I'm at 21 degrees of Brix in some of my rows. Another week of hot weather, maybe less, and harvest could begin. What the hell difference could a few weeks mean if we promise to keep equipment out of the affected area? We'll only harvest those areas that you give a clean bill of health."

"It doesn't matter what Dr. Karger says about the rest of our vines," Sandra said tiredly. "The picking crews will refuse to bring their equipment into any part of our vineyards. They won't have any choice, really. We're just two of their clients. The rest of the growers will be scared to death at the thought of allowing contaminated equipment onto their clean land." Sandra shook her head slowly. "Once the word goes out, I'm finished in the Napa Valley."

She turned her back on us and looked out over Deep Purple's acres as though saying good-bye.

"Then Dr. Karger can bloody well keep his mouth shut until he knows the extent of the infestation," I said. "Either that or I'll hit

him with a civil lawsuit that will tie him up in court for the next ten
years."

"You can't do that," Karger said, shocked.

I smiled. "Try me."

11

Traven and Karger walked about thirty feet up the row and stood talking in low voices. I don't know what Traven offered him—or rather, how much—but in the end Karger agreed to quietly determine the extent of the infestation before he started calling out the alarm, as long as we agreed not to allow harvest equipment into any area that hadn't personally been cleared by him.

We left Karger in the dusty vineyard, pulling more envelopes out of his pockets as he headed into Deep Purple's famous rows.

Without a word the four of us piled back in the Jeep. Sandra and Traven agreed to get together for a strategy session, but I could see that she wasn't up to it yet. She was pale and dazed, and even though her skin was misted with sweat, it was cool to the touch. Like most farmers from the beginning of time, Sandra had been counting on the next harvest to pull her out of a financial hole. If Karger changed his mind about talking or found that the infestation was too extensive, there would be no harvest.

Traven drove quickly back to Highway 29, trailing a plume of tan dust. He fought his way into the creeping traffic like a professional chauffeur. As we crawled south at six miles an hour Fiora looked at the open land and the solidly packed highway.

"This is as bad as Pacific Coast Highway on Sunday afternoon," Fiora said. "Why hasn't the state put in a four-lane highway? It's not like you would have to condemn residential property to build it."

"Napa's agricultural land is too special to turn into highways and tourist motels," Traven said. "It deserves better, and it's going to get it."

Fiora looked skeptical. "Newport Beach fought the freeway for a decade," she said. "Now they're going to have it shoved down their throat. Fighting development is a losing battle."

Speculatively, Traven glanced at Fiora in the rear-view mirror. I had the distinct feeling that he didn't disagree with her summation, but he didn't necessarily like it, either.

We drove a mile south on the blacktop before Traven made a right turn onto a broad, straight private road that bore no name.

"Is this your property?" I asked.

"Not yet. I have just under eight hundred acres scattered around Deep Purple. The château and winery are on a separate hundred-acre parcel just up over the low hills ahead."

It was tempting to ask what all that was worth. I didn't. There was no need to be crass as long as Fiora was around to do the calculations for me. That was one of the reasons I had brought her to Napa.

Even so, I had continued to hope that Sandra's problem was less fiscal than physical. Now I frankly wondered if I would be any use to her at all. It was clear that someone was trying to ruin Sandra—professional torch jobs don't come cheap—but it was even clearer that Sandra needed a fast-track money shuffler more than she needed an out-of-work violinist. Even I was forced to admit that Sandra had to sell out or go under. If anyone could put together rich investors for that kind of sale on short notice, it was Fiora.

Unfortunately it was also obvious that Sandra still didn't realize that phylloxera had changed every fiscal equation. Selling out was her only alternative to going under. The best favor I could do her was to convince her to give up and auction off her dreams to the highest bidder.

The idea of being auctioneer made rage prowl around the basement of my mind. Years ago Sandra had healed me. Surely there was more I could do than wring my hands at her funeral.

The Jeep popped over the shoulder of a round, oak-studded hill at the west edge of Napa Valley. Suddenly we were on the edge of a small side valley that contained one of the most beautiful estates I've ever seen. It had to be remarkable; I heard Fiora draw a sharp breath in surprise, and she is less easily impressed by landscape than I am.

From where we were, the small valley looked as immaculately manicured as a putting green at a world-class country club. The carefully trimmed vineyards on either side of the winery had been cultivated with such an even hand that the furrows were perfectly aligned. Occasionally the vineyard rows parted around the trunks of mammoth oaks that I suspected had been left in place for visual relief. Cost had not been a consideration in designing this landscape.

At the center of the valley there was another rounded hill. It was much like the one we were on, but lower. The gentle slopes were festooned with oaks and a few twisted old olive trees whose leaves fluttered like tiny silver pennants in the small breeze. The oaks were big enough to shade the winery building, which had been mortised into the hill. The winery was constructed of soft white stone. This was real stone, too, not stucco.

I remembered Sandra saying that Traven lived in a stone-by-stone reconstruction of a French château. It was an odd house, half barn and half castle. At first glance the building was beautiful in its immaculate green setting. But when you placed it in the context of the spare golden hills that rimmed the valley the building looked almost uneasy, out of place. Like Traven, the château had a feeling of theatricality, as though reality were only a stage set to be arranged and rearranged at will.

"I brought the stone in from Bordeaux, from an abandoned winery that was more than three centuries old," Traven said. "It gives my valley a touch of genuine history, don't you think? I had to sandblast it, of course. It had the wrong finish entirely for what I wanted to achieve."

Fiora and I made appreciative noises. It seemed the polite thing to do.

From this distance the pale stone walls had both a smooth glow and a feeling of texture, like nubby raw silk. Centuries of weathering had been sandblasted away, making the stone look both new and aged at the same time. Quite a trick, but then it's easier when you have more money than any sane man could spend.

The closer we came to Traven's home, the more obvious it was that Traven knew how to dress his hundred acres of reality. The entire building was surrounded by a half dozen acres of the greenest, cleanest lawns I had ever seen. Off to one side, surrounded by grace-ful curtains of trailing willows, a rock-lined pond was afloat with so many water lilies that I was reminded of Giverny. The carefully designed lawn was punctuated with bursts of color—flower gardens and burnt-purple ornamental plum trees and redwood decks that were sheltered beneath canopies of blooming vines.

Traven pointed out the English maze off at the base of the hill to the side of the house. I couldn't see the fountain at the center of the big maze, but I believed it was there. The estate was a modern-day old-time castle, a mixture of styles that was striking if not altogether successful. What it achieved most clearly was an impression of money.

Traven grinned with proprietary pleasure at our reaction. "I guess the place does look pretty good, doesn't it?" he said. "I've been so damned busy getting everything ready for the party that I haven't had a chance to stand back and purely appreciate it."

As though on cue, a Hughes JetRanger helicopter came buzzing in on a flat run from the southeast and settled on a side lawn. It was painted in the dark maroon that was Traven's signature color.

"I'm going to fly some of the guests in from the city," he said, gesturing off in the direction of San Francisco. "The JetRanger can handle about six at a time. The pilot will earn his pay tomorrow."

Traven turned to Sandra. "Are you still going to be able to handle my party?" he asked gently. "You've had a hell of a rough couple of days."

"I'll be fine," she said, but her tone wasn't very convincing.

As the Jeep rounded a small bend at the bottom of the hill we came upon a crew of Mexicans and two large, four-wheel-drive tanker trucks. The trucks were equipped with high-speed pumps and pressure hoses. The men were hosing down the grapevines beside the road.

Traven rolled to a stop next to the crew. A dark-skinned *indio* with a heavy belly and a sweat-stained straw cowboy hat threw Traven a halfhearted salute and tried to make his men look busy. It was a bit like whipping a burro, more gratifying than effective, for the men continued to work at their own measured pace. I didn't blame them. That sun was one hot bastard.

A drift of cool mist from the hoses seemed to revive Sandra. Traven noted her new interest instantly.

"I'm having the dust washed off the first few rows of vines for the party," he said. "You don't think that will hurt the fruit, do you?"

Sandra smiled wanly and shook her head, as though the only vines she could think of right now were her own.

I watched the men with the hoses and wondered if there was a crew of maids with soft cotton towels to dry the vines and wax their leaves. Whatever else anyone might say about Traven, he put his money where his dream was. He had come to Napa to stay, and he had built a monument to his sense of homecoming. It was an expensive conceit that he had constructed. Considering the value of Napa land and the cost of the building itself, I had no doubt that I was looking at ten million bucks' worth of the most expensive toys that money could buy.

And if Karger had his way, Traven was going to get a chance to spend a lot more of his money in the near future. Replacing the grapevines on more than a full section of Napa vineyard was going to be a hell of an expensive undertaking. It may have been a measure of Traven's money that he seemed more distressed by the prospect of Sandra's loss than by his own. Maybe he did indeed have four hundred million dollars in holdings.

Up close, the stone building was even more imposing than it had been from across the valley. It looked as solid as Spring Mountain. Big leaded-glass windows had been set in the thick stone walls. The natural blond oak of their casements matched the several balconies that had been built to take advantage of the view.

Another garden crew was at work planting flats of daisies and periwinkles, dahlias and morning glories and bright-faced pansies in beds around the lawn. I was reminded of Disneyland, where the flower beds are dug up and replanted with blossoming plants once a week, and every surface is painted no less than once a month whether it needs it or not.

That's what Traven had done. He had taken his piece of the world stage and transformed it into a Disneyland for adults. It fit right into what Napa Valley had become—Traven's hundred acres of grape land was the new, all-rides ticket for the urban cognoscenti. Like Disneyland, Traven's estate was pleasant and attractive. But it wasn't the sort of place that would be comfortable to live in. It was a hundred acres wide and half an inch deep.

Traven braked to a stop in front of the house. "Well," he said, "now that you're here, what do you think of the old barn?"

I climbed out and surveyed the house. "It's a real showplace."

Traven smiled in pleasure. "Exactly! That's what I'm after. The most beautiful winery making the best wine in the most magnificent setting in Napa Valley. Come on, I'll give you the hundred-dollar tour."

I looked at Sandra.

She looked right through me, then said, "Thanks. Walking around again might help me to work out some of the logistics for the party."

Right. One tour, coming up.

Traven led us through big oak double doors at ground level. The air was still and faintly perfumed with the sweetness of wine aging inside the dark, cool building. The work area was barnlike, with fifteen-foot ceilings and pristine concrete floors. As my eyes adjusted to the level of the light I saw a dozen huge oval casks in a double rank down one side of the building. On the other side was a gallery of perhaps a hundred blond oak barrels stacked three high on sturdy oak cradles.

"Chardonnay and Cabernet," Traven said. "That's all we make here, and it's all we're going to make. But we're going to make the best. Those barrels are Limousin oak from France, damn near six hundred dollars apiece. And we won't use any casks bigger than fifteen hundred gallons here. Our wines are all handmade."

To prove his point, he stopped us and grabbed a wine thief—a bulbous, hand-blown glass tube with a tapered tip at one end and a glass loop like a trigger guard at the other. He tapped the erect bung out of one of the oak barrels, thrust the tip of the wine thief inside and clapped his thumb over the tiny air hole, sealing a golden column of Chardonnay in the tube. He decanted the wine into glasses with a subtle flourish.

"This hasn't been fined yet, but it'll give you an idea," he said.

The wine was faintly cloudy and sharp with the taste of the fruit and the oak from the barrel. Beneath that sharpness there was the beginning of something more complex. I never have been much of a judge of the future of barreled wine. On the other hand, there was no percentage in being rude to one of Sandra's friends.

"Lots of body there," I said.

Traven smiled with pleasure. "You really think so?" he asked. "That's great. Some people think it's a bit too acidic, but I think it has promise, real promise. We'll bottle it in a few months and give it an extra year of bottle age before we release it."

"Sounds like you're going for the top of the market," I said.

Traven frowned. "Marketing is less important to me than quality," he said. "I want to make a real contribution to the Napa wine image."

We got the mandatory tour of the rest of the place. It was beautiful and immaculate. Too immaculate. I kept remembering the rich, sweet stickiness of working wineries.

"Where do you do your crushing?" I finally asked.

Traven gave me an odd look, then smiled. "You've been away from Napa for a long time, haven't you? We harvest with machines that pick and crush in the same operation. It's all done in the field. Then we bring the must in to the fermenters in stainlesss steel tank trucks." He paused, then added, "Actually, we have a building down in Napa where we do our fermenting in stainless vats. There just wasn't enough room here for everything."

What he was saying was that his winery was even more a false front than NaVaMoVi. I couldn't help thinking about some of the small country wineries that once had populated the valley, and about the glass of thick, grapy wine Sandra had poured for me at lunch. That was the stuff that was truly handmade. It certainly had never touched stainless steel.

I was sure that the wine Traven had previewed for us would become excellent in its own way—refined and sophisticated and carefully designed for international tastings. Yet in another way Traven's wine was artifice, like his winery, like the too perfect estate with its matched maroon cars.

But then I've been accused more than once of having retrograde tendencies and primitive tastes. And in the end that's all that wine is. A simple matter of taste.

The tour ended on the upper floor of the stone building, which held Traven's living quarters and the executive offices of the Traven Winery. The lavish restorative detail of the château's exterior was duplicated here. He ushered us into a huge, comfortable living room that looked out through large french doors onto the rolling satin lawn, the immaculate vineyards and the valley beyond. The view was idyllic. The only other humans in sight were the leaf-washing crew and a few scattered gardeners. There was something almost medieval about the isolation.

A pair of white-jacketed Mexican houseboys appeared and took Traven's quick instructions for sandwiches, fruit salad, mineral water and wine. Traven motioned us toward a long, overstuffed couch that faced the best view, threw himself into a comfortable leather recliner nearby and turned towards Sandra with the air of someone who can no longer delay the inevitable.

"I've been thinking about it," Traven said, "and I'm afraid we're sitting on a powder keg. Frankly, we may face a quarantine tomorrow or the day after. Karger wants to be Traven Winery's resident bug specialist, but he has his own reputation to consider. Even giving us a few days of leeway could cause him a lot of trouble with the state agriculture people."

"Why a quarantine?" I asked, forcing Traven's attention away from Sandra. She wasn't up to making decisions right now, so there was no point in hounding her. "How the hell could harvesting grapes spread root lice?"

Traven kicked back in the chair and frowned at his boots. A fine patina of dust lay on the heavily tooled surface of the leather. His fingertip traced one of the whorls, then he absently wiped his hand on his jeans.

"I've done a little research on the subject since Karger first told me about his suspicions a few days ago. Phylloxera are descended from some kind of airborne parasite that originated in Central or South America. Now, in California's dry air, we *believe* that they can't spread except through contaminated soil or rootstock." Traven's frown deepened as his soft drawl continued without pause. "But we can't be sure, not a hundred percent, take-it-to-the-bank certain. That makes growers real nervous, because the only sure cure for phylloxera is to kill the host—the vines themselves—and then fumigate the hell out of the soil."

Traven grimaced and looked out at the immaculate vineyard rows that lapped at the golden hills like a calm green sea.

"At least, it used to be a cure," he said. "Who knows how tough this new strain will be? Frankly, if I were a neighboring grower I'd demand that the soil be left fallow for a few years, then replanted and watched damned carefully for a few more years." He turned back to me. "Hell, if you want the truth, I'd demand that the land never be used for commercial grapes again until an absolutely surefire cure for the new phylloxera is found."

"That sounds like overkill," I said flatly. "From what Karger said, the infestation didn't begin last week or even last year, which means that harvest equipment has already been all over the infested area, probably for years. Any contamination that was going to get spread around on tractor or gondola wheels already has been spread. It doesn't make sense to ruin Sandra's chance of pulling Deep Purple out of bankruptcy by slamming the barn door on horses that are long gone."

Traven smiled but there was no humor in him. "What you're saying is scientifically correct and quite rational to an outsider. But phylloxera isn't a rational subject for grape growers. It's the agricultural equivalent of AIDS—contagious and invariably fatal. The growers whose vineyards are healthy won't be reasonable or rational in their demands for checking the epidemic. I can't blame them. In their place I wouldn't be either."

I looked at Sandra. She nodded, her expression empty.

Traven leaned forward and took her hand. "I'm sorry, honey. I didn't think how my words would sound to you. Don't worry about it. We'll find a way to beat the damned bugs. And if it's money that's bothering you, don't worry about that either. We'll work something out, just the two of us."

"I can't sell Deep Purple," she said, her voice drained of all vitality. There was determination in it, though. Sandra had never lacked nerve.

"I know how tough this is for you, but you've got to face reality," Traven said softly. "Excuse me for being blunt, but it's common knowledge that you're having a tough time of it financially. Right now you can't afford the cost of fighting phylloxera. I can." His voice dropped. "I won't take advantage of your bad luck, honey. If you really don't want to get out from under your high-interest mortgage we can work out some kind of refinancing at a lower rate."

Though Sandra made no sound, tears started to stream down her pale cheeks. At best, Traven's offer was a stay of execution. She couldn't meet any payments no matter how low the interest. She would have to sell and she was beginning to realize it. It took no genius to see that facing reality was tearing her apart.

"That's very generous of you," I said to Traven, "but Sandra won't have to sell out. Money won't be a problem for her. I'll cover the costs of fighting phylloxera and help her get back on her feet."

Though Fiora said nothing, I could feel the protests crowding against her tongue. In order to help Sandra I'd have to strip money

out of every source I had. Tough. Sandra needed that money a hell of
a lot more than I did.

Sandra took my hand and cradled it against her cheek. Her skin
felt hot now, wet with tears, soft. Slowly she released my hand,
shaking her head as she did.

"I can't let you do that," she said huskily. "But thank you,
Fiddler."

"Sandra—"

"No," she interrupted, her voice soft and very, very stubborn.

Before I could say anything more Traven started talking.

"I didn't know you were interested in investing in Napa Valley,"
he said in a clipped voice.

"I'm not, but I am interested in helping a good friend."

Traven's shrewd eyes took in my sandals, shorts and hairy
chest. He was too polite to say it, but it was clear he wondered
whether I had the cash to back up my promises.

Fiora opened her purse, pulled out a business card and handed
it to Traven.

"I represent several investors who would love to put some
money in here," she said. "Judging from the traffic on the highway,
there are plenty of business opportunities."

Traven's face changed as he studied the card. His genial expression faded into something a good deal less friendly. "I've heard of
your firm," he said. He looked at Fiora coolly. "You're aware, of
course, that development is out of the question?"

Honey-colored eyebrows rose in delicate contradiction. "I have
learned, Mr. Traven, that nothing is out of the question when enough
money is at stake. The fact that Napa Valley has been artificially
withheld from development makes the valley more, not less, attractive to high-risk investors." She smiled. "As a former oil man, you
should know all about long shots paying off."

"You ever heard of dry holes, darlin'?" he drawled. "I sure as
hell have."

Fiora smiled again. I winced. Traven was going to regret that
"darlin'." Fiora smelled condescension the way a terrier smells rats,
and she responds in the same way to the scent.

"The risk is always equal to the potential reward," she said in a
calm, go-to-hell tone. "My clients know that. I'm sure all the people
who invested in your dry holes knew it too."

Traven didn't like that at all. He leaned forward suddenly. "Napa doesn't need cut-and-run condos for people who have no understanding of the valley's heritage and potential. The highest residential density anybody can squeeze out of this valley is one house per forty acres of land. That's the law. There's no profit for development there. If you're thinking of a motel on Deep Purple, forget it. The Planning Commission hasn't approved a new motel in the agricultural zone for more than five years. You could build a bonded winery, of course, but there are too many of them already. No profit there either."

Traven glanced over at Sandra, patted her hand as though to reassure her and said, "In other words, we know this valley is special and we intend to keep it that way. We sure as hell don't need Beverly Hills hotshots to tell us how to use our land."

"Century City," Fiora corrected gently. She looked rather pointedly at the manicured vista and then back to Traven. "Don't confuse us with the movie crowd, darlin'. We're real."

12

Unfortunately the threat of quarantine was even more real than Fiora's money shuffling. Traven would do what he could, but even if he had as much money as he wanted people to believe, he still had to bow before time, the tides and more bugs than he had bucks.

Then another possibility came to me. Fire is fought with water —and sometimes with fire. It's the same with experts. You buy yours, I'll buy mine, and we'll see each other in court. If Karger started pushing for official sanctions I needed a way to push back. I needed an expert who didn't turn white and get the shakes at the word "phylloxera." Most of all, I needed more fingers to put in the dike until harvest time.

As soon as we got back to the guesthouse I put in a call to the Ice Cream King of Saigon.

I'm one of the few people who can get away with calling Benny that. The name is an ironic reference to the only formal job Benny ever held. He was born in Christchurch, New Zealand, and in the late 1960s was hired by a U.S. multinational as a quality-control engineer in their South Vietnam operation. The job description said he was in charge of the dairy-products plant that supplied ice cream to a half million American GIs and dependents.

In truth, Benny had another job as well, but there was no written job description for what he did on his after-hours gig. By day he checked five-gallon tubs of chocolate, vanilla, strawberry and flavor-of-the-month. At night he was a GS-13 communications expert, coordinating an up-country spook microwave system for the Central Intelligence Agency and taking his pay in gold to a numbered Hong Kong bank account.

Benny is too pragmatic to brood over things that are beyond his control, like the botched war that cost him the use of the lower half of his body. What's more, he gets impatient with people who do brood about it—either the war or the paralysis. He once said to me, "If the Disabled American Veterans ever solicit me for membership again I'll burn my U.S. citizenship papers, go back to Christchurch and spend the rest of my days helping Greenpeace blow up the sodding militarists."

The Ice Cream King lives in what used to be a beach-front duplex in West Newport. He turned one half of the duplex into a workshop. That's where he fabricates everything from surveillance radios for the Drug Enforcement Administration to gear for special-weapons teams and crazy rock climbers. He is technologically eclectic. That means he takes an odd cut at all sorts of problems, using materials most of us can't even pronounce. He has one of the most active and inventive minds I've ever encountered. When I've got a technical problem, or when I just want to drink beer with a kindred soul, I call up Benny.

Only barely civilized, Benny lives alone despite the fact that women are frankly fascinated by him. He returns the favor as often as he feels like it but has refused to attach to just one woman. He has a well-hidden fear of dependence that drives him to extraordinary proofs of personal endurance. He does wheelchair marathons. He surfs on a short board and has been known to beat the hell out of loudmouthed jerks twice his size; he simply locks the wheels of his chair and fractures ribs with a single blow.

Other than Fiora, Benny's the only person in the world who could ask for any favor from me, including cold-blooded assassination, and get it without question.

Unfortunately Benny has a major character flaw. Normal social amenities mean nothing to him. He doesn't flout them. He just doesn't notice them. He not only marches to the beat of his own drummer, he has his own damn band. He sleeps only a few hours a night, usually around dawn. Sometimes he calls me to talk or to drink beer when the hours before sunrise take on too many shadows. Most of the time he spends his extra waking hours reading omnivorously. Philosophy, poetry, particle physics or potboilers, all come and go from his hands. But not his mind. If he's seen it, heard it or thought it, it's his for life. He can tell you his first-grade teacher's birth date.

And he answers the phone when he's goddamned good and ready.

So I let the phone ring well past the normal ten. The record so far is sixty-seven, but who's counting? He'll answer it sooner or later.

Benny was panting when he got around to putting the phone out of its misery. I smiled, hoping that I'd finally evened a bunch of old scores.

"I hope I'm interrupting something interesting," I said.

"I only wish you were," he grumbled. "You caught me in the middle of a 200-pound bench press. I'm getting too old for free weights. I damn near dropped it on my own neck when the bleeding phone rang. I finished the set anyway. How's paradise?"

"It has more than the mythical number of serpents. Bugs, too. That's why I called you."

"It better be insects, mate. I hate snakes."

"You're in luck. Phylloxera. Know them? Tiny, look like yellow bedbugs."

There was a three-beat pause while Benny rummaged in his memory.

"Family Phylloxeridae," he said. "Nasty little plant lice of all sorts and types. It's been years since I did my obligatory life-science courses, but if I recall, the bugs like grapevines."

"Bingo. Got anything on your database network?"

"I can get you anything in print. What do you need?"

I told him about Sandra's problem. There was another long silence interspersed with the sound of a computer keyboard being stroked.

"Vastatrix," he muttered. "That's the louse she's got."

The keys sounded for about a minute more.

"There are quite a few abstracts on vastatrix in the scientific databases," Benny said. "They have a lovely history. Damn near destroyed the Frog wine industry a hundred years ago, which for my money is a worthy undertaking. Not much new material, though. Looks like they've been brought under control in the past several decades. Bleeding scientists spoil all the good things. . . . Hello, what's this?"

I listened to Benny breathe for a few minutes.

"There are a few recent journal articles," he said finally. "Mostly theoretical modeling of vastatrix gene structure. Someone called Eric Karger seems to be the bloke to talk to."

"I have. I didn't like what I heard. I need an expert who can burn him down. At the very least I need to take the steam out of the roller he's using on Sandra."

"How much time?"

"None."

"Call me after midnight."

I spent a lot of time constructing and discarding several plans of action. In between, I called Fleming and questioned him about the arson investigation. He told me that there were no new leads and none of the old ones had gone anywhere. When I pointed out that Sandra wouldn't get any insurance settlement until she was cleared of suspicion of arson, Fleming told me things were tough all over and hung up.

So I circled back on Sandra and repeated my offer of a loan. She simply shook her head. She had planted her own vineyard, now she would damn well harvest what came.

About the only pleasure I got out of that day was remembering Fiora and Traven. She had needled him right to the bone and then watched the results with professional interest. Anger is a tool in negotiations, just like flattery. Traven had kept his temper fairly well, all told. Despite his allusions to cut-and-run condo developers, if he knew Fiora's firm at all, he knew that she didn't waste her time with low-cost, high-volume schlock. However, I got the clear feeling from Traven that the idea of breaking Napa Valley ground for anything less than the Taj Mahal was sacrilege. It's an understandable point of view—he already had his piece of paradise. He didn't want a lot of peons moving in and mucking it up.

I didn't particularly blame him for that, either. On the front porch of the guesthouse, away from the hot steel and gasoline fumes of the highway, the valley was fresh and silent and self-contained. The hills were gold and green, elegant in their evening serenity. Tendrils of brilliant white fog seethed silently over the crests of the hills, and the rest of the sky was a blue as deep as time. The late sunlight was the color of a particularly rich Chardonnay, a splendid topaz that you could almost taste. As the sun sank into the last segment of its downward arc, the light would change through rose to Cabernet to a burgundy that was only a few shades of darkness removed from night itself.

But not yet. Now it was still the time of Chardonnay and silence.

In the distance a hawk turned in slow, hungry circles, watching the valley floor through the clear golden air. The bird knew that rodents were moving all through the valley. It could sense the presence of prey as surely as it sensed the currents of air beneath its wings. But the hawk didn't know whether hunting light would run out before the prey revealed itself.

It was the same for me. Sandra's "bad luck" kept rustling and stirring through the valley, gnawing at the foundations of her life. Too many "coincidences." Not enough time. Nothing tangible except hunger and empty talons. Quarantine would be Sandra's nightfall, unless her imported raptor got lucky or the rodents got unlucky.

A flock of crows passed, calling in the stillness, and then it was silent again. The screen door opened behind me. There was a pause before I heard the click of the front door lock taking hold. We might be in paradise, but the habits of civilization were deeply ingrained. There was the soft whisper of the screen door closing and Fiora's footsteps crossing the porch to stop by my chair.

"It's too beautiful an evening for you to look so grim," she said. "You've been here less than a day. What did you expect—a miracle? You're good, but you're not that good. No one is."

I looked at her.

"There are times," she continued, "when I wish your eyes were brown or green or blue or even black. Any color but gray. Right now they remind me of February in Montana."

Before I could think of a suitable answer I heard the flicking whisper of rapid wingbeats as a bird passed close by. I turned quickly toward the sound, drawn by something I couldn't name. I was both surprised and exhilarated when I saw a falcon skimming the nap of the land at barely subsonic speed. He arrowed through the windbreak of thick-trunked eucalyptus without hesitation. Then he turned and came back, settling on a high, naked branch as though Fiora and I weren't there.

I see so few falcons that I couldn't identify this one. He was about eighteen inches long and his feathers were dark and heavily barred, as though he were wearing an expensive Harris tweed. He sat erect, motionless, watching the vineyard beyond the trees with a hunter's intensity. It took me a moment to see what had attracted the falcon's interest. Far off toward Traven's land, a flock of mourning doves was coming toward us. They flew low and fast and skittish, darting and flaring unpredictably.

The falcon fell from its branch. With two sharp motions of his wings he was upon the doves. His approach was fast, stylish and too direct. He pulled up in the face of the flock and reached forward with both talons as though to snatch a dove from the air. Birds scattered like smoke in a gust of wind, gray and insubstantial and elusive. The hungry falcon returned to his perch and sat motionless again, waiting.

"Nature, red of tooth and claw. I'm not sure I want to watch this," Fiora said quietly.

"It's tough on the doves," I agreed, "but falcons don't have an easy life either. They spend a lot of time failing."

"Who are you rooting for?" she asked.

"Both. There are a lot more doves than falcons."

"But the doves are beautiful," Fiora objected. Then reluctantly she admitted, "And so is the falcon, damn it."

I smiled slightly and took her hand. One of the things I love about Fiora is her odd blend of wistful romanticism and intense Scots pragmatism.

In the fading light another flight of doves came in from the direction of the dry creek, skimming a few feet above the vines. Their path brought them past the falcon. He waited, waited, waited, until I thought that perhaps he wasn't hungry after all. The doves were almost abreast when he dropped off the limb and fell like a sword. There was a sudden, silent explosion of feathers as the falcon struck and the dove died between one heartbeat and the next. Falcon and prey vanished between the green vineyard rows.

Fiora drew a deep breath and sighed for the lost dove.

"You wouldn't have the falcon starve to death, would you?" I asked softly.

"No, but I'd have bought him a hamburger if I'd known he was that hungry," she retorted. "And yes, my loving primitive, I know where hamburger comes from."

"You sure?"

"The supermarket."

"I don't know how to break this to you," I began.

"Then don't," she interrupted firmly. "Now what was all this about buying a restaurant?"

Sometimes Fiora's mind is like the flight of a dove—quick, incredibly agile and erratic as hell. But, like the falcon, I'd had a lot of practice following her twists and sudden turns.

"I thought we'd check out the only surviving highly promoted haute cuisine in Napa," I said. "See if it would be something your clients might think of as a good investment."

"It's been awhile since I looked at anything as small as a restaurant. They never were my specialty. You're not really thinking of buying, are you?"

"No, and I doubt that Cynthia is thinking of selling. I just want your opinion as to whether her fancy restaurant was a good investment *before* Sandra's run of 'bad luck.' "

Fiora's eyes narrowed as she thought over the possibilities. "All right. For starters, call and see if they have a table for us. If they do, they're in trouble."

"I may be primitive but I don't fart in public or drink wine through a straw. I've even been known to use a salad fork on special occasions."

"I wasn't referring to your company manners," she said. "Any fancy restaurant that isn't full on Saturday night is not doing much volume."

Cynthia's restaurant passed Fiora's first test. We couldn't get a table until Sandra called Cynthia. I didn't want Sandra to do it but she insisted that it was preferable to having us underfoot and hungry while she and her tardy kitchen crew did advance work on Traven's party.

Sandra's call turned the trick. We drove quickly through the thick evening light. Nouveau Printemps was tucked away on a dry hillside above the Silverado Trail. The reward at the end of a long, twisting drive was a multimillion-dollar view. The redwood and glass building was cantilevered spectacularly into a volcanic wall.

"This view adds twenty percent onto the tab," said Fiora, "and it was worth every nickel it cost her."

As we pulled into the parking lot Fiora started counting.

"Well?" I asked as we walked away from the BMW.

"Between fifty and sixty cars. Subtract a generous twenty for the staff and you've still got forty cars. For our purpose we'll say three diners per car." She glanced at her watch. "It's not even seven o'clock, but I'll bet there are a hundred and twenty patrons inside and parking lot space for as many more. Unless Cynthia has unusual overhead or a crew of crooks she should be making her monthly nut without much problem."

The restaurant was what is called "country casual" in Napa. Open-beam ceilings and lots of smoked glass, fresh flowers and crisp white linen, and a stated preference for jackets on male guests. A jacket on a warm summer night is the kind of affectation that irritates me. Under other circumstances the dress code alone probably would have kept me out of Nouveau Printemps. It was a reminder that modern restaurants have become a kind of participatory avantgarde theater. The show's the thing and the food is irrelevant, so long as it's witty and trendy and not offensive.

I guessed without looking that Cynthia's menu would have a pronounced French accent—caul-wrapped calf's brain and fava beans and pot-au-feu with prices in the gold-card range. I was right. The food was French in the same careful, derivative way that Traven's castle was. As usual, I wondered why people were so intent on aping a declining civilization. I don't buy the "long history of civilized cuisine" argument, either. The Chinese have a history of cuisine and civilization that vastly predates Christ, much less De Gaulle, but I haven't noticed knockoffs of the Forbidden City decorating Napa's hillsides.

When I gave my name to the maître d', I was handed over to a white-coated waiter who ushered us out to a patio table where two could sit comfortably if both of us ordered nothing bigger than a glass of wine. We were told that our table would be ready as soon as possible.

The wine list was as thick as a desk encyclopedia and weighed damn near as much. I was thumbing through it when I recognized Guy Rocheford returning to an nearby patio table. It was obvious from the empty bottle of Moët & Chandon White Star and the scattered appetizer plates that Rocheford and his table partner had been waiting for some time.

The other man had his back to me. There was something familiar about the line of his neck and the set of his shoulders. When he moved slightly at Rocheford's return I recognized Karger. Without his boots, hat, work gloves and jeans he looked very different, almost stylish in an understated, academic way. Rocheford looked like a continental fashion plate, but more androgynous than his American counterpart. I remembered what Sandra had said about a wife and kids and wondered if she had been misinformed. The Frenchman had a bit of the *pouf* about him.

"Isn't that Dr. Karger?" Fiora asked softly.

I nodded and watched Rocheford sit down again. The two men were at ease with each other and the setting. They greeted other diners and chatted with them about the state of the vines and the harvest and the weather. From time to time Rocheford sipped from a tall, fluted glass of Moët. I decided that he would probably burn natural gas in Newcastle, too.

Karger excused himself and vanished in the direction of the rest rooms, giving me a clear view of Rocheford. His face had the look of a man who was on the downhill slide between relaxed and plastered. It made me wonder if the bottle of champagne in the ice bucket was the first or the second of the evening.

Normally I don't drink Cabernet before dinner, particularly not a "big" Cabernet. On the other hand, sitting in a too warm jacket and watching Rocheford swill French wine in the Napa Valley just kind of pissed me off.

"How would you feel about Deep Purple?" I asked Fiora, loud enough to be overheard.

From the corner of my eye I saw Rocheford's head whip around. You would have thought I'd just asked for live escargots. He rolled his eyes heavenward, asking to be spared from the bourgeoisie.

Fiora looked surprised but nodded anyway.

"An excellent choice," the waiter said. "We have several vintages of Deep Purple."

He opened the wine list and pointed toward the Deep Purple entries. I found the vintage I wanted immediately.

"We'll take the one that blew out the Paris tasting," I said casually, waving away the wine list.

"Save your money, *mes amis,*" Rocheford called out, looking up from his champagne glass. "That wine was past its prime six months after it was bottled. American wines simply do not have the depth of French wines."

The waiter cut a sideways, uneasy look at Rocheford. Apparently his feelings about Deep Purple were well known.

"It's a point of view," I said neutrally. "What would you recommend I drink instead?"

Rocheford studied me skeptically for a moment, then shrugged. "If your palate is refined, you will enjoy the Château Rocheford 1969. It will give you a standard against which to judge the mediocrity of Deep Purple's wines."

"Rocheford . . ." I said slowly, like a man searching his memory. "Rocheford . . . Didn't that take second place at Paris? Or was it third?"

"That tasting was a cheap publicity stunt," he said, dismissing it with a wave of his hand. "It is ludicrous to pit a French wine meant to be cellared for decades against an American wine that was made to be drunk right from the crusher." He took another sip of his champagne.

"Do not misunderstand," Rocheford continued. "Deep Purple has its own unsophisticated charms. It is not a great wine, however. It is barely even a good one." Rocheford's face settled into bitter lines. "The wine world would be better off if Deep Purple had never been planted. Its vines should be pulled out by their roots and burned."

"Oh no, not again," groaned Karger from behind us, but the humor underlying the words said that no one took Rocheford's diatribes seriously. "Every time you drink Moët you get angry all over again. For God's sake, you were only a child when the tasting was held."

Karger sauntered between the two tables, hands in the pockets of his pleated pants. On him they looked comfortable rather than purely stylish. I could tell the exact instant when he recognized us. His steps faltered. I turned in time to catch a hint of red on his tanned cheeks. I don't blame him for being embarrassed. He had no way of knowing whether Sandra's friends would be civil about Rocheford's unsolicited lecture.

"I consider his remark a case of enlightened self-interest," Fiora said, smiling at the two men. "That's my specialty."

I simply smiled. Unenlightened self-interest was my specialty, but I saw no reason to point that out.

The waiter reappeared with the speed and urgency of a hummingbird at a feeder. "Your table is ready, messieurs. If you will follow me."

There was as much demand as request in the waiter's words. He clearly wanted nothing further to interrupt the tranquillity of the patio. With an apologetic smile in our direction, Karger helped hustle Rocheford into the dining room. As soon as Rocheford was properly launched into the dining room Karger returned his hands to his pockets and walked along behind, nodding to other patrons and stopping to chat with a few.

"He's unusually politic for a scientist," Fiora said, following my glance. "Most of the ones I've helped set up in business had the social graces of a muddy clam. Wonder if he's planning on starting up a business in Napa Valley?"

"Sounds like he already has. Traven isn't getting Karger's services for free."

The appetizers arrived with unusual speed. They were beautifully presented and geometrically precise in their placement on the polished china plates.

"Does the gentleman still wish Deep Purple?" the waiter asked.

I looked at the plate of pâté. It was very fine-grained and wrapped in its own ribbon of fat. I tasted it, mentally shrugged, and shook my head. Cynthia's pâté was good, but not great. I suspected the rest of the meal would be the same.

"I'll try one of the Rocheford reds," I said.

For the next few minutes I just sat and watched the valley below us. Fiora watched the staff and the flow of patrons, saying nothing.

It was the same throughout the dinner. Fiora was present but she wasn't there; she was thinking about money and all the tricks you can make it do. Normally being shut out like that was guaranteed to piss me off. Not tonight. Tonight I had asked her to go into work mode. In the silence I could practically hear her calculating the overhead against the price of the entrees and the turnover in the dining room.

As I had guessed, the food was good but it had paid the price of feeding a hundred people at a time. Mass production doesn't allow attention to fine detail. Or maybe it was just that the Rocheford 1976 Bordeaux was simply too good for the meal. Guy Rocheford might have been a prick, but the boy's family really knew how to make wine.

"What do you think?" I asked Fiora as I started up the BMW.

"Cynthia is a hell of a businesswoman," Fiora said. "The average seating only takes about ninety minutes from soup to cheese and the average ticket is probably a hundred and fifty dollars with wine. She keeps the prime dining time reserved for the local high rollers and wedges in a seating on either side for the tourists who don't know about eating at a fashionable hour. Any fancy restaurant that can hustle three seatings a night and still price its wine list at two hundred and twenty-five percent of retail is making money."

"Do you think she was doing that well before Sandra closed?"

"Even at two thirds this volume the restaurant would be successful." Fiora yawned. "What about Rocheford and Karger?"

"What about them?"

"Didn't it seem a little odd," she asked dryly, "that the two men in Napa Valley who want Deep Purple to be pulled out by its roots were having dinner together tonight? If I were Sandra, I sure as hell wouldn't count on any secrets being kept between now and harvest."

The thought hadn't occurred to me more than twice a minute all through dinner, but there wasn't a damn thing I could do about it except hope that Traven's clout was enough to ensure Karger's silence.

Fiora and I drove home through the pleasant, warm evening. As soon as I tried the front door of the guesthouse I knew I had something more immediate than Karger to worry about. The door was unlocked.

"Go back and wait by the car," I said to Fiora in a low voice.

Her face went very still. She turned and retreated without a word. Another reason I love that woman is she'll get back in the wagon without an argument, most of the time.

I went in the back way, very quietly. Nobody was inside, but someone had been. A note lay on the bed.

I must speak with you. Meet me in Calistoga tonight.

I looked at the address and Beltrán's signature for a long time before I went out to get Fiora. She watched me change into jeans and a dark T-shirt. She said nothing, even when I tucked the Detonics into its holster at the back of my belt and slipped on a black windbreaker.

She said nothing when I went out the door, either, but her eyes reminded me of broken promises every step of the way.

13

The moon was rising, filling the valley with thin silver light and ebony shadows that shifted with every tiny breeze. I drove with the windows rolled down. The smell of harvest and crush was rich enough to make you drunk. I swore under my breath as I thought how much easier Sandra's life would have been if she had just grown Chardonnay rather than Cabernet grapes. Chardonnays were mostly picked by now. The harvest wouldn't have solved all her problems, but it would have kept her out of bankruptcy.

Beltrán was to have spoken to Don Cummings, the wine maker for the Friars, hoping to force an early pick at Deep Purple. Usually it was only the weather that drove a vineyardist crazy, but this year Beltrán had more to contend with than rain. If he couldn't get the wine maker off his ass, Deep Purple's harvest would be remembered as the Lost Vintage.

I wondered if Karger had found evidence of infestation beyond the few acres bordering Traven's land and then I wondered what the scientist had let slip to his dinner partner. Rocheford wasn't reasonable on the subject of Deep Purple. He'd be delighted to spread the bad word to half the valley, just for the pleasure of watching Sandra's black Cabernet grapes shrivel and raisin in the autumn sun.

If the word got out, the Department of Agriculture would be all over Deep Purple. They wouldn't condemn Sandra's entire vineyard just because one small corner was lousy, especially with Traven throwing his weight around behind the scenes. But unless the official bill of health was issued with incredible speed, Sandra's grapes would be past their prime, good for nothing but feeding starlings and rotting between the rows. And she would be bankrupt.

Air that was neither warm nor cool blew over my face, bringing with it the scent of harvest. Usually I'm not the envious type—vengeful, maybe, but not envious. Yet I looked at the headlights of tractors towing crushers into the vineyards and I felt something that could only be described as jealousy. In a few vineyards people were still picking, rushing frantically to catch the grapes at their bursting peak.

Gondolas rattled by me on the highway, going the other way, reeking of the rich perfume of broken grapes. Empty gondolas were being positioned next to the fields where men and machines would swarm before dawn, harvesting the grapes of growers who had been shrewd or lucky enough to plant early-ripening varieties. Sandra and the other Cabernet and Merlot and Carignane growers had a lot of sweating left to do. The same weather patterns that had brought an early spring, hot summer and early harvest to the Napa Valley could also bring an early round of rain.

Other than harvest traffic, there was little moving on the road. The crowded tasting rooms and boutiques and French deli shops were closed. The tourists had staggered back to the city or to the very few motels that lay at Napa's edge. It would begin all over tomorrow, the bizarre mix of leisurely tasters and frenzied harvest crews.

Maybe tomorrow it would finally be Sandra's turn to reap the rewards of all her work. The sugar levels were low but an early pick would be better than none at all.

The air warmed as Highway 29 headed north, pitching up subtly, rising on the shoulders of Spring and Diamond mountains. The marine influence waned with each quarter mile farther north. It was a dramatic demonstration of microclimates. There were still vineyards around, but not as many and not nearly so famous. The almost overwhelming perfume of crushed, ripe grapes gave way to the more subtle scents of dry grass and dust and pavement slowly cooling beneath the moon. It was a relief not to be reminded with every breath that some farmers had gotten lucky and others were waiting for the dice to stop rolling.

Calistoga's claim to fame had never been wine. The town is known for the mineral water from the hot springs and geysers that hiss and growl and finally burst through the earth with a scalding scream. At one time Calistoga was quite the upscale spa, complete with hot-springs swimming pool, mud baths and assorted witch doctors to hold your aching hand. But that was fifty years ago. People no longer come here to "take the waters." Now the waters are shipped out in little bottles to your local grocery. As a result Calistoga's intersections, gas stations and closed shops still had the feel of old Napa, the California of twenty years ago, back before the Paris tasting set Deep Purple up as a target for French chauvinists and Napa Valley wine pushers. The old hotel where Sandra and I used to stay had been gentrified but at least the job had been done with some respect for the underlying structure. It was not as though the place had been hauled in, brick by brick, from somewhere else.

I drove through the town quickly. Beltrán's address was one of the old, crumbling auto courts that nowadays are rented out to illegal immigrants rather than arthritic spa-goers.

Six young men were standing around a choice '65 Chevy Impala in front of the auto court. The car blocked the driveway that led into a court whose cottages looked like they hadn't been painted since Prohibition. My headlights caught the milk-white glint of Budweiser cans. Trendy Americans drink Corona or Dos Equis but *Mexicanos* prefer Bud. As I passed by, rancho music from the Chevy's radio poured into my car along with the hot air. A few heads turned, but once they saw that I wasn't official the *vatos* lost interest.

And they were *vatos,* no doubt of that. Only crazy kids could harvest from dawn to dark, drink beer until midnight, then get up before sunrise and do it all over again. Older, wiser men—*norteños* to whom the trip to the United States for harvest was a job rather than an adventure—were already in bed.

I circled the auto court on back streets. There was no way to get in to the cottages except past the *vatos* and the driveway. I doubted that the arrangement was an accident. Harvest is a favorite time for Border Patrol raids, because most of the field crews are composed of illegals.

I parked the BMW in front and got out. The boys holding up the Impala gave me a long stare. They couldn't think of a good reason for a gringo to walk their streets at night. As I approached they shifted around, glancing at me quickly and then looking away if I met their gaze.

"Anyone know which cottage is Ramón Beltrán's?" I asked. "He's expecting me."

For a moment no one answered. Then a young kid popped out of the dark. "I'm Pablo Beltrán. I'll take you to my uncle for a buck," he said brashly.

Before I could accept, one of the *vatos* reached out, cuffed the kid and berated him in Spanish, asking if the boy would sell his uncle's life for a dollar.

Pablo yelped. "Hey, Chuy, that hurts, damn you!"

Pablo struggled loose and stood defiantly, fists raised in proof that his big brother didn't scare him. In Spanish, Pablo added that the people who wanted to kill Beltrán were from Sonora, not America. Chuy grabbed a handful of Pablo's hair, shook several times and yelled in Spanish that gringos can pull triggers too.

I began to understand why Beltrán had a wary look about him.

Chuy dropped the kid and turned toward me. He had long hair tied Apache style with a red bandanna. I had eight inches on Chuy but he had shoulders the width of the Chevy's chrome-plated bumper.

"Who are you?" Chuy demanded in heavily accented English.

I answered in Spanish that has a regrettable border accent. Low class, but quite comprehensible. I told Chuy my name and that Beltrán had asked me to come. Then I told him to go and check with Beltrán.

Chuy did a little double take at the Spanish but stood his ground.

"I'll wait in the car," I said in English.

Chuy gave me another thorough look before he gestured to Pablo, who vanished into the small courtyard darkness like a ghost. I sat in the car with the window down, listening to the rancho music, wondering why country songs always sound the same no matter the language or culture.

I also wondered why a Mexican illegal had to worry about hit men in Calistoga, California.

After a few minutes I saw a flash of white in the courtyard shadows. As Beltrán emerged from the darkness I snapped on the dome light so he could see me and be reassured that I was alone. He circled around the car, got in and sat down. Pablo passed by my side of the car, heading toward the low-rider again. I popped a dollar bill between my fingers and handed it to him.

"Muchas gracias," I said.

" 'S okay, man," he said. "Give me five and I'll fly for a six-pack."

I glanced at Beltrán, who nodded. I dug out a ten. "Bring some for Chuy and his friends, too. Being *vatos* is thirsty work."

From the corner of my eye I caught the flash of Beltrán's teeth as he smiled. I suspected he had set me up, just a little payback for being blind-sided in a quiet vineyard. I didn't blame him.

The ten leaped from my fingers and Pablo vanished into the night.

"Where the hell is a twelve-year-old going to buy beer?" I asked Beltrán without turning my head.

"There's a Mexican grocery around the corner," Beltrán said. "They'll trust him. This neighborhood operates under Mexican law, not American."

"I imagine you know a bit about Mexican law," I said. "You were a cop, weren't you?"

Beltrán's teeth flashed again in the darkness of the car. "So were you, I think. An honorable job, no?"

There was a bitterness in Beltrán's voice that was at odds with his smile.

"It can be an honorable job," I said, shrugging, "on both sides of the border."

"More often here than in Mexico," Beltrán retorted coolly.

I waited, letting the silence gather, taking my rhythms from the culturally different ones of Beltrán. It wasn't difficult to picture Beltrán as he must have been once: a clean cop in a dingy little government substation in Mexico. Cops have a different role there. They're expected to dispense curbside justice on a variety of minor offenses. They are empowered to summarily mediate in civil disputes. They are true figures of authority. They are also vastly underpaid and equally corrupt—by American standards. But Mexico isn't America. They have their own system down south and it works for them.

Beltrán was a man who had once wielded real power. Now he was a handsome, tough and very wary majordomo for one of Napa's oldest families. I wondered how long he had been here and whether Sandra had any idea that Beltrán was at least half in love with her. Then I wondered whether he had any idea himself.

Pablo reappeared at the car window. I took one six-pack and waved off the change. The aluminum cans of Budweiser were sweating heavily in the hot night air. Pop tops hissed as we opened them. The beer tasted better than Bud had any right to taste.

Silently Beltrán dug a pack of Marlboros from his shirt pocket, offered a cigarette that I declined and lit his own. The match smelled sulphurous but for once the tobacco smoke smelled sweet rather than harsh. Beltrán smoked with controlled, intense style. It's something you seldom see in the United States anymore. Mexicans don't seem to be afraid of lung cancer.

"You are a friend of Miss Autry," Beltrán said, exhaling smoke into the night.

There was no real question in his voice. He was simply confirming something that he had seen in the way Sandra and I treated each other. A cop's instincts die hard, if they ever die at all.

"Yes."

He was silent for another moment. "What do you think of the professor, this Dr. Karger? Is he a man of knowledge? Does he know what he is doing?"

"You work in the vines. You should know more about that than I do."

Beltrán shrugged expressively. "It is the men I know best, not the vines. Señor Autry hired me because when I say, 'Do this,' the men do it. I have learned much in my years here, but it is still Señor Cummings who says, 'Prune here and here, and spray there and hold back the water in the last eight rows, and wait and wait and wait for the pick.' *Ai chingada,* how that man waits!"

Beltrán made a sharp gesture of frustration. He was the vineyard man; Cummings was the wine maker. They were fighting the age-old battle between the farmer who feared early frost or unseasonable rain and the maestro of wine who waited and waited and waited, hoping to achieve the absolute peak of ripeness.

"If it helps," I said, "Traven thought enough of Karger to pay him a hefty consulting fee. Sandra says he's a recognized authority on phylloxera from one of the best agricultural universities in the world."

There was a short silence. Beltrán drained his beer can, crumpled it absently and sat juggling it in his hand.

"You have been asking questions about people who might desire to harm Miss Autry," he said calmly.

"Yes."

"The valley . . ." He hesitated. "It is a place of old families and old jealousies. Like Mexico, you understand?"

"Vendetta?" I asked, feeling my blood light up at the hint that there might be some game for me to hunt after all.

Beltrán shrugged. "Not the vendetta of blood, no. You Anglos are too cold and pale for that."

I smiled slightly but didn't argue. I try to let people believe whatever comforts them. Beltrán smiled too, as though he guessed what I was thinking.

"Deep Purple is a place of much power, much . . ." He paused, obviously looking for a word.

"Prestige?" I suggested.

"*Sí,*" he said. "People admire, but they also envy. Sandra—Miss Autry—does not always understand this."

"Are we talking about Cynthia Forbes, Bob Ramsey, Guy Rocheford, Vern Traven or somebody I haven't discovered yet?" I asked dryly.

Beltrán's cigarette flared, then sank into an ash-coated ember. He exhaled harshly. "The first two are the same," he muttered. "Ramsey is a *pinche cabrón*. The *huera* is a fitting mate for him."

"I hear he gave Sandra a rough time over the divorce."

"*Sí.* That is why I ask to speak with you. I knew that Sandra— Miss Autry—"

"Leave it as Sandra," I said. "She wouldn't be insulted to know that you think of her as a friend."

The cigarette burned fiercely before Beltrán flipped it out the window with a hard snap of his fingers.

"I would say this to no other man," Beltrán continued reluctantly, "but I can see that you would protect her if you could."

"If she'd let me."

Beltrán smiled sadly. "*Sí,* that is a problem, is it not? With Ramsey, she was a kitten spitting at a tiger, not knowing how cruel a tiger can be."

"What happened?"

"Blackmail," he said calmly.

"What?"

He nodded. "You see, Sandra was very unhappy when she found that her man had been in Cynthia's bed more than he had been at home. I do not live here even a year, but I knew that Sandra's husband had another woman. Everyone knew but Sandra. Finally there was a big fight."

I stiffened suddenly.

"He did not beat her," Beltrán said. "That is not his way. He told her how it was so much better with Cynthia. You understand? He made Sandra feel small as a woman."

I understood. I flexed my hands absently, wondering how Ramsey's neck would feel.

"In the end she went to another man, an old friend," Beltrán continued. "He gave her . . . comfort. Ramsey found out. He hired someone who took pictures. He showed the pictures to Sandra and said that he would publish them in the paper unless she sold Deep Purple to him." Beltrán bent his head and lighted another cigarette with swift, almost savage motions. Smoke wreathed him as he spoke. "I found Sandra crying among the vines. She told me what had passed, and she told me that she would have to give up Deep Purple. The man, the one who had comforted her, would have been ruined if it was known that he had taken a lover, even for such a short time."

There was a long silence. I waited. Beltrán was the kind of man who spoke at his own pace or not at all.

"Late that night I waited for Señor Ramsey to come home from his whore. We talked. He agreed that it would be better for him if he divorced Sandra and went back to his grapes in Sonoma."

I remembered Beltrán's lethal knife and his unexpected strength. I hoped that both had figured prominently in his "talk" with Ramsey.

"I have not told Sandra that I spoke with her husband. I ask you not to tell her. Yet I thought you should know. He is a man who would stoop to blackmail."

That didn't surprise me. On the other hand, it had been a few years since the divorce. Feelings that once ran hot would be running a lot cooler now. Much as I disliked Ramsey—and much as Beltrán obviously loathed him—Ramsey wasn't the only one who wanted Deep Purple. Vern Traven's offer to Sandra had been gently done, but the intent was the same. Not blackmail, but default on a loan. Either way, Sandra lost Deep Purple.

Then there was Guy Rocheford, a good hater if I ever saw one. It had been a long time since the French tasting, but his feelings hadn't cooled one bit.

I looked down at my watch. Midnight, straight up. Time to call the Ice Cream King.

"Anything else I should know about?" I asked.

"Deputy Fleming," Beltrán said, exhaling. "He is Bob Ramsey's friend. They played football in school. Now they drink and hunt deer together. Even a very hardworking policeman would have little chance to find the man who burned Sandra's restaurant. The deputy, he is lazy, I think."

"Yeah, I got that impression. Happens to a man who's on the same job too long."

Beltrán nodded, opened the door and slid out. With the dome light on, he saw the watery ring his sweating beer can had left on the leather. Carefully he flicked away the water.

"The car, it is very beautiful," he said.

I could tell that he had something he wanted to say but he didn't know quite how to phrase it.

"It belongs to Fiora," I said.

"Your wife?" he asked.

"My ex-wife," I said, "but still my woman." There's a crucial difference, especially in Mexico.

"It is a fine thing for a man to have a woman," Beltrán said, shutting the door and stepping away from the car. "A very fine thing."

Beltrán crossed the street like a ghost and vanished into the darkness of the crumbling auto court.

I started the car, backed out into the street and turned toward the center of Calistoga. Chuy raised his Budweiser in silent acknowledgment of the six-pack as I drove by. I flashed the headlights in reply.

Everything in town was shut up tight, but I finally found a phone booth beside a darkened Texaco station at the edge of town. The closed glass booth still held the heat of the day. I stood inside long enough to punch in a 714 area code number. While the phone was ringing I stepped outside of the booth as far as the cord would let me, seeking anything that resembled a breeze. I pulled a beer from the windbreaker's front pocket, popped the top and waited for Benny to answer.

While I waited I ran through Beltrán's words. Other than the fact that he would be glad to stick his pruning knife into Ramsey, I hadn't learned much useful. I had already known that Ramsey was a prick and Fleming was a lazy hound looking for a soft spot to sleep in the sun.

It was the phylloxera that really worried me.

"You took your bloody time," Benny said by way of answering the phone.

"It's four minutes after midnight," I said. "Two of those minutes were taken up waiting for you to answer the phone." I took a swig of beer. "Is Karger bulletproof?"

"No one is, boyo," Benny said. "Haven't you been listening to me all these years?"

I heard the sound of Benny ruffling through papers.

"When you boil off the bullshit," he continued, "Karger is selling a theory that traditional methods of controlling phylloxera are losing their punch."

"Anyone buying?"

"A few professors are publishing quibbles based on things so esoteric it takes another professor to understand them."

"Shit, Benny. I need something more than a quibble to stop Karger."

"Academic reputations are made or broken on quibbles. So are fortunes, in agribusiness."

Now that was a chord I liked to hear.

"Tell me how a scientist can get rich off of piss-colored bugs," I said.

"How? Fast, that's how. Some bloke with a new idea about how to breed cows that will give more milk or grapevines that give perfect, machine-harvestable fruit can make serious money. Even if he doesn't have an idea that can be translated into a patent." Benny continued, rattling papers, "A bright technologist can pick up millions in private grants from growers' associations, chemical or insecticide companies or biotechnology concerns. Technology is bucks, and today's trick scientists are tomorrow's millionaires."

"In other words, a scientist like Karger would have more than an academic interest in proving that he was right."

"You bet he would," said Benny. "As a matter of fact somebody like Karger might have extra incentive."

"Why?" I asked.

"Well, he's from Stanford, right? Stanford is a big-time school but in the field of agriculture it's way behind California's land-grant universities. The top names are all at the University of California campus in Davis. A guy like Karger, with a radical theory, would have to sweat his balls off to gain any acceptance at all."

"A man working that hard might be tempted to stack the odds in his favor," I said.

"Sodding right, mate. And I've figured out a few ways it might be done. Listen up."

I took a drink of beer and listened up. Benny is good, so good that I'm grateful he's on the side of the angels. Otherwise I'd have to take him out in the desert and shoot him. Benny without a conscience would be too dangerous to have around.

By the time he was finished, so was my second beer.

"No wonder people hate experts," I said, crumpling the beer can. "They can get away with too much. All they have to do is overstate the problem and people line up with money in their sweaty hands. Hell, Karger can get rich just examining vineyards for phylloxera that might never have been there in the first place."

Benny grunted. "Right, and if he's on the trail of some promising, as-yet-unfunded research on the problem, grant money will rain down on him like a green monsoon."

"Have I ever told you how brilliant you are?" I said. "Benny, you're a genius. You're the only—"

"Oh no," he interrupted. "Too many times, Fiddler. Too many times."

"Too many times what?" I asked innocently.

"Too many times you have worked that scam on me."

"What scam?"

"The scam that begins, 'I've got a real problem, and *you are the only one in the whole world who can help me.*'"

"Oh, that scam."

"Too right, mate," he said.

"Well, shit. It always works on me."

"You're more bored than I am."

Ouch. "Does that mean you won't sniff around Stanford and see if you can get someone to go off the record on Karger?"

"Oh, I'll do it. I'm already packed."

"You are?" I asked, surprised.

"Fiora called me an hour before you did. Said you were wearing your Detonics but it wouldn't be enough." He paused. "She been dreaming again, boyo?"

14

I finally got some sleep that night, though it was the restless kind. I dreamed about Uncle Jake. The setting was Montana, back before either of us discovered that there was a place called California; but the dialogue was all in Spanish, which neither of us learned until years after we'd left Montana. Everything in the dream was disjointed. I awoke several times feeling out of phase with reality.

The last time I awakened was about six-thirty. Fiora was still in bed, which was unlike her. The sun had been up for hours. She was lying on her side, her head propped on her hand, and she was watching me with clear, thoughtful eyes. Groaning, I closed my eyes again.

"I see you made it back in one piece," she said. "Anything I should know about?"

I lifted one eyelid and looked at her. She was still watching me. In the early morning light her eyes were deep green with bright flecks of gold, far too intense for my peace of mind. The sheet she had tucked over her breasts shifted lower with every breath she took. As neither of us bothers with clothes in bed, it was fascinating to watch the navy-blue sheet slipping down over skin the color of sun-warmed honey. She breathed in again and suddenly sleep was the farthest thing from my mind.

For an instant my arms felt too heavy to move. Beneath the sheet I slid my hand across the bed until it encountered taut, warm belly. By habit, my fingers moved up until they rested comfortably on the hollow between Fiora's rib cage and hipbone.

"Beltrán just wanted to tell me that Sandra's ex-husband is a prick," I said.

Fiora made a sound that could have meant anything.

I opened both eyes to meet her level look. She is always so clear and sharp in the ungodly hours after dawn. She says she gets her best thinking done then, which is why I was a bit worried when I opened my eyes and found her staring at me as though I were an unusually stubborn problem she had to solve before breakfast.

"Sandra came over looking for you last night," Fiora said.

My hand tightened on her smooth hip. "What's wrong?"

"Nothing new. She was just lonely and unhappy and in need of a broad shoulder to put her head on."

"Fiora—"

"It's all right, Fiddler," she interrupted. "I understand."

"Do you?" I asked, tracing the curve of her body with an index finger. "You know I'm only here to help an old friend, not to catch a spark from an old flame. I've got all the fire I can handle in my life right now."

Fiora let out a long breath and put her head down on the pillow next to mine. "I've been thinking about that too. I know that's what you believe with the top of your brain, the civilized part," she said. "But what about the underneath part, way underneath? That's the part of you I've never been able to reach. It's the primitive part of you that loves danger and the hunt. It's the part of you that responds to Sandra's desperate plea for help, even when she hasn't specifically asked for anything. Especially then." Fiora looked at me with troubled green eyes. "And I'm not sure what arouses that instinctive, primitive part of you."

"You have no problems at all in the arousal department," I said, but it was too late. Fiora had been thinking for hours and now I was going to find out exactly what she had been thinking whether I wanted to or not.

"Sometimes you're gentle and refined and thoughtful and caring and all those other civilized things," Fiora continued. "And sometimes you aren't. You're more at home with violence than any man I've ever known. It's simply a part of you, like your gray eyes and the warmth of your hands." She smiled almost sadly. "You have very warm hands, Fiddler. They always feel as though you've been holding them over a campfire."

This time I was the one who refused the sensual bait.

"Everyone is both civilized and savage, whether they admit it or not," I pointed out. "Including you. The two parts just aren't very well integrated in most people, probably because civilization tries to deny the primitive. But it's there. You know it's there and you don't like it. You never have."

It was an old discussion between us. Sometimes it was an old and passionate argument. I knew my lines by heart and so did she. Yet, even though the words were old, the pain of deep disagreement was always new. We keep after it because sometimes, rarely, we manage to learn something new about each other and ourselves somewhere between the automatic words and the fresh pain.

Fiora slid her hand up my arm, across my shoulder, and let her palm smooth down my chest. As she spoke, she kneaded the mat of hair and muscle like a contented cat.

"Sometimes I think I never should have made you rich," she said. "If you had to work for a living you wouldn't have time to go wandering around looking for windmills and dragons and unlucky maidens."

I closed my eyes, letting Fiora's words rush by like clear water. What she was saying mattered less than the subtle huskiness of her voice and the heat of her hand sliding down my chest.

"And too often I'm so goddamn busy that I don't have time to play fair-haired maiden for you," Fiora admitted. "So you have to go out looking for some other fair-haired maiden to rescue. And that makes me edgy and then you get defensive and we have a fight and one of us gets mad and there you have it—a thoroughly jumbled existence."

I drew a deep breath through my nose, making it sound like a snore.

Fiora's hand slid lower. Much lower.

"Am I boring you?" she asked. "If so, I'll get up and let you sleep."

The muscles of her haunch flexed when she slid a leg out from under the sheet as though she were getting out of bed. I took a healthy grip on her thigh to keep her from following through on the threat.

"Then I'm not boring you," she murmured.

"You have my full attention—"

"Yes, I noticed," she said, moving her hand under the sheet.

I breathed deeply and tried to ignore her. "—and you're confusing the hell out of me, but you're not boring me."

"Perfect," Fiora murmured, relaxing full length against me.

I had the feeling she wasn't talking about boredom. Her tongue was warm as she teased my ear and her breasts were nestled against my shoulder. Her nipples had begun to rise and harden. They were pressing against my arm like soft, hungry tongues. Beneath my hand her body was taut, humming like a tightly drawn wire with the fierce, almost secret intensity that makes Fiora unlike any other woman I've known.

"Fiddler?"

"Any time," I said, picking her up and settling her in place. "As long as the first time is now."

She didn't answer, unless that odd sound she made as we fit together was meant to be a word. Then she opened her eyes and looked at me, into me, all the way to the core, and I could feel her intensity burning through me. In that instant I wondered what her dreams had been, what she had seen that made her look at me as though she had to sink as far into me as I was in her. Then she began moving and touching and tasting and I didn't want to think about anything anymore.

It was a long time before we untangled and showered together and dressed. I had just finished pulling on some clothes when there was a gentle rapping at the door of the guesthouse. Sandra stood on the porch, looking as though she had been up for several hours, none of them pleasant. She smiled rather wanly and held out a basket to me. It was full of fragrant, freshly cut flowers.

"One of Vern's boys just delivered these," she said. "Vern said he wanted Fiora to have them first thing."

As I turned to call Fiora, her small hand appeared from behind me and took the basket.

"They're spectacular," Fiora murmured, eyeing the flowers the way you're not supposed to eye gift horses. "I wonder what he wants?"

Sandra made a vague gesture and turned to go. "There's a note with them. I'd better run. I've got thirty hours of work to do in the next eight."

"Wait," I said.

I reached into the flowers and pulled out a deep pink rose. It was the color Sandra's cheeks would have been if she hadn't been too worried to sleep. My pocket knife made short work of the thorns and long stem. I tucked the rose through one of the buttonholes on Sandra's white work shirt.

"Now you'll have time to smell at least one flower," I said.

Suddenly Sandra's golden-brown eyes got too bright. She hugged me close and hard before she headed back across the lawn to the big house, where kitchen workers were even now circling, looking for their boss.

When I turned around Fiora was watching me with eyes that were almost as haunted as Sandra's had been. After a moment she looked away and read the card that had come with the flowers. Wordlessly she passed the card to me. The handwriting was masculine, highly stylized, almost hieroglyphic.

> *Fiora, I was too hasty and far too harsh yesterday. Please accept these as a partial apology. The rest of the apology awaits you and Fiddler at breakfast this morning. Any time before nine. Vern.*

There was a postscript.

> *Please do come. It could be enormously profitable, as well as a lot of fun.*

I looked up and saw a single, honey-colored eyebrow raised in the rankest sort of skepticism. "Fun," she said, deadpan. "Goody. Do we go?"

With a shrug, I accepted the inevitable. "Sandra needs Traven's clout right now. It won't kill us to be nice."

Fiora smiled. "You do realize that 'nice' is found between 'nasty' and 'obnoxious' in the dictionary?"

"Maybe you'd better stay here," I said.

Suddenly Fiora gave me a warm smile.

"I'd rather be with you," she said softly. "Don't worry. I'll be good. Despite the green-eyed monster that lurks in the basement of my mind, I like Sandra too much to deliberately hurt her. Even over you."

As soon as the BMW dropped down into Traven's private valley I guessed what form the rest of Traven's apology would take. The hot-air balloon was just beginning to flutter and fill on the front lawn of the Traven estate. In the few minutes that it took us to drive up and park, the balloon grew out of the grass like an immense burgundy-colored mushroom.

A ground crew of six men used the balloon's burner and a bank of commercial-sized fans to fill the envelope. As we watched, the gas bag became lighter than the cooler air surrounding it. Slowly the balloon lifted off the ground.

The wicker basket that was the gondola still lay on its side. As the gas bag rose, it slowly righted the gondola. A member of the ground crew sprang aboard and kept the burner cranked up high, pouring heat into the expanding envelope. There was something both stately and comic about the balloon, but it was very pretty in the morning sun.

Traven emerged from the house as if on cue. He was carrying a huge hamper with him. His shirt was maroon silk with pearl buttons. His riding pants were black. Knee-length English riding boots shone in the slanting sunlight. How the hell he managed to avoid looking ridiculous, I'll never know. Maybe it was just that, against the backdrop of the ruthlessly manicured estate, he looked perfect, an actor carefully costumed for the coming performance.

As Fiora and I got out of the car Traven gave us a big, come-ahead wave and gestured toward the balloon straining up into the bright morning sky.

"Looks like we're being taken for a ride," Fiora said under her breath.

"Bite your tongue."

When we got up to the balloon Fiora smiled widely and thanked Traven for the fresh flowers. She was in work mode again, as thoroughly costumed in her own way as Traven was in his.

"Your timing is perfect," Traven said, turning toward me. "Step aboard."

I lifted Fiora over the lip of the basket and levered myself in after her. The kid on the burner let go of the lanyard, grinned at Traven and hopped out. Traven handed me the hamper of food and got in with the grace of a man to whom the awkward gondola was very familiar. At Traven's signal the ground crew released the balloon. Slowly we began to rise.

"Isn't it a great day to be alive?" Traven said enthusiastically, admiring the estate and the balloon and the endless, open sky. "Let's get some altitude on this thing and then we can talk."

As Traven pulled on the lanyard, the propane burner burst into life. We rose up into the clean morning air. Balloon ascents are noisy. The burner makes a hollow, rattling snarl that I found grating in the few minutes before I learned to ignore it.

The balloon hit a small rising air current and our rate of climb began to increase. Despite Traven's theatrical clothes, he was no fool in a balloon. He sensed that new current of air instantly and shifted to take advantage of it. Letting go of the lanyard, he allowed us to rise quietly on the back of the natural thermal.

In five minutes we had floated a hundred and fifty feet above the vineyards, which put us well above the highest trees and out of the reach of anything except the hawks and the crop dusters. Men and equipment moved through the fields below us, harvesting the Chardonnay vines that Traven had stair-stepped into the edges of his valley. Fiora leaned over the edge of the gondola and made appropriate noises at the cultivated beauty unrolling beneath us. Finally she turned back and gave Traven her most polished smile.

"This is the most beautifully dressed stage I've ever seen," she said. "If I could walk out of my front door each morning and commute to work by balloon, I'd want to make sure things didn't change too much."

Fiora's oblique apology was accepted in the spirit that it had been given—obliquely.

"Something this grand does make people overprotective," Traven admitted. He smiled at Fiora, then at the rich color and swelling curves of the balloon and finally at the equally rich color and curves of the vineyards below. Still smiling, he opened the hamper and produced a magnum of Schramsberg Blanc de Noirs 1981. "Let's drink to the Napa Valley and its unparalleled life style."

The champagne was so cold that moisture had beaded up on the dark green body of the bottle. He handed the wine to me while he bent over the hamper again. I peeled the lead capsule and twisted off the wire birdcage. Sensing Fiora's attention, I looked at her. She was watching my hands and smiling as though she were remembering our morning. For an instant I was tempted to chuck Traven headfirst into his too perfect vineyards and finish the rest of the voyage alone with Fiora.

The cork popped with a sound as round and full as the balloon. The bottle smoked as carbon dioxide and the rich smell of yeast curled up. Traven handed Fiora three crystal tulip glasses etched with the Traven Vineyards logo and I poured the pale, bubbling wine into each. With deft motions Traven unloaded the contents of the hamper onto the small sideboard that was mounted on the inner edge of the gondola. There were gigantic, long-stemmed strawberries and a covered basket of croissants and muffins still warm from the oven. We touched glasses and drank. The champagne was perfect, haunting. The strawberries were nearly as big as teacups, succulent, overflowing with juice and flavor. The croissants tasted as light as the air we floated on.

As Fiora said, Traven really knew how to dress a stage.

I looked off toward the southwest, where the hot summer sun was dissipating the morning clouds over San Pablo Bay. Traven swirled the tulip lightly in his hand, releasing a burst of the champagne's aroma. Without missing a beat he lifted the glass to his nose, inhaled, then sipped and drew a breath lightly through his mouth.

The assured gestures of a wine cognoscente should have been at best ostentatious and at worst ridiculous, like the clothes he wore, but Traven had made the role his. There was no longer a difference between the actor and the person, the stage and the world.

"I kind of hate to spoil a nice morning, but time's flyin' a lot faster than this ol' balloon," Traven said.

I could feel Fiora come to a point beside me. She used to say that when a Texan's drawl deepens you should grab your wallet and run. When Traven bent over and rummaged in the picnic basket, Fiora shot me an amused glance across his back. I wondered how many business breakfasts like this she had scripted herself.

When Traven straightened, he had the morning newspaper in his hand. I hadn't seen a headline that big since Neil Armstrong landed on the moon.

PHYLLOXERA MENACE INVADES NAPA VALLEY

15

I showed it to Fiora. She gave me a sudden, dark look but said nothing.

"It's impossible to keep a secret in a small town," Traven said, his tone halfway between apology and irritation. "But this was unexpected."

I started reading. The by-line on the story was "Peter Chapman, Napa *Register* Farm Writer." The breathless style of the opening paragraphs suggested that context wasn't Chapman's main concern, drama was. The biggest bang for the buck. Chapman probably wasn't going to remain a farm writer on the *Register* for very long. He wrote with the fervor that would probably win him a spot on the *Chronicle* or the Los Angeles *Times* before long.

> *A shudder of concern passed through the Napa Valley wine-grape industry yesterday when it was learned that a plant pest which once destroyed millions of acres of French vineyards has been discovered in at least two Napa vineyards.*
>
> *Phylloxera, a root louse that sucks the life from grapevines, has been unearthed in one of the valley's most historic vineyards and in a major parcel of Cabernet Sauvignon grapes immediately adjacent to it.*
>
> *If the louse has, indeed, managed to establish itself, the entire varietal wine industry in the Napa Valley may well be at risk, according to experts and grape growers.*
>
> *"We are all in terrible trouble. This is exactly the problem that almost killed France a century ago," said one prominent vineyardist who asked that his name not be used.*

There was something about the phrasing of that paragraph that made me look up quickly at Traven.

"The reporter called me last night, just before press time," Traven said heavily. "He was fishing for confirmation from me. I did the best I could to duck it, but, hell, underneath all this"—he waved a hand at the balloon and the valley—"I'm a roughneck, not a goddamned PR type. After I hung up I called Eldon Lee, the editor of the paper, and tried to get the story pulled. That didn't work, but I did get Eldon to tone it down somewhat and to keep our names out of it."

"Toned down?" I said, looking at the headline again. Then I kept reading, wondering how the hell the original could have been worse than what I was seeing.

> *The* Register *learned from several independent sources that the existence of the infestations was confirmed yesterday afternoon by an outside consultant, Dr. Eric Karger of Stanford University.*
>
> *Contacted last night at his temporary lab and office in St. Helena, Karger refused to comment. He said any release of information would have to come from the growers who are his clients.*

I looked up at Traven again. "Did you get any idea from the reporter who his sources were?"

"None," he said. "This Chapman is a shrewd little cock. He's pissed off most of the growers in the valley at one time or another. I don't know why the paper uses his stuff. Eldon defends him, says he's a hell of a reporter. Personally, I think he's a loser."

"The standards by which you judge human beings don't apply to journalists," Fiora said, giving me a sideways look.

I wasn't about to argue that one.

The story jumped to an inside page and I went with it. There were several paragraphs of background about the decimation of French vineyards a century ago. Then Chapman executed the kind of shrewd jump-switch that said he had pretty good background sources.

> *Napa Valley grape growers have kept the dread parasite at bay by grafting their varietal vines onto rootstock which*

*is capable of resisting phylloxera. It is feared, however,
that a new strain of the insect has developed, a strain
which attacks the previously resistant stock.*

I looked up at Traven. "Your man Karger has been talking to
the press," I said. "He's the only possible source for this paragraph
about rootstock."

Traven looked surprised. "Do you really think so?"

I nodded. "At the very least, he's talking to Chapman on background."

"Not any longer, he isn't," Traven said quickly.

I shrugged and went on reading. It didn't much matter what
Traven did to Karger now. It was too late. The cat was out of the
bag, the horses were out of the barn, and the balloon was well and
truly up.

The next paragraphs told me how right I was.

*The affected vineyards are adjacent to Highway 29 in
the central part of the Napa Valley. Both are planted in
Cabernet Sauvignon, one of the most widely planted
grapes in the valley. The smaller parcel is owned by an
old-line grape-growing family whose wines are among the
most famous in California.*

*The larger parcel is under the control of a newcomer
with his own line of premium varietals.*

The story petered out into some paragraphs on other plant di-
sasters that afflict grapes and a series of innocuous quotes from the
county agricultural agent and the head of the growers' association.
The pained neutrality of the quotes told me that Traven had been
good for something, at least. He had kept the official agriculture men
out of Deep Purple's vineyards. How much longer he could do that
was a moot question.

Traven flicked a manicured fingertip against the newspaper.
"Poor Sandra. She told me last night that she thought she had just
about talked Art—you know Art Jenkins, Napa Valley Growers Service and Trust?—into rolling over the loan despite the fire. Seems
Fiora had run the numbers a new way for Sandra and they really
looked good."

I looked at Fiora. She hadn't said anything to me about that.

Apparently she had been doing more in Sandra's kitchen than filling quiches.

Fiora nodded. "They did look good. I don't know why the accountant she had was being so conservative."

"It doesn't matter now," Traven said, glaring at the paper. "After this, Art wouldn't lend money on Deep Purple if I underwrote the loan myself." Traven made a sound of disgust. "At least I managed to hold off the cry for quarantine. It took a little yelling but folks finally agreed that there's no point in running off half cocked. The least we owe the daughter of Howard Autry is a few days for Dr. Karger to find out if the problem is widespread."

I looked down at the champagne in my glass. The slanting rays of the sun were already hot, even before nine. The wine was warming and flattening. Soon the only significant difference between champagne and piss would be the alcohol content. Traven held up the bottle and gestured toward my glass. I shook my head. He toyed with the basket of giant, long-stemmed strawberries, selecting one, taking a bite of it and then flinging the remainder away. He did that several times before he turned back to us.

"Well, what's done is done. Now it's up to me to save what I can. Sandra loves the land but she's just not being realistic about what can happen." Traven shot a look at Fiora. He grinned a bit ruefully and suddenly looked about ten years younger. "Living in Napa Valley kind of takes you away from reality. You reminded me of that yesterday. Then there was that damned reporter. I've been living in a fool's paradise, thinking that nothing would ever change here. Well, it will. The only businesslike thing to do is accept it and try to keep the changes to a minimum."

Traven picked up a huge strawberry and balanced it on his palm. The tip of the fruit had been bruised. It oozed red juice onto his hand. He frowned and pitched the strawberry overboard without taking a bite. Absently he rubbed his damp palm over his pants. It was the gesture of a man who had grown up in work-stained jeans.

"Sandra is a lovely woman," Traven said finally, "but she's living in a dream world and she just doesn't want to wake up. Under normal circumstances I'd do what I could for her and then walk away and leave her to her dreams. But I can't do that any longer. Deep Purple touches Traven Vineyards on three sides. Whatever happens to her happens to me and my way of living."

Without looking down, Traven snapped his wrist lightly, sending the wine swirling in the glass. There were a few bubbles. The champagne, like the cool of the morning, was largely spent.

"Sandra," Traven said, sighing over the name. "Sandra won't face the truth until it's way too late to help her, much less Napa Valley. She'll be forced to sell out and then she'll do it in a rush and at a loss and she won't have the valley's best interests at heart when she looks for a buyer. She'll just be trying to survive, and who can blame her for that?"

Traven sent Fiora another fast look, but there was more apology than antagonism in the glance. He had learned.

"Now don't misunderstand me, ma'am," he said softly. "I'm sure if you got your hands on that property you'd do your best to put up a really classy resort—I mean diamonds, not rhinestones—or a bunch of top-end shops like Rodeo Drive. Class all the way. Nothing but the best. And sooner or later you might be able to get your zoning changes through and building would begin."

He smiled. It was the smile of a man who understood how those things happened, a man who had helped a few of those things happen from time to time himself. "It would take years, but it would come sure as God made little green apples," he said. "Your firm has a lot of clout, and my people tell me that you're a big part of its success."

Clear-eyed, intent, Fiora watched Traven with the calm of a person who has heard all the business pitches before, the flattery and the truth and everything in between.

"I'm still a reasonably young man," Traven continued, "and I came to this valley to stay. No matter how classy and rich they might be, tourist resorts or shops just aren't estates or vineyards. That's what Napa wants for itself and that's what I want too. We won't get it if Sandra lets you underwrite her agricultural costs."

As though to emphasize his point, Traven leaned on the lanyard and set a roaring blast of heat into the balloon's dark envelope. After about thirty seconds he let go again.

"Let me be sure I understand you," I said, trying to make my tone businesslike rather than angry. "You're saying that we'll take advantage of Sandra when she's desperate and—"

"Not at all," Traven said quickly, cutting across my words. "I know you're her friends. You'll do everything you can for her. It's just that you can't do as much as I can. I've looked into you, Fiddler. You've got money but, to be indelicate about a very delicate—"

"You have a lot more money than I do," I said impatiently. "So?"

"So you could carry Sandra for a while, but sooner or later you'd have to get out from under. Either you'd take Deep Purple in payment for old debts—and you know Sandra would be the first to insist on something like that—or Fiora's firm would sell the land for Sandra and get your money back that way." Traven shrugged. "Hell, man, I'm selfish. I'll be the first to admit it. I want to control the destiny of the land that controls the destiny of Traven Vineyards."

He turned back to Fiora, telling me that he had long since figured out when business was the topic she was the power to be swayed.

"On the other hand, I know what business is like. I don't expect you to do me any favors for free. I'm used to paying for experts, and I'm used to paying top dollar. It's worth it."

Fiora made a neutral sound, the kind that tells someone she's listening but she hasn't heard anything to respond to yet.

"I want you to tell Sandra the plain truth," Traven said.

"Which is?" asked Fiora when Traven paused.

"That, much as Fiddler wants to help her, he doesn't have the cash," Traven said bluntly. "But I do. I can buy off her loan from the bank before they foreclose. I can refinance her land, using some of mine as collateral. Hell, I'll buy the damn land if it comes to that. Just so no outsiders go getting their fingers in Napa's pie."

"Go on," Fiora said.

She had switched from her neutral "I'm listening" face to her "I'm intrigued" expression. The latter comes with a faint smile of approval designed to encourage the poor slob across the desk to proceed full speed ahead and damn the land mines. Along with the poker face, it's an expression that all Harvard MBAs must master before graduation.

It's also the expression that irritates the hell out of me. It always has. I don't know why. I do know that it never fails. It makes me want to grab Fiora and peel that cool, calculating veneer off and get to the fierce, responsive woman beneath.

Fiora's expression didn't bother Traven one bit. He smiled slightly, nodded slightly and all but clicked his champagne glass against hers. I got the distinct feeling of being the audience, the outsider. It's not a feeling I like, not with Fiora.

"If you bought Sandra out, you'd stand an outside chance of making a killing," Traven said, "but I promise you I'd fight any development plans. Nothing personal, you understand. I'd just be looking after my own interests like you were looking after yours. But I'm sure you'll agree that my opposition would increase your downstream risk appreciably."

Fiora said nothing. It was poker-face time.

"But on the other hand," Traven said, "if Sandra let me underwrite a new loan for her, or buy the land outright, I'd be more than happy to see that you could turn an immediate profit with absolutely no downstream exposure."

Fiora nodded as though she knew what was coming. "Go on," she said.

"If somebody just explained the facts of business life to Sandra, I'm sure she would agree to let me take care of her."

I started to object but Traven raised his hand to me.

"Now before you react, hear me out," he said. "I'd guess that Sandra is probably in debt to the tune of half of her equity in Deep Purple. Say . . . three million, plus or minus. Of course, I'd want her to have a cash bonus on signing so she could take care of her other debts. Say five hundred thousand. That brings the whole package in at three point five." He nodded to Fiora. "The usual finder's fee for a deal like that is three hundred and fifty thousand dollars."

"Plus or minus," Fiora said smoothly.

Traven leaned on the lanyard, buying altitude at the cost of silence. After a long burst of flame he turned back to Fiora and nodded very slightly, like a gentleman bidding at a private auction.

"Call it four," Traven said. "Naturally, I wouldn't expect Sandra to cover that finder's fee, or even to have any knowledge of it. She feels indebted enough already, to all of us."

There was a fascination to it all, like watching a sidewinder angle up on a mouse. Strip any sentiment from the process and you can admire the muscular grace of the snake, the speed and cleanness of the kill.

Traven was a sidewinder. He saw what he wanted and he was going after it. When he got to it he wouldn't play around. He would eat it. Then he would sleep it off until the time came to hunt again.

Not very sophisticated, perhaps, but snakes have thrived for millions of years.

Yet I happened to know the particular prey in question very well. Listening to Sandra being cut up and portioned out made the primitive part of me killing mad. I did what I could to keep the lid on my basement instincts.

"What kind of time frame are we looking at?" Fiora asked.

I turned my back and stared out over the gondola. Two hundred feet below us, paralleling us on a dusty farm road, a maroon truck kept pace with the balloon. Behind that was a maroon car, rapidly getting dusty. The glossy vineyard spread out in all directions until it lapped at the brushy hills. Everything was laid out for inspection, rows of vines washed and polished as though waiting for the gods to give their stamp of approval.

Slowly I tipped my glass and let the wine pour out, wondering if the grapes would think that gods pissed champagne. That was one more thing I'd never know, right along with how Fiora could stand to participate in all the genteel, civilized violence. For me, the fact that the score is kept in money rather than blood somehow makes the process more vicious, not less. Fiora doesn't feel that way; it is blood that repels her, physical rather than fiscal violence.

I turned back and watched the woman I loved, wondering if I'd ever learn anything new about her or myself.

"The sooner you can get Sandra to sign, the better," Traven said bluntly.

"I couldn't give Sandra any recommendations without researching matters more," Fiora said.

"What you gave the bank yesterday is all the research anyone needs," Traven countered. "I don't like pushing this hard, but things have gone sour so quickly that I can't hold this offer open more than a few hours. Especially after that newspaper article."

"When did you have in mind?"

"Tonight. At the party."

Fiora looked thoughtful, then slowly shook her head. Honey-colored hair burned as sunlight ran through the strands. She appeared as innocent as an angel, incapable of vice or violence. But then Volker had looked that way, too, and he had been capable of every vice, every violence.

"I can't promise anything," Fiora said finally. "Sandra won't have time to consider the offer seriously until after the party to-night."

Traven shrugged. "Do what you can. But I have to tell you that as soon as I get down on the ground I'm putting out feelers for another kind of settlement."

"Of course," Fiora said. She turned toward me, saw my empty glass and said, "More champagne?"

"No, thanks. Must be getting airsick. You know how it is with me."

Fiora's eyes narrowed. It must have been my tone. She knew that I had a real limited tolerance for the kind of bloodless yet still lethal throat cutting that was the meat and drink of the business she so loved.

"Then we'd better get down, hadn't we?" Traven said solici-tously. "Actually, I should be getting back home anyway. Lots to be done before the party tonight."

I didn't argue about hanging around to enjoy the view. A con-versation like the one I'd just heard strips the romance right out of the wine country. The only thing I felt like was taking a shower. Knowing that you're in love with a honey-blond tiger shark is one thing; watching her in action is another. The fact that Fiora felt the same anger about my more direct methods of solving certain prob-lems was no comfort. I knew all about our differences. What I needed to know was how to live with them better.

Traven pulled a hand radio from the picnic hamper. He spoke a few words, then turned and pulled on a rope that opened the vent panel at the top of the balloon. Hot air rushed out of the envelope and we began to settle. By the time we were a hundred feet above the ground the maroon pickup truck was beneath us. Traven slowed our descent with another blast of hot air. Twenty feet off the ground, he poured on the heat again and arrested the descent perfectly. We settled into the grasp of the ground crew like a feather.

I couldn't get out of that beautiful balloon fast enough. Fiora took care of the obligatory small talk while we were driven back to the recreated, sandblasted château. I nodded to Traven politely enough but didn't say a word as I drove Fiora out of that perfect valley just as quick and as hard as I could.

From time to time Fiora gave me quiet, sideways glances, but all she said was, "Unless you have something planned, why don't I drop you back at Deep Purple and take the car? I've got some things to do in town."

"Looking for a dress to wear to Sandra's funeral? You might try your sharkskin suit and flensing knife," I suggested. "And a gutter for the blood. Christ. And you complain about my brutal, primitive nature. At least the folks I hit have it coming. What the hell has Sandra ever done to—"

Abruptly I stopped talking, knowing that I was being unreasonable, irrational and unfair. It wasn't Fiora's fault that she had a clearer grasp of reality than Sandra's generous, naive nature allowed. It also wasn't something that I particularly wanted to change about Fiora. It was just that sometimes Fiora's unflinching Scots pragmatism irritated the shit out of me, and now was definitely one of those times.

Fiora gave me a hard-edged look. "You've really got it bad for Sandra and the Napa Valley, don't you?"

"What does that mean?"

"It means that you're still so shot in the ass with your romantic memories of the way it used to be when you were here with Sandra that you can't see anything else. You want to help her but Vern's right—you don't have the money. That makes you mad as hell and you're taking it out on everything around you." She leaned forward. "But I *can* help Sandra, Fiddler. And I have. Sandra's going to be all right now, and you haven't been beaten or shot or had your hands mangled until you can't even button your own shirt." She drew a harsh, broken breath. "But you can't see that, can you? All you can see are the tears Sandra won't cry when she looks at you and remembers how it once was!"

We drove back to Deep Purple in silence.

16

Irreconcilable differences. That's what the court document said, however many years ago it was.

Still there. Still potent.

We had learned to avoid confronting those differences in anger. Most of the time.

I pulled off the highway at the entrance to Deep Purple's long, winding driveway. Fiora got out and came to my side of the car to take over the driving. As I got out, I tried to think of something to say. Nothing came but the truth, the three words that said so much yet never seemed to say enough. I bent quickly and lifted Fiora's slender, fierce body against mine in a hug.

"I love you."

For an instant she was stiff. Then she hugged me hard, told me that she loved me and got in the car. I could still feel the force of her arms as I watched her drive away.

The sun was blistering. I walked quickly along the soft asphalt of the new road leading to the ruined restaurant. The petroleum smell of the blacktop was pungent, overwhelming the earthy smells of the valley. The leaves of the Cabernet vines rattled and scraped dryly, like sheets of parchment or dried bones. The sound seemed more insistent today than it had yesterday, as though the vines were impatient to be relieved of their rich burden. A hundred yards away Don Cummings, the Friars' wine maker, moved down Deep Purple's rows, sampling grapes at random, squeezing a drop of juice onto the glass slide of his refractometer and reading the sugar level against the sun. I watched as he held the instrument to his eye, then lowered it and shook his head. Harvest was still out of the question.

When I rounded the last curve in Deep Purple's drive I knew that harvest had never been farther away. Sandra was standing motionless on her front steps, frozen in the act of wiping her hands on her apron. Ramsey towered over her, gesticulating. Karger was at the bottom of the steps, watching with the detachment of a man accustomed to seeing reality through a microscope.

In front of them, half filling the yard, was an audience of frightened farmers. I had seen their trucks on nearby farm roads. They were neighbors who lived close enough to the terrified at the thought of Deep Purple infected with phylloxera. Other men were wine makers or cellar masters or their friends. They, too, were frightened.

Karger did nothing to reassure them. He stood with one foot on the first step of the old porch, his arms folded, his eyes downcast, studying the cracked cement at his feet. His whole attitude was that of a man who could hear the arguments better if he didn't see them as well.

A movement at the base of a huge shade tree caught my eye. The man was in his early twenties, had hair over his collar and a mustache whose ends grew to his jawline. He was tall, thin, and watched the action as though it were a sporting event. He wore unremarkable clothing—blue jeans and an open-collared shirt. I recognized his type even before I saw the 35-millimeter camera slung over his shoulder and the spiral notebook stuffed in his hip pocket. Peter Chapman, small-town reporter/photographer on the way up.

The faint smile on Chapman's face told me that he was enjoying the scene. There was no particular maliciousness in the fact. It was just that reporters live on drama the way phylloxera live on grapevines. Chapman was smiling because he could already see another page-one by-line for himself. He had probably composed the lead in his mind already, something along the lines of: "Angry Napa Valley grape growers yesterday confronted the owner of a phylloxera-infested vineyard and demanded that she protect their holdings from the spread of the dread parasite."

I shouldered quickly through the group and deliberately brushed past Ramsey with enough force to interrupt his harangue. I didn't stop moving until I was standing between him and Sandra.

"You look like you could use a friend," I said very quietly to her.

She smiled weakly, let out a long breath and sort of sagged against me. "Help me," she whispered. "Oh, Fiddler, please help me!"

I turned and faced the group, keeping Sandra at my side but a little behind me.

"What's the problem?" I asked, careful to keep my voice calm. They were good men, most of them, but frightened. I don't trust good, frightened men. They're unpredictable.

Ramsey's mouth flattened into a mean line. He wasn't a good man, so I wasn't worried about him. I knew just what his impulses would be and how I would handle them—and him.

"This doesn't involve you," he said curtly. "This is wine business, and I don't mean the business of drinking it, which is all you know about."

"Beats selling dirty pictures."

For a moment Ramsey didn't get the reference to his aborted attempt at blackmailing Sandra. Then his face went white before it flooded with red. He leaned even closer to me.

"Listen, you nosy son of—"

"I'm listening," I interrupted. "So is the Napa *Register*. You going to tell either of us something new or are you going to stay with the tried and tacky methods you know so well?"

The promise of a confrontation had lured Chapman out of the anonymous shade into the sun. He had circled the crowd and edged up to the porch so he could hear what was being said. Slipping the camera into position, he held it at the ready, sensing a good action shot coming up.

"You're on private property, Chapman," I pointed out. "You'd better have permission before you shoot a picture."

He lowered the camera and looked uneasy. Most people don't know that there's no need to suffer the assaults of the free press quietly. Technically, at this moment Chapman was a trespasser. He knew it and so did I. The only reason I didn't run his ass off Sandra's property was that I had a use for him. He was going to publish all the arguments Benny had given me against taking Karger's word for the seriousness of the phylloxera situation.

I turned back to Ramsey. "Actually, I've been thinking about getting into vineyard financing. Deep Purple looks like a good place to start."

Ramsey didn't like that. His reaction made me wonder if he had tried again to cut a deal with Sandra and failed.

"Are you buying into a vineyard or a bed?" Ramsey asked, but he was bright enough to say it so softly that only Sandra and I could hear.

I shrugged. "I know it comes as a surprise to you, but most men don't have to pay for sex."

With a feeling of detachment I watched the signs of rage in Ramsey's face. The decision to throw a punch registers first on the face, then in the fists. I wasn't looking for a fight, specifically. On the other hand, if he was looking, I was right here.

Ramsey took a few deep breaths and brought himself back under some kind of control. "If you buy into Deep Purple you're buying into trouble. It's rotten with phylloxera."

"Is it?"

"Can't you read?" Ramsey retorted, waving a copy of the paper under my nose.

"I didn't believe everything I saw in the newspaper even when I worked for one. How about you? Bet you still believe in the tooth fairy, too."

For a minute I thought Ramsey would swing. So did he. I don't know which of us was more disappointed when he controlled himself.

"Are you saying that this article isn't true?" demanded one of the growers who had crowded up to hear what we were saying.

"You know how it is with half-truth," I said. "Like half a brick, you can throw it twice as far."

The man turned toward Karger. "What the hell is going on? Does Deep Purple have phylloxera or not?"

"Speak right into the microphone, Karger," I said sarcastically. "You caused this little dustup."

Karger gave me the kind of look that said he'd like to see me on a glass plate under a microscope.

"The cause of the problem isn't me," he said carefully. "It's a plant parasite."

"But you're the off-the-record expert whose words are separating the *Register*'s ads today," I retorted. "So why don't you do your little phylloxera dance for us? On the record, this time."

Karger didn't like it but he couldn't ignore me without looking bad.

"As I told Miss Autry yesterday, we could try a variety of approaches," Karger said stiffly. "There are chemical agents that have had some limited success in other phylloxera-infested crops. I can immediately name three insecticides that might be helpful."

"How successful have these three insecticides been?" I asked.

Karger stroked his chin thoughtfully. "Very limited success," he admitted finally. "And they have the unfortunate side effect of rendering the fruit unusable for several harvests."

That sent a murmur through the growers. No crops meant no income. Very few growers could survive one season like that, much less several.

"In other words," I said, "you're telling us that the known treatments for phylloxera aren't successful and have a lot of nasty side effects."

Sandra looked worried. I seemed to be digging a deeper hole for her. I hoped that Karger would think so too.

Karger nodded. "I'm afraid that's about right."

"So the only treatment that makes sense is to pull Deep Purple and Traven's vineyard out by the roots. Right?"

Sandra wrapped herself more tightly in the apron when Karger nodded again.

"I'm sorry," he added, looking at her.

"That's some very radical surgery, Doctor," I said.

"Only as radical as necessary," he replied, studying me warily.

"Necessary?" I asked, making sure that my skepticism projected all the way to the back row. I paused while Chapman flipped over a new page and got his pencil lined up again. No point in overrunning the hound that's going to bring your fox to bay for you. "There's a few other things that are necessary first," I continued. "One is a thoroughgoing study of the extent of the phylloxera infestation. Assuming, of course, that the so-called infestation exists at all on Deep Purple." I shifted my attention to the growers and spotted the Friars' wine master, who had been drawn out of the vineyard by the crowd. "Ask Don Cummings. He'll tell you that there has been no steep drop-off in Deep Purple's production."

Chapman stopped writing and glanced up at me. I realized that he didn't understand what I was driving at.

"The first evidence of a phylloxera infestation is a decline in grape production," I said quietly to Chapman whle the men in the crowd turned to Cummings for confirmation. "No drop-off, no infestation." Not quite true, but hell, what did Chapman care?

Chapman nodded and continued scribbling.

"You would have to do a very careful study before you could draw that conclusion," Karger said quickly.

"Really?" I said in a loud voice. "You haven't done a thorough study, yet you're recommending that one of the most famous vineyards in the world be destroyed."

"I haven't recommended that," Karger said harshly. "I only said that it might be necessary in order to save the other vineyards in Napa Valley from devastation."

There was a surge of muttering as the growers heard their worst fears repeated out loud.

"Maybe. And maybe you're just blowing it out of proportion," I said, looking at the restless growers. "Reputable scientists print the results of their work in academic journals. Quacks have to resort to the daily press. Think about it."

That got a reaction I hadn't counted on. Karger turned the color of salt. He opened his mouth but no sound came. It was as though I had knocked the breath out of him.

"Are you calling Dr. Karger a quack?" Ramsey demanded, seeing that the field had been temporarily abandoned.

"You know him better than I do, Ramsey. Does he fit that description?" I turned to concentrate on the growers. "At the very least, Dr. Karger is only one expert. There are several more who have studied phylloxera. I'm arranging for one of them to check Deep Purple at my expense. He will check any other vineyard on the owner's request, also at my expense. It's the least I can do for Sandra and for the Napa Valley."

Karger made an odd, whistling sound, as though he were fighting for breath. I gave him a look and then ignored him.

"But until my expert gets here I have some other things I want you to think about," I said, holding onto the audience. "There was an outbreak of phylloxera in the Barossa Valley."

"What does Australia have to do with Napa?" snapped Ramsey.

I looked past Ramsey to the growers. "It might make these guys feel better to know that they aren't the only growers caught in the technological crunch."

I had them now. No more muttering and shifting, just avid attention.

"Barossa was like Napa," I said, "an ecosystem very delicately balanced on the cutting edge of man's knowledge of grapes and all the things in the world that like to prey on them. Let's face it. If God had intended single cropping, He would have left predators off the Ark. But it didn't work out that way, so we resorted to chemicals and intrusive cultivation and crossbreeding and close cloning to allow us to cover the land with a single crop."

I paused to let Chapman catch up, but not for too long. I didn't want to lose the audience.

"Things go along fine most of the time, but then one little element gets out of balance in that delicate ecological equation and away we go. It's happened before and it will happen again. It's nothing new and certainly no reason to panic." I smiled. "You don't shoot a beautiful woman just because she has herpes."

There were a few low chuckles in the crowd. It was a good sign. But Karger had regained his second wind.

"What if the herpes could spread to every woman in the valley?" he demanded. "What would you do then?"

"Well, Dr. Karger, I've read your study on the potential shift in the resistance paradigm of phylloxera. So have a lot of other experts. Most of them don't agree with you. Several of them feel that, if phylloxera vastatrix has mutated as much as you say, it probably has changed in other ways as well."

I switched my attention back to the crowd. "Any geneticist will tell you that mutations are at best trade-offs. The organism wins something and it loses something. Maybe this new phylloxera will have a low viability or an inability to tolerate existing pesticides or any one of a hundred other things that could make the new strain controllable."

There were mutterings through the crowd again, but there was a new current in the sounds, an excitement that was born of hope. Not for the first time in my life, I felt like bowing down and burning incense at the Ice Cream King's altar. Or his computer's. The only difference between magic and science is the level of education in the audience.

Chapman was still scribbling notes. Without looking up, he said, "Karger claims that there are only two options—insecticide or pulling out the vineyards. Would your experts agree with that?"

The kid had the makings of a great reporter. He already knew that there was only one thing better than a disaster story. That was a disaster story with a happy ending.

I grinned. "I know one of them who would say that's the kind of reasoning that lost us Vietnam. Napalm or nuclear arms but nothing in between. Hasn't Dr. Karger heard of nonintrusive biological control?"

I could see Chapman write the phrase in big block letters. It had immediate appeal, even if he had no idea what it meant. I just hoped to hell Benny had known what he was talking about when he briefed me.

Karger made a sound that could have been a cough or a short laugh. "Biological control? Bugs eating bugs? You've got to be crazy. It's never been proven truly effective on a commercial basis."

"That's a pretty broad statement," I said. "Maybe you'd like to qualify it before you see it in tomorrow's headlines."

"Past research has shown that insecticides—" Karger began.

I interrupted by talking louder than he was. "Most of the agricultural research in the United States is financed by the chemical industry. Not surprisingly, control methods that aren't based on insecticides don't get much support. That doesn't mean that they don't work. And it certainly doesn't mean that they won't work on an entirely new, previously untested strain of phylloxera. Does it, Dr. Karger?"

"Well, of course, without experimentation, no method of control can be categorically ruled out, but—"

"Exactly," I cut in. "And you just admitted that you haven't completed your tests. So all of this is just hot air. I don't know about you gentlemen," I added, looking at the growers, "but I think the sun is raising all the hot air the grapes need right now."

There was another murmur of laughter. Several men began to withdraw toward the pickups and the harvests that awaited them.

"When your expert comes into town," Chapman said, "have him give me a call. He's worth at least a Sunday feature."

Chapman folded his tablet and shoved it in his pocket. Whether Karger knew it or not, this round of the debate was over. It had been a draw, which was all I had hoped for. A draw bought some time.

The remaining growers sensed the stalemate too. They began to break up into smaller groups and to argue among themselves. Ramsey got off the steps, collared Karger and began talking earnestly with him. I could feel Sandra trembling as she leaned against me.

"It's okay," I said, stroking her hair soothingly. "It's all over for a while."

"He told me I had to d-destroy Deep Purple," Sandra whispered, fighting to control herself now that the crisis was past. "He said that I would r-ruin the whole valley."

"That's just one man's opinion. There are other men, other opinions. Nobody's going to railroad you into destroying Deep Purple."

Ramsey heard that. His head came up fast and I could see the angry glitter in his eyes as he stalked back onto the porch.

"Listen, Sandra. Maybe you'd better back up and take another look at the situation," he said harshly. "No matter what your loud-mouthed lover thinks, Dr. Karger is a recognized expert in his field."

"There are other experts," she said, turning away from Ramsey. "There's only one Deep Purple."

"Don't you dare turn your back on me!" Ramsey snarled. As he spoke, he grabbed Sandra's arm with his right hand, his fingers digging into her flesh. "Just because you own Deep Purple you think that you're God's gift to—"

That was as far as Ramsey got. I took his left hand and forced his little finger back against his palm in what the cops call a "come along" hold. Maximum pain, minimum publicity, and no damage at all if you apply the hold right. Ramsey yelped and let go of Sandra.

"Good-bye, Ramsey," I said, releasing him. "The next time you come here, be sure you have an invitation." I looked at Karger. "You too. You have anything to say to Sandra, say it to me first."

"Just a minute," Karger said. "How can I study—"

Sandra turned on him like a cat. "Study? What's this shit about studying? Not ten minutes ago you stood there telling me that I had to destroy Deep Purple. You damn near had me talked into it. You didn't say anything about studying then, did you?" She took a deep breath and leaned toward Karger, fists clenched at her side. "If you set foot on my property again I'll shoot you for trespassing. Do you hear me? The next step you take on Deep Purple will be your last one!"

"Easy, Sandra," I said, putting my hand on her shoulder. "He hears you. He's leaving."

And Karger was, taking Ramsey with him. From the corner of my eye I caught a motion. Someone else was leaving too. I turned slightly and saw Beltrán at the corner of the house, watching Ramsey with a hatred that was palpable. Beltrán looked at me, nodded slightly and faded back into the vineyards he had come from. Sandra didn't notice. She was watching Karger's retreat with a combination of rage and confusion.

"He would have let me destroy Deep Purple. He as good as *told* me to pull out my vines. And then you came and asked questions and he starts talking about more studies! Why?"

I didn't bother to list the half dozen or so reasons Karger might have for stabbing Sandra in the back. Hearing them wouldn't do her any good. She was about at the end of her endurance as she stood there trembling with anger and fear and watching me with golden-brown eyes. The only thing I could do for her was to open my arms and offer her a big hug, trying to reassure her in a way that went deeper than words.

She was tall and she smelled sweet, like fresh-baked bread, and she hung onto me and cried with wrenching sobs. I closed my eyes and held her familiar body, rocking back and forth very slightly, telling her by my physical touch that she wasn't alone.

I don't know how long we stayed that way. I do know that when I looked up again Fiora was there, watching us with sad green eyes. She said nothing. She didn't have to. I remembered too well what she had said about me and damsels in distress.

She was wrong about me in some ways.

And in some ways she was right.

17

By the time Sandra was ready to go back to the thousand last-minute details involved in catering Traven's huge party, Fiora had quietly left for the guesthouse. When I got there she was on the phone. She wasn't contributing much to the conversation, just a "Say again, Jason," or "Good," every now and then. She was writing in her green spiral notebook, scrawling the incomprehensible squiggles that were her own personal brand of shorthand.

Money-shuffling mode.

I grimaced and turned toward the bathroom. We still had Traven's party to get through. I showered and shaved. Then I tried to trim my mustache, which is usually Fiora's contribution to my good grooming since I never have learned to transpose mirror images of myself. Before I was finished snipping and swearing Fiora hung up and came into the bathroom. She took the scissors from me, picked up my comb and began ordering the chaos.

"There's an envelope for you on the bed," she said, looking at my mustache critically. "It just came by courier."

"What's in it?"

"Everything useful Jason could find on Vern Traven, Sandra Autry and the Napa Valley wine industry in the last five years."

"Why—"

"Shut up and hold still unless you want your lip trimmed along with your mustache."

I shut up and held still.

"It's the standard preliminary research I'd have ordered up if I were thinking of going into business with Traven or Sandra," Fiora said. "Dow Jones database search, Lexis-Nexis, Dun & Bradstreet, microfilm prints of local and San Francisco newspapers, copies of property tax records, that sort of thing." She tilted her head to one side, took a few more tiny cuts at my mustache and said, "That should take care of it."

I put my hand under Fiora's chin and tilted her face up until she met my eyes. Her skin was warm and smooth. I could feel the pulse in her throat. It was beating too fast. She was as tightly strung as a violin.

"You didn't have to do that for me," I said.

"I don't mind trimming your mustache," she said, deliberately misunderstanding.

"The information, not the scissors. You know, I had really hoped down underneath that this would somehow turn out to be a vacation for us, a quiet time to be together in a place that I used to love. But the Napa I loved seems to be gone and whatever has taken its place isn't very quiet at all." I searched Fiora's eyes, hoping to see understanding instead of tension and shadows. "I'm sorry, love."

Fiora closed her eyes for a second and then opened them again. Nervous tension was clear in the lines of her face. "When is Benny getting here?"

"Any time. He's stopping by UC Davis first, hoping to find something useful to undercut Karger. What I did this morning was blue smoke and mirrors. We need something more substantial."

"Are you ready to leave?" Fiora asked. Her tension was reflected in her voice. Something was riding her hard. I didn't think it was the fact that I had held Sandra while she cried.

"What's wrong?" I asked softly.

Fiora looked at me, taking in the open-collared shirt and slacks and leather shoes. "You're not dressed yet."

"What? If you think I'm going to wear a suit and—"

"The Detonics," she said, cutting across my words. "It's not on your belt."

I knew it wasn't. I also knew it should have been. And I knew how much Fiora hated to see me wear it. I was avoiding putting on that gun because I wanted to ease the tension between us, not increase it.

"Put it on," she said. "Wear it. All the time, Fiddler. From now until you leave this goddamned valley. It's not enough, just like that file isn't enough. Hell, add Benny and it still isn't enough, but it's all I can do. I wish—" Fiora stopped talking abruptly.

"What?" I asked, pulling her into my arms. "What do you wish?"

"Nothing new," she said, resisting the embrace. "You do what you have to in order to live with yourself. I do what I can so that if it all comes apart and you're hurt I'll be able to live with myself afterward. I couldn't bear spending the rest of my life wondering if I could have made a difference. But what I do isn't enough," she said, her voice tight, desperate. "It's never enough. So you do what you do and I do what I do and sometimes living with each other is hell."

Fiora straightened suddenly and pushed me away. "Read while I shower. It's getting late."

I watched her while she shed her clothes, wondering what she had been dreaming lately.

"Remember. You were wrong about me and the fire," I said. "I walked out of it unhurt. Well, I crawled out of it, but I wasn't hurt, was I?"

The bathroom door closed with an audible click.

It took me a few minutes to look at the papers Jason had sent and see print instead of Fiora's worried, angry eyes. I skimmed pages quickly, setting aside any that piqued my interest. Except that I couldn't really skim the stuff. By the time I finished even the roughest kind of sorting through, Fiora was out of the shower and dressed. If she thought this packet was "preliminary" research, I'd hate to wade through the in-depth variety.

When I looked up Fiora was standing in the bathroom doorway watching me. She was wearing a dress that was the shimmering electric blue of a wild artichoke flower. The dress was a simple, clingy thing that shifted and floated on the least current of air. Her hair was like the dress, silky and long and clinging to everything it touched.

"Beautiful," I said simply. "The dress isn't bad either."

Fiora smiled but beneath that immaculate, sophisticated surface she was coiled like a spring. The primitive, fey part of her that she hated to acknowledge was worried for me, for us. I was wound tight too, guilty and angry and frustrated as hell. I couldn't walk away from Sandra's trouble and live with myself, even though I knew how unhappy I was making Fiora right now.

Fiora knew that. She even accepted it. What she couldn't accept was living with her breath held, waiting for the other shoe to drop, and me with it. Fiora had the persistence and hunting lust of a hungry wolf in her own arena. But here in my world, where the blood was real . . .

Like I said, we'd been here before. There was nothing new about it. There was nothing new to say about it, either. I looked at the papers spread across the bed and wondered if there were a Lexis-Nexis database for unanswerable questions.

"Now, if you were as smart as you are beautiful, you'd tell me what the hell all this means," I said, gesturing toward the papers.

Fiora closed her eyes, shuddered visibly, then took the conversational lead that I had offered.

"Jason gave me the overview," she said, sifting quickly through the papers. "The newspaper pieces tell you that Napa Valley is in trouble. A lot of California's wine country is in trouble. Too many grapes, too much competition and too much bad wine."

She pulled out Xeroxes of clippings and stacked them to one side. "In the last decade dozens of vintners like Vern have been dropping millions of dollars into boutique wineries that produce fancy varietals for a market that is, to put it mildly, quite limited. See?" she said, pulling out one sheet.

Jason had written *Wall Street Journal* and the date across a Xerox of a news story. That was all I saw before Fiora whisked the paper to one side and began rummaging again, talking as she sorted.

"What did it say?" I asked.

"Table wine sales in the United States have been declining for the past three years," she said. "Those are the same three years that all the late 1970s plantings here and around California started to produce. That means the wine industry is facing a shrinking market and an increasing supply at the same time. Especially among the varietals, the high-ticket wines."

She shrugged. "Bad news, Fiddler. There's a real squeeze on. Some people are going to take a bath in the next few years. They'll be lucky if they don't drown."

"Who's going under? The growers? The wineries?"

"Mostly the newcomers," Fiora said, "whichever end of the business they're in. The newcomers are the ones who bought land high and will be forced to sell out low. Old valley types who didn't borrow heavily at high interest against inflated land prices will be okay. They won't have a big debt load to service during the deflation.

When it's over, there will be fewer wildcat wineries and land values will be more realistic."

"What about Sandra?"

Fiora hesitated. "The good news is that she didn't borrow up to the limit on her land. The bad news is that a burned-out restaurant isn't worth anything as collateral, and with the phylloxera . . ." She didn't finish. She didn't have to.

"Shit."

"I know you don't like it," Fiora said quietly, "but in order to survive Sandra has to have a lot of money. You don't have enough to save her and she wouldn't take it even if you did. Frankly, until the phylloxera issue is settled, I can't advise any but the most speculative of my investors to buy—and then only at a fraction of the land's value. That leaves bankruptcy or Traven."

"I thought you didn't like him."

"If liking was a requirement, damn little business would ever get done."

"I don't trust Traven."

"Nobody trusts a business partner. That's why we have so many lawyers."

"Deep Purple is Sandra's home."

"Sandra is young enough to build another home. Traven's money will give her a stake. That's more than most people get."

"You're assuming she'll default on the loan."

"She'll have no choice."

Fiora was right and I knew it. I just didn't like it.

"What about Traven?" I demanded. "He's a newcomer. How come he's not in trouble?"

Fiora bent over again and rustled through the pile of Xeroxes. She came up with several sheets that she handed to me. They were copies of copies of documents bearing the legal chops and hieroglyphics of the Napa County Recorder's Office. It took me about thirty seconds to get to the bottom line. Vern Traven was the legal owner of his perfectly dressed stage and the blocks of land that sprawled all around Deep Purple.

"Interesting, huh?" Fiora asked.

"A deed is a deed."

"Yeah, but you don't see many like these. Until a year ago the land was absolutely unencumbered," Fiora said. "Then he was forced to take out a loan on it to help cover his losses."

"I knew that son of a bitch was a fraud. He's going to take advantage of Sandra, get his hands on Deep Purple and use it to 'make a contribution to the wine world,' " I said bitterly, remembering Vern's words. "Hell, he probably doesn't even have the money to bail her out!"

"Fiddler," Fiora said patiently, "people take out loans all the time. Owning a piece of land is useless unless you make the cash value of the land work for you. Vern may not be worth a tenth of the four hundred million he was a few years ago, but he has more than enough unused credit to take care of Sandra."

"You sound like you admire him."

"As a businessman or as a person?" she retorted.

"I don't separate the two."

"Try it. A whole new world would open for you."

In the electric silence Fiora ran her fingers through her hair, a sign of the tension vibrating just beneath her polished surface. She let out a long sigh and then began to speak quickly, as though somewhere there was a clock running and there was little time left.

"I agree that if Sandra's problems have been caused by someone Vern Traven is a likely candidate. He certainly stands to gain if she defaults to him on a loan. He'll control a significant block of Napa Valley land, whereas now he has only scattered parcels. Owning the vineyard will have a pronounced halo effect on the wines he sells. Traven is hardly unaware of these things."

"Yet you'll recommend to Sandra that she take his offer," I said.

"Would you rather have her bankrupt?" Fiora retorted. "With the phylloxera, that's her only choice! Besides, what in God's name is wrong with making a business deal that benefits both parties?"

A reasonable question. I didn't have a reasonable answer. I just had a gut certainty that I had failed Sandra. She had been harried and chivied and brought to bay and had asked me to help her. For an instant I wished that she had asked me for help sooner, before the game had run its course. In the forty-eight hours I had been in Napa, I had come to believe one thing: human greed rather than bad luck was behind Sandra's troubles.

But I couldn't prove it before she went under. Traven knew that the time to tighten the screws had come and he was twisting them hard. There were only a few hours before Traven's deadline ran out, yet Sandra had refused even to consider the offer when I had approached her that morning.

"How bad off is Traven in Texas?" I asked.

"Dun & Bradstreet gives him as good a rating as any of the small-to-medium oil companies. He already survived the major shakeout that came when oil prices took a dive and he's in a good position to snap up his former competitors at bargain prices. He needs a good harvest in Napa to keep his margin, but there's nothing new about that. All farmers need that."

She tapped her fingernail absently on the papers. "Traven is the kind of guy investors like. He's lucky. He's the original 'victory from the jaws of defeat.' In fact there are rumors out now that he's got something planned that will pull his oil company way up in the black. It could be just hot air, of course, like his maroon balloon. Rumors launched in the right place at the right time can be worth several points on any deal, and Traven has a reputation as an opportunist rather than a planner."

I stared at the papers for a long time but no brilliant solution came to me. I pushed the papers away, grabbed my Detonics and shoved it in the holster at the small of my back. When I shrugged into the suit coat Fiora was waiting by the door. I got in the BMW and started the car. Neither of us said much on the way to Traven's bash. There really wasn't anything new to say. Sandra had lost. Traven had won.

And the Detonics was digging into my back.

As I coasted up to the long, sloping front lawn of Traven's showy château, a crew of white-jacketed Mexican field workers was at work policing the lush swaths of green. They weren't after stray cups or cigarette butts, though. One by one, they were picking up the oak and olive and sycamore leaves that had fallen overnight. I wondered if they were finger-combing the English maze as well, or if too many of them got lost that way.

The burgundy JetRanger came beating in from the direction of San Francisco. As I watched it settle toward the side lawn I looked at the green walls of the maze and wondered whether Traven had dyed the dragonflies that doubtless clustered around the fountain in the center of the maze. It wouldn't have surprised me. He had done everything else to ensure the perfection of his artificial world.

The helicopter descended loudly to its manicured landing pad. A batch of laughing party-goers scrambled out, hanging onto hairdos and skirts in the forceful propwash. Two white-jacketed attendants met them and led them toward the maroon canopies where three hundred early arrivals were already partying.

Traven must have hired an army of the white coats. Two of them had the doors of the BMW open before I stopped rolling. They were parking the cars along the vineyard road, which meant that the cuffs of the men's burgundy pants were already coated with powdery Napa dust.

When Fiora and I walked up to the château Traven was nowhere to be seen, but several members of the household staff were on hand to greet early arrivals. I asked after Traven and got a wave toward the back of the house.

He wasn't there but Sandra was. She seemed to be running an open kitchen, the kind of place that invites spectators. There were twenty people in the huge kitchen. I eased into the melee, losing Fiora in the process. On one table women put the finishing touches to heavy trays of summer fruit—nectarines, peaches, seedless grapes, a few early pears, the first Golden Delicious apples, and melons. Another crew was basting dressed rabbit in a red wine sauce. Two women were unwrapping platters of tea-smoked duck slices. Bowls of fragrant, freshly chopped salsa stood heaped and waiting to be taken outside. Two men laughed and talked in Japanese while they shaved abalone steaks into sushi with Sandra's sharp knives.

Sandra herself was just outside the back door, supervising a crew of *vatos* who were unloading chicken from marinade barrels filled with lime juice, cilantro and beer. Other men were hauling washtubs full of pork ribs and a dark barbecue sauce out of a van and down the sloping lawn toward the fire pits.

"You've got a regular United Nations here," I said when I caught Sandra's attention.

"Just Pacific Rim, actually," she said. "I'm not going to serve a single European dish today. I don't know if anybody but you will catch on, but it's the most radical culinary statement anyone could make."

As Sandra smiled at me, her golden-brown eyes shone with pleasure. She was in her element here, cooking up a new world. I hated to ruin it for her.

"Is Traven around?" I asked.

"No. The housekeeper said he was with a bunch of men. Business."

"It may be business that involves you."

"No," she said firmly. "I called him after you talked to me. I told him that I just couldn't—"

"Sandra, we're missing a barrel of chicken," called one of the men, cutting across Sandra's words. Before she could answer him, two more of her workers descended, plucking at her sleeves, demanding her attention.

"I'm sorry, Fiddler," she said. "Give me a couple of minutes. I just can't talk now."

I started to object but she was gone. I went after her, only to be ambushed by a fast-moving tray of fresh vegetables. I sidestepped but Sandra was screened from my view by a group of guests wandering through. The men were looking around the kitchen as though they had just fallen through a rabbit hole. The women looked with frank envy at the kitchen help. I admired the knives laid out by the cutting tables.

Fleming came through the kitchen, looking dour and skeptical. He was dressed for the party but he looked as though he were on duty just the same. Probably he was. Lots of cops moonlight as private security. And let's face it—any time you invite one thousand of your most intimate friends to a "pre-harvest gala," you're bound to come up with a few jerks who need watching.

Especially if you start with the likes of Vern Traven.

I followed a washtub of marinated ribs down the sloping lawn, looking for Traven. What I found was Beltrán. He had talked Sandra into an old-fashioned approach to cooking the meat, so she had put him in charge of overseeing the coals. He was sweating like a foundryman. Someone handed him a bottle of beer. He finished it in one long draft.

"What's the latest word on the harvest?" I asked.

Beltrán wiped his face on a towel, looked at me and shook his head. "Not yet. A few days more, maybe."

Too late. *Shit.*

I surveyed the crowd, looking for Traven's tall, lean shape. Beltrán threaded the washtub of ribs onto huge skewers. He did it very deftly, finding the soft, meaty area between the bones without fumbling or hesitation. I looked at my watch, shaded my eyes and stared toward the parking lot. There were cars of all kinds and sizes, but no vans, no sign of Benny. He should have been here by now.

"Are you expecting trouble?" Beltrán asked.

"Why?"

He didn't answer, except to glance toward the small of my back. The Detonics is about the size of a two-inch .38, tiny by the standards of 9-millimeter pistols, and my coats are cut to conceal it. Beltrán, however, had been trained to look for weapons.

I smiled and gave Beltrán the elaborate, Mexican-style shrug. "It's only a tool of the trade," I said, "like pruning shears or a *flic* knife."

"What trade is that?"

"Snake charmer."

Beltrán's grin flashed. He threaded the last of the ribs. "Tell me, *jefe,*" he said. "Have you ever eaten roasted rattlesnake? It's even better than *cabrito.*"

"Keep the fire hot," I said. "I'll see what I can do."

"*Seguro que sí,*" he said. "*Ándale pues.*"

He turned away and began calling orders in Spanish to his crew. I recognized Chuy by the red headband. He was swinging a mop full of sauce, basting ribs that were turning and sweating over slow mesquite coals.

I made a few more circuits of the party before I settled on a second-floor balcony. If Traven showed up—or Benny—I'd spot him quickly. I could also keep an eye on the area where Sandra and her crew were working and see the parking lot as well. A young waiter materialized, deposited a glass of white wine on the circular table beside me and told me to have a nice day.

From where I sat the center of activity was the balloon. It had been turned into a carnival ride. Guests were taken aboard the basket for a short ride up to the end of a fifty-foot tether. They floated for a moment or two, leaning out and waving and calling to their friends, and then the kid on the burner signaled the ground crew, who hauled the balloon back down to earth. A line of guests was forming, as though the balloon were Space Mountain.

From two floors up, Traven's party came across with the impersonal air of a company picnic. I tried the wine. Like the party, it was carefully planned, solidly executed and relatively boring. When I leaned back the Detonics dug into my spine. When I leaned forward to check the parking lot the sun glared full in my eyes. When I stood up I wanted to pace but the balcony was too small for that. I sat down again and felt the Detonics prod me.

Voices approached. One of them was Traven's. I turned just enough to see him walking down the hallway past the french doors. With Traven was a prosperous-looking, barrel-chested man sporting a styled head of white hair and a pin-striped business suit. He had the look of a small-town banker or prosperous businessman.

"You go ahead, Art," Traven said. "I'll catch up in a few minutes. Be sure to try the white wine. I'm particularly proud of it."

Traven stood at the balcony door and stared at me as though I were painted the wrong color.

"You should have been happy with your half million," he said in a cold voice. "But no, you had to play cute. Well, you played cute with the wrong man. You didn't drive the price of Deep Purple up. You didn't drive it anywhere except right into the ground."

He spun around and was gone even as I came to my feet.

18

Before I could reach him Traven had rejoined the silver-haired man called Art. They shook hands like fraternity brothers and separated. Art went immediately toward the kitchen. He stopped a waiter, asked something and was directed toward Sandra.

Whatever this guy had to say to Sandra, I wanted to hear. I wasn't quite fast enough. He was leaving the kitchen by the time I arrived. He wore an undertaker's expression—professional solicitousness—but he walked quickly, as if he had an uneasy conscience.

Sandra looked worse than she had when Traven told her about the phylloxera outbreak.

"What happened?" I asked.

She stared at me for a moment without focusing. When she spoke she sounded like a computer voice spliced together from a pool of recorded words. "I'm going to lose Deep Purple."

"What did Art say?" I demanded.

She closed her eyes. "I've missed too many payments on my loan. Art could have taken over Deep Purple any time in the past year, but he knew my dad and he—" Sandra's voice broke. She cleared her throat and kept talking.

"He's had all the default papers signed and ready to go for months. But he promised to wait until harvest was over. Now he can't. He's worried about the phylloxera. If the price of land crashes because of it, the bank will be hurt. He has a buyer for Deep Purple, but only if he starts foreclosure right now. He has an agree—agreement in principle, whatever that is." Sandra took a ragged breath. "I can't really blame him. He's been out on a limb for me. It's just that —that—"

"Traven," I muttered, understanding too late what he had done. When he couldn't railroad us into getting Sandra to sell quickly, he had railroaded the bank instead.

Suddenly Sandra swayed as though her footing had changed without warning. I grabbed her shoulders.

"Don't quit," I said. "You told me that one night a long time ago, up there in that hot little room in the Mountain View Hotel. Now I give it back to you. Don't quit."

She tried to smile as she touched my face with fingers that shook. "Those were good times, weren't they? Like the wine Dad used to make. Thick and rich and strong. No one makes it like that anymore."

For a moment Sandra put her head against me and held me as though it were years ago, when she was just at the beginning of her dreams and I was at the end of mine. I held her the same way. Finally she straightened and stepped back, letting go of me.

"Thanks. I'll be okay now," she said.

Sandra walked back toward the kitchen. I stood watching the empty doorway for a long time. She didn't come back out.

I went looking for Traven. I had gotten as far as the balloon ride on the front lawn before someone grabbed my arm.

"Hey, Fiddler! Great to see you! You musta been bit by the wine bug too," the man said, pumping my hand hard.

Jerry Bernard was an aerospace entrepreneur from Tustin. I had done his wife a favor a few years back. He thought that made us buddies.

"Yeah, Jerry. Great to see you. Excuse me."

It was as though he hadn't heard me. He held on to my hand and smiled. I looked at the wineglass in his hand. It was covered with greasy fingerprints and had been filled several times.

"Isn't this a great little place Traven's got here?" Jerry asked. "Makes you really want one of your own." He knocked back a swallow of wine. "You trying to get in on the Napa land rush too?"

"I don't have the down payment for a vineyard, and neither do you, unless you've just decided to sell that software company of yours."

"What d'ya mean?" he said. "I just heard a hot rumor about some land being cut up for development. A house and a real small vineyard, just enough to make your own wine. Wouldn't it be great to put your own personal label on the cases you give clients at Christmas?"

"That's one of the reasons I don't have clients," I said curtly, staring over his shoulder, looking for Traven.

"Five, maybe ten acres and a weekend house," he said in an eager voice. "That's all you really need. Now how much can that cost?"

"I hate to tell you this," I interrupted, reclaiming my hand and turning away, "but the game's been rigged so that it can't be done. If it could, there would be a waiting list from here to LA."

"You bet there would be," he called after me. "You could be in on it too, if you help me track down the rumors. Hey, we could be neighbors!"

The idea gave me hives. Then I felt the hair stir on the back of my neck.

"Wait a minute," I said turning around fast. "Do you have some kind of deal cooking up here?"

Jerry gave me a faintly drunken conspiratorial wink. "Not yet, buddy, but I will." He clapped me on the shoulder. "Watch me."

I stood on the manicured lawn, watching Jerry get swallowed by the crowd. Traven was still nowhere in sight. There were other familiar faces, though. I began picking out the ones I could recognize. A former state assemblyman who had retired a couple of years ago—taking with him an unexpended campaign chest of more than a half million bucks—stood next to a Beverly Hills entertainment lawyer who owned race horses and Rolls-Royces. The female star of a daytime soap noshed with two Palo Alto cowboys who had invented the most promising artificial intelligence programming system in Silicon Valley. A congressman strolled by, a glass of wine in one hand and a barbecued rib in the other. A busty blonde in a white, spaghetti-strap sundress hung on his arm. The congressman leaned over, looked down the front of the dress and muttered something he thought was funny in her ear. She responded with the kind of giggle that made you believe in euthanasia.

I wasn't the only one watching the passing parade. Chapman was there with his notebook out, jotting down the names of the rich and famous. He had the subtly askew stance of a man who hasn't counted his drinks too carefully. Not drunk. Just relaxed.

"You seen Traven in the last ten minutes?" I asked.

"Nope. Quite a party he throws, isn't it?" Chapman asked, gesturing around. "I counted at least a half a billion in venture capitalists alone, to say nothing of three senators and a governor—our very own. Yes indeed, friends and taxpayers, there's a lot of wheeling and dealing being done here tonight."

"Yeah," I said bitterly, thinking of good old Art the banker. "I guess this is how the wine 'bidness' really operates."

Chapman laughed. "If I didn't know where my bread was buttered, I'd write up a story about the Board of Supervisors meeting in violation of the Brown Act. That's why you haven't seen Vern Traven. He's upstairs with them."

It took me a moment, but I remembered that the Brown Act was a quaint California law that prohibited private meetings by public bodies.

"You sure?" I asked.

The young reporter gave me a sidelong look and a cynical smile. "I'm sure. Three supervisors—a clear quorum—are sitting down over champagne with Traven right now," Chapman said, pointing toward Traven's living quarters. "But somehow I doubt that I'd get the story into the paper, since my boss is up there with them. It's not the first time, either. Everybody is all worked up about the phylloxera situation."

"So?"

"Soooo . . ." Chapman smiled and worked his fingers at chest level as though he were typing. While he pantomimed, he did his impression of the local six o'clock TV anchor. "County supervisors are expected to act as soon as next week to prevent the spread of the devastating parasite called phylloxera through the gracious and peaceful Napa Valley."

" 'Gracious and peaceful'? Do you work for the newspaper or the Chamber of Commerce?"

"In this case they're one and the same," Chapman said, shrugging. Then he twiddled his fingers again, shadow-typing the second paragraph as he intoned:

"The supervisors are expected to pass an emergency ordinance granting special development privileges to owners of infected vineyards. These development privileges would be an incentive to strip out those vineyards and thereby prevent the spread of the parasite, which threatens the more than thirty thousand acres of vineyards in beautiful Napa Valley, and potentially all of the vineyards in California as well."

I barely followed the flow of words. My mind had stuck on just two of them. Development privileges. Suddenly Jerry's glassy-eyed drivel about five acres of vineyard and a weekend house began to make sense. Traven the opportunist at work. He had used the public panic over phylloxera to stampede the local power structure into development concessions—concessions that his own construction company would no doubt exploit.

Not only that, but he'd managed to turn his party into a selling tool. Here were a thousand of the rich and powerful, just the sort of folks who had enough spare cash to consider a weekend home in the midst of Napa's famous vines. Guys like Jerry.

And then I wondered if the whole phylloxera infestation weren't as phony as a whore's smile.

No wonder Traven had worked so hard to keep the official agriculture inspectors out of Deep Purple and Traven Vineyards. He hadn't been helping Sandra and himself hang on until harvest—he'd been working like hell to get his own ducks in a row. And the biggest of those reluctant ducks had been the acquisition of Sandra's land, the piece that would give him highway access, a famous name and an integrated unit of land to develop.

"They're going to lift the agricultural preserve restrictions on infested land," I said to Chapman. "A thousand acres of five-acre homesites, right in the heart of the Napa Valley."

Chapman shot me a look of amusement. "You already knew?" he said. "Oh, that's right. Your friend Sandra ought to come out ahead on this deal, too. Even though it will probably end up at fifteen acres instead of five." He frowned. "Too bad I can't go with the story now, before the big papers get wind of it, but nothing's final until the supervisors say it is, and old man Peters swings a lot of weight. He's dug in like a tractor and the rest of the supervisors want it unanimous, so that if the voters kick they'll kick everyone. Peters will come around in a few weeks," Chapman added. "He always does. Until then, nothing will get in the paper."

In a few weeks Traven would own Sandra's land or the reality of foreclosure proceedings would have stampeded her into accepting Traven as a financial angel. Assuming that he didn't screw her out of the land entirely—an assumption that I wouldn't have put a penny on—she would get a cash settlement and the death of her dreams for Deep Purple. Or she might get nothing at all. Not one damn thing.

No blood, no violence, just the kind of fiscal and psychic defeat it takes people years to crawl out from under. If they get out at all.

My mind started running the numbers because it was better than thinking of what Sandra would look like when her land became a batch of weekend vineyards. Roughly a thousand acres would be developed, counting Traven's valley blocks and Deep Purple. Cut it up into small parcels that could be sold to guys like Jerry Bernard, cash-heavy guys with an insatiable thirst for something that would set them apart from the other scufflers who'd made their first five million.

It was hard to estimate the market for parcels like that, but I knew plenty of realtors who would love to try. Not far down the road from my cottage in Crystal Cove, somebody spent a few hundred thousand dollars hacking postage-stamp lots out of a hillside between Coast Highway and the ocean. The lots were sold off at more than four bucks a square foot. Land only, no house.

Now I grant you that good old Jerry couldn't afford a vineyard at four dollars a square foot, but he'd be glad to shell out a million bucks or more for a Napa Valley weekender with his own little vineyard. With a smart accountant, he'd probably be able to write off most of the costs under the Hobby-Farming Tax Act.

Of course a developer would probably have to throw in a community swimming pool, golf and tennis courts, maybe even a riding stable. All the Sun Belt amenities. But two hundred building sites would offer more than enough profit margin to repay the cost of those upscale essentials.

The result would be gracious and peaceful and breathtakingly expensive. It might even be almost as pretty as the Napa Valley used to be, certainly prettier than the rumpled, sweaty old farming community that once had been here. For a while the mini-estates might even be as pretty as the romantic wine-country pictures people carry around in their heads.

Unfortunately, in the end Traven's acres would look like every other expensive planned community—pointlessly winding walkways and carefully calibrated slopes for visual relief, eucalyptus and day lilies and sprinklers that only came on after midnight.

What God might have done if He'd just had Traven's taste.

I looked around at the crowd drinking mediocre wine and sharing in the "pre-harvest gala," a foretaste of the good life for everyone who had the money to buy a spot on Traven's list. This manicured valley with its hand-washed vines and imported château was an elaborately dressed stage, a hundred-acre model home all perfect and glowing in the late afternoon sunlight; and in its center was Traven, his *vigneron* role as carefully tended as the vines themselves.

He was a hell of an actor. While professing to love the Napa life style, he had broken the farming monopoly on a thousand acres in the fertile heart of the valley. But Traven was a very special kind of actor, the kind known as a scammer. The difference was shown in the size of the stage he worked and the price of the admission tickets the unsuspecting audience bought.

Traven owned what amounted to a special license to develop the only available residential property in one of the world's most commercially romantic settings. It was as though he had just created a thousand acres of vacant beach-front land in Malibu, or an equal amount at the corner of Fifth Avenue and Fifty-seventh Street in Manhattan. He had opened Napa Valley up to development, but only for him. He had created an exception that no one could take exception to. A thousand acres of vineyards sacrificed to save thirty thousand, with the rest of California's wine-growing future assured for good measure. Pre-harvest gala indeed.

Traven figured to harvest millions.

As I watched the sun slide behind the hill, throwing indigo shadows across the land, I wondered how the assemblymen would enjoy their weekenders, and whether the governor would have his own private label.

Both the beauty and the hell of the scam was that Traven hadn't done anything criminal. Not quite. Nothing you could prove, which amounts to the same thing. Everything is legal until a cop figures out how you did it. Then only some things are legal. Traven's scam arguably came in the gray area of civil law, where cops are as close to helpless as a man with a gun can be. The gray area is where too many stock deals are made and where nearly all of the late unlamented tax shelters abide.

Gray is legal until proven otherwise. That's not the same as illegal. That made Traven an entrepreneur rather than an outright crook. He was merely taking advantage of the opportunities that presented themselves to him. Never mind that he was manufacturing said opportunities at the expense of people like Sandra. Wasn't that the essence of entrepreneurship—cunning and the nerve to see a scheme through to its conclusion?

If I didn't like the conclusion I could try to interest a local cop like Fleming or a county district attorney in the case. Fleming would tell me to go to hell and a DA wouldn't be interested in putting a disgruntled outsider's questions in front of a jury of Traven's peers.

That left civil rather than criminal court. Taking Traven to civil court would be like getting into a pissing contest with a herd of elephants. At best, I'd get an out-of-court settlement that would equal my lawyers' fees. At worst, I'd get to pay Traven's lawyers out of my own pocket, along with paying my own lawyers as well.

There was only one possible slip left between the cup and Traven's lip. If the phylloxera infestation could be proven to be a hoax, Traven would be the one on the wrong end of the pissing contest.

I turned and studied Chapman, wondering if he would be of any use to me. Family Journalist, genus ambitious, species *small town.* He was a bright kid who thought he had already seen it all twice. He was both fascinated and repelled by the naked exercise of power. He regarded everyone, including himself, with careful disdain. Young enough to still have ideals but not old enough to know what to do with them. An awkward age. Useless, too.

"Is Dr. Eric Karger at this soiree?" I asked Chapman.

"I saw him around back an hour ago. Haven't seen him since. He was looking for Sandra."

The maroon JetRanger lifted suddenly, beating the air until it echoed, drawing every eye. Beyond the rising chopper, Benny Speidel came rolling across the grass toward me. He was using what he called his off-road wheelchair. The soft, wide tires required enormous upper-body strength but he was making the chair fly. With his flowing head of black hair and full beard, he attracted almost as much interest as the helicopter. His piratical grin gave me hope.

I pointed toward a place away from the clumps of guests, who had gathered around the barbecue pits, the bars and the tables set out among the flower gardens. The long evening shadow of the maze darkened the grass fifty feet away. There was no one between me and the hedge; the novelty of being lost in the greenery had quickly worn off on the guests. They avoided the maze now, and the empty sweep of sloping lawn that led to it.

"Got that little shit, we did," Benny said when he came within earshot. "Lord God but I hate someone who uses his education to bugger his fellow man."

"Make it march. Things are going to hell fast."

I must have been a bit grim around the edges, because Benny locked the wheels of his chair and settled in right where he was. We were well away from the crowds, three quarters of the way to the maze that looked black in the twilight.

"The question of phylloxera resistance has been kicked around for at least a decade," Benny said. "The problem is a hell of a lot bigger in some of the other viticultural regions of the state. We're talking about the potential loss of thousands of acres over in Monterey County, and similar problems in Lake County. And when I say kicked around, I mean like a soccer ball. Lots of theories and no consensus."

"You mean some experts would back Karger's conclusions and some wouldn't?"

"Yes."

"Shit," I said, disgusted.

"There are rootstock propagators and vineyard managers with hundreds of millions of bucks riding on the outcome," Benny said, ignoring my comment. "They'd love to have the issue resolved. Hell, Ernie and Julio Gallo threw a couple million into a research pot recently, and they aren't even Napa Valley landowners."

"Benny—"

"Hang on, mate," he said. "The route to understanding is sometimes indirect. That's what makes it fun."

He took a deep breath. I waited.

"With so much money involved, more and more researchers have been jumping into the field—people like Karger, who is basically a laboratory man, not a field entomologist. About three years ago he started propounding some fairly radical theories and attracting a lot of attention and research money. So much money, in fact, that a few of his competitors—blokes at Davis, for instance— got worried and started studying his research results very carefully."

I didn't say anything, but I must have grinned. Benny smiled in return.

"That's right, mate. The little sod fiddled his field tests. He never did anything so crude as inventing results. Too clever by half for that. But he introduced extra phylloxera into an environment where they already existed, giving the little buggers a boost. It was like salting a proven gold mine. He didn't invent any facts but he sure did gild the bejesus out of the ones that already existed. It makes for nice, dramatic test results, the kind that look suspicious to fellow scientists but impressive as hell to a layman handing out grants."

"What happened?"

Benny laced his fingers together and cracked his knuckles enthusiastically. "People started replicating some of his experiments and getting different results. He was always careful, so nobody was able to really pin a rose on him, but finally the Davis boys documented enough discrepancies to raise a stink. That's when the whispering began. Stanford got wind of what was going on. The school quietly told Karger to look elsewhere for tenure."

"That was all? No court-martial and drums and snipped buttons?"

"Do you believe in flying reindeer too?" Benny asked acidly. "Stanford has its own reputation to protect, boyo. They certainly don't want to be associated with a scientific scandal. Officially Karger is on sabbatical. He isn't expected back."

"So he's scrambling like hell to establish himself a big reputation, or make himself a big chunk of dough, before the word gets out about his lack of tenure."

"Right. Now all you have to do is bend the ear of the local reporter. Karger and his phylloxera scare will be lining birdcages all over the valley by this time tomorrow. Sandra will get a clean bill of health, harvest her crop and live happily ever after." He cocked his head at me. "You're not coming in with the chorus, mate."

Before I could tell him why, a woman's scream rose above the distant hum of party noise. The scream came from down the hill and to the side, where Traven's maze loomed out of the sunset.

I was running before the scream ended.

19

I didn't bother trying to find a trail. I went through the maze greenery as though it were a line of scrimmage. The fountain at the center
was cunningly illuminated so that only dancing water was revealed.
Two women were standing at the edge of the wide, dark pool, back-
lighted by the hidden floodlamps. One of the women was Sandra.
The other was Fiora. When I ran up to them, both were as pale as
Sandra's apron in the dusk.

"What's wrong?" I demanded.

"Put that away," Fiora said. Her voice was a stranger's,
stretched right to the edge of breaking. "Quick, before some cop
comes and shoots you by mistake." She was looking at the pistol in
my hand. I had no recollection of having drawn it. I holstered the
gun and put my arm around Fiora. She was shaking.

"What is it?"

"Sandra—the pond."

Benny arrived, having found his way through the maze. Bits of
greenery sticking to the wheelchair told me that he had used force
when finesse was too slow. He pumped past me and stopped by
Sandra. She stood partly in shadow at the edge of the pond. Her
mouth was open but no sound was coming out.

"Sandra," I said sharply.

Very slowly her eyes focused. "Fiddler?" she whispered. "Someone—I think—" Helplessly she gestured toward the fountain pool
and the lush growth of lily pads. "In there."

I went to the pool. Beyond the tiled edge, some of the lilies were
broken, as though a wading drunk had crashed through them. The
wader was now face down and motionless in the water, a parody of
the dead man's float.

The bottom of the fountain was slippery as a fish. I waded out
three short steps, just far enough to confirm my worst fears.

Karger. He hadn't been drunk, though, and he hadn't drowned, but his floating position wasn't a parody. He was quite dead. A handle extended from his light sport coat. Blood had seeped through the cloth until a dark stain showed in the upper left quadrant of his back. The stain looked black in the low light, but I knew it would be blood red in daylight.

My first thought was of Beltrán and his *flic* knife. But the handle was wrong, too big. This was a small chef's knife with a five-inch blade, sharp enough to dry-shave the hair on the back of your hand. I had handled it, or one of its mates, yesterday. It was identical to the one I had seen slicing tough abalone steak this afternoon. It was Sandra's knife.

I turned and looked at Sandra. She was standing by the tiled edge of the fountain, staring at the knife handle.

"Why are you here? Why aren't you cooking?" I asked quietly, the first question that a suspicious cop would ask her.

"I—" Her voice broke.

"Talk," I said urgently, bending over Karger. Already I could hear people straggling down the long, sloping lawn toward us.

"I didn't do it," she said in a rush.

"Shit, I know that! Who told you to come here?"

"Karger."

I got a grip on Karger's soggy jacket. "What did Karger say to you? When?"

Sandra gulped air and then seemed to get a grip on herself. At least she was able to talk coherently.

"He came to me about a half hour ago, wanted to talk to me but I was too busy. I agreed to meet him down here. He said he could help me save Deep Purple. When I got here I saw—that."

"What about the knife?"

I heard a deep shout from somewhere beyond the maze. Fleming, probably. Hurriedly I knelt and wrestled with the body as though I were trying to find signs of life. What I was doing was frisking the poor son of a bitch. He had known too much about phylloxera and land schemes. Now his corpse would be used to send Sandra to jail so that she wouldn't have a chance to get her part of all the millions that would be made from the destruction of Deep Purple.

Unless I could find something useful before Fleming bulled his way through the maze. For that, I'd need keys. Karger's keys.

"The knife, Sandra." I had another ten seconds.

"Mine have initials on—on the handle."

Sweet. Really sweet. I'll bet her fingerprints were on the handle, too, right next to the engraved S.A. that I could see dimly in the floodlamp.

"What's going on?" shouted Fleming.

Close, but not yet through the maze despite the fact that he was taking some crashing shortcuts. In two seconds he'd be able to see the clump of people around the fountain.

The keys were in Karger's pants pocket. It would be bloody hell getting them out without being seen—the pockets of the baggy, pleated slacks seemed to go all the way to his knees.

"Benny, Fiora, cover me."

Fiora's scream was loud and shrill. She stepped back, recoiling from the body, and screamed again. Benny moved to comfort her. Anybody who wasn't deaf was suddenly watching the hysterical woman and the man in the wheelchair who was trying to calm her.

I grunted and clawed the keys free of the soaked pants and palmed them into my own. Then I gave the body another fast look, knowing it was all that I'd get.

From the position of the knife, it was clear that Karger had been taken from behind and without warning. The sharp, heavy blade was parallel to his spine. The stroke had been powerful enough to slice through two ribs that were immediately adjacent to the entry point. Death had probably been instantaneous. His face showed no fear and there was comparatively little blood around the wound.

"Hey! You in the water! What the hell's going on!" Fleming shouted.

"I'm trying to see if he's still alive," I snapped.

Fleming was in the water and next to me before I could say another word. He gave the body and the knife one quick, expert look. He'd seen bodies before. Knives, too.

"How did you find him?" he demanded.

"Face down in the drink. I can't find any signs of life."

Blunt, powerful fingers dug into the region of Karger's carotid. When that didn't show a pulse, Fleming got a grip under one of Karger's limp arms and levered upward.

"On the grass," he grunted.

Together we hauled the corpse to solid land. It wasn't easy. Dead men weigh twice as much as they ought to, and they don't cooperate.

"Back off," he ordered.

I went over and stood next to Fiora. There were already three or four people gathered around, nervous and fascinated expressions on their faces as they stared at the body. The crowd was getting bigger every second as people bushwhacked their way in. Traven's maze would never be the same. New arrivals muttered and whispered while Fleming checked vital signs with a few well-executed moves. He was as calm as a coroner.

While Fleming was busy I spoke very softly to Fiora. "As soon as you can, fade into the crowd. Cooperate, but get out before he thinks of material witnesses."

Fleming's head came up when he realized that I was talking and he couldn't understand the words. "Shut up or you'll be in more trouble than you already are."

"You're the man with the badge," I said quietly.

He stared at me for a minute, then checked Karger again. He was as dead as ever. With a grimace Fleming wiped his hands on his tailored slacks before he reached into his hip poclet for a walkie-talkie. He spoke into it tersely, requesting a coroner's wagon and a crime lab team. When he pulled out a small flashlight and spotlighted the knife the crowd gasped. He ignored them as he scrutinized the handle. When he stood up he looked at me.

"Was anyone here before you?"

I answered honestly, because a single look at Sandra's face told me she wasn't up to deception.

"Sandra and Fiora. They—"

"Don't say another word unless I ask a question," he ordered curtly.

He looked at the crowd as a uniformed deputy came running up. "Was anyone here before either of these women?"

No one answered.

"All right. Jackson, move this crowd the hell out of here, everybody except these four here." He looked at Fiora. "I want you over there, out of earshot," he said, motioning toward a corner of the maze. "Now."

Fiora looked at me. I nodded slightly. It's standard technique to interview witnesses separately.

As Fiora walked away Fleming turned toward Sandra, giving her a hard look. "Taking a break from cooking, Miss Autry?"

Sandra glanced sideways at me. I couldn't help her right now. If I so much as blinked Fleming would have me standing under a tree fifty yards away.

"Dr. Karger came to me in the kitchen and asked me to meet him down here," Sandra said. "But when I got here I saw him— there." She gestured toward the reeds.

"Uh-huh." Fleming looked down at the body. He didn't have to say that he didn't believe her. He couldn't have made his opinion clearer if he had shouted it. "Anybody else hear that conversation?"

"No."

"Did she come down here with you?" He looked toward Fiora.

Sandra shook her head. "No. I didn't even know she was around until I saw him and screamed."

"You were alone when you got to the pond?"

"I—I guess so."

"What did you argue about?"

"What?" Sandra looked confused.

"Karger and you," Fleming said curtly. "What did you argue about?"

"How could we argue? He was dead."

Fleming grunted and tried another tack. "This morning you threatened to kill him."

"But—"

"There were witnesses," Fleming said impatiently, cutting across Sandra's attempt to speak. "It doesn't make sense that you'd threaten to kill a man in the morning and then agree to have a private little talk with him in the dark that night. So let's try it again, Miss Autry. You say Dr. Karger wanted to talk to you so you met him here. Maybe you were a little nervous about meeting him way off here in the dark. Maybe you got to thinking how much bigger than you he was. Maybe you picked up a knife and put it in your apron pocket. That is your knife in his back, isn't it?"

"Don't answer," I said.

I didn't stop moving until I was standing next to Sandra. She took my hand and looked up at me with frightened eyes. She didn't say a word.

"That isn't very smart," Fleming said. "Failing to cooperate in a field interrogation looks fishy to a jury."

"This isn't a field interrogation," I retorted, "it's the local version of Amtrak. Sandra's getting off the railroad right here, right now."

"Don't bet on it," Fleming said.

He walked over to where Fiora stood. I followed.

"How long was Miss Autry out of your sight?" he asked Fiora.

"When?"

"From the time she left the kitchen until you saw her at the pond."

"She wasn't out of my sight. She couldn't have killed Karger. The body was in the water when she got here."

"Uh-huh. You must have real sharp eyes to see through all the corners in this here maze. Seems unlikely that you kept Miss Autry in view every second. You're a good friend of hers, aren't you?"

"I never met her until a few days ago."

"Uh-huh."

Without another word Fleming turned and went back to Sandra. "You're under arrest for suspicion of murder," he said. He pulled out a plastic card and began reading Sandra her rights.

"Even you have more imagination than that," I said. "You've got a witness who just said that Sandra didn't do it!"

Fleming finished reading and then turned to me. "I've got physical evidence, motive and opportunity. The rest is up to the lawyers. I've done my job." He turned toward the uniformed deputy who had made it through the maze. "Cuff her and book her into the jail. Put her in the holding cell in the detective bureau until I get there."

The uniformed deputy stepped forward, producing a pair of handcuffs from the case on his utility belt.

When Sandra saw the shiny glinting metal she looked at me with confusion, disbelief and the beginning of real fear. "Fiddler? I haven't done anything wrong! Help me! Can't you help me?"

And there wasn't a damned thing I could do.

"From now until a laywer comes to see you, give them nothing but your name and address," I said distinctly. "Fleming's a lazy old bull who will do anything he can to close a case. Don't believe a word he says. Say nothing to him. Not one word. Got that?"

Dazed, she nodded, and her eyes fastened on me as though expecting miracles.

Fleming took the handcuffs from the uniformed deputy, stepped behind Sandra, gathered her hands and roughly pinioned them.

It's standard procedure to immobilize suspects like that. Under normal circumstances I probably wouldn't quarrel with the idea. The cop has a job to do. But as I heard the cuffs close and ratchet down to the size of Sandra's slender wrists, I had to turn away in order to keep from doing something really stupid.

At least the uniformed deputy had the decency to remain civil. "Come this way, miss," he said, taking Sandra by the elbow. "Stand back, folks," he said to the people who had followed him through the trampled maze and were now staring at Sandra with a combination of curiosity and horror.

"It will be all right, Sandra," I said roughly. "I promise you."

Words. Just words and the cold steel of handcuffs against her warm skin.

Head down in humiliation, trembling with fear, Sandra was led away. A man stepped out of the maze's concealing shadows. I recognized Beltrán's lean body even as Sandra spoke his name. For an instant she pulled against the cuffs. He understood and went to her. His hand touched her hair for a moment, then the deputy led her away.

Fleming turned and walked over to me, deliberately standing too close, getting in my face. His breath stank of whiskey rather than wine. I stared back, saying nothing, doing nothing. Then I gave him a smile that could have been seen thirty feet away.

Fleming's face went white with anger.

He gave it a long ten-count. Then he gave up trying to goad me into giving him an excuse to use the spring-loaded sap that bulged in his hip pocket. The crowd slowly pivoted and watched him walk away. Gradually the knot of party guests unraveled into twos and threes, people talking and staring at the fountain and the body and the other people like themselves who still couldn't believe a murder had taken place.

I had no such problem. I walked over to Benny and Fiora, unfastening my belt as I went.

"Follow the deputy and Sandra to the jail," I said quietly to Benny. "While they're booking her, round up a local bail bondsman. Lay a grand on him up front," I said, pulling two five-hundred-dollar bills from the zipper compartment of the belt. "Tell him he'll be the one to write whatever bond is finally set. Then get him to tell you the name of the presiding judge of the superior court in this county. For a thousand, he'll be glad to give you the judge's home phone number as well."

I turned to Fiora. "When you have the judge's number, call George Myford in San Francisco. Tell him he's retained for the specific purpose of getting bail set. We'll talk later about whether he gets a full retainer for representing her in the case-in-chief."

Fiora nodded. Her face was pale and set, but it was anger rather than fear. Fleming had not been a class act.

"Change you clothes before you use those keys," Benny muttered. "The shirt's too light by half."

"Go teach your grandmother to suck eggs."

Benny grinned and began wheeling out of the maze along the broad flagstone pathway. Fiora followed.

Another deputy materialized and began shooing people away from the crime scene. Better late than never, I guess. One of the people being herded out of the maze was Beltrán. I followed him out, then motioned him off to a quiet spot beneath one of the old oaks. He asked no questions, simply listened with complete attention while I told him what had happened. He said nothing, did nothing, but there was no mistaking the primitive rage that vibrated through him. When I finished he was silent for about a minute.

"The knife," he said finally. "It is nothing. Anyone could have stolen it. The kitchen and the barbecue area"—he shrugged—"¿cómo se dice? A circus?"

"Close enough. But ask around anyway. Find out if anyone in the kitchen crew noticed a knife missing, and when, and did they see anyone actually take one."

"You have a suspect?" Beltrán asked.

"Traven," I said quietly, "but I doubt that he would do it himself. He'd hire it out. Whoever did it was strong," I said. "Even using one of Sandra's knives, it took a lot of upper-body strength to slice through two ribs with a single stroke at that angle."

"Then it was not Sandra."

"But we're going to have to prove it. Meet me back at Sandra's place as soon as you can. I may need you to run down something else. Okay?"

"It is done," he said simply.

My feet squelched every step of the way that I jogged to the front of the house. A ten-dollar bill bumped my car up out of the parking lot in record time. I stopped at Deep Purple long enough to change everything but the Detonics. I also got an address out of the phone book.

I dodged harvest equipment all the way to St. Helena. I no longer saw the richness of the land spread out beneath the moon. All I saw was Sandra's fear and her shame, as though it were somehow her fault that Fleming had his mind made up the second he saw who was standing by the pond.

I slowed down inside the city limits. The less attention I drew now, the better. Most of the old Victorian houses were darkened. Even in town, people tended to keep farming hours. The streets were deserted as I cruised by Karger's house. There were no official vehicles parked outside, no unmarked detective units parked down the block. At least Fleming was consistent in his laziness. It wasn't hard to stay ahead of a cop like him.

Two blocks down and one over, I found an inconspicuous place to park. I turned off the headlights and coasted in along the curb. I pulled the bulb from the dome light before I eased out of the car. The sidewalks were buckled and cracked from tree roots, the crickets were in full voice and fans droned in most houses, drawing in the cooler night air and providing a nice cover of white noise to mask my footfalls.

I circled Karger's block once, like a man on an evening stroll. The few houses that weren't dark were illuminated by the flickering, vaguely colored vapors of the television screen. No shadows moved against the windows. No one peered out to see who might be walking by. I cut down an alley, hopped a fence and was in Karger's backyard.

The easy part of any burglary is getting in. The hard part is keeping a stranglehold on your imagination. It makes you believe that every sound means discovery and disaster. Every scampering cat is a cop on the beat. Every soft sound is a pit bull measuring your leg. Every breath of wind is a door opening behind your back.

There was a cracked cement walkway leading from the alley to Karger's back door. I had a little flashlight in my hip pocket but I didn't want to show a light around unless I had to. I also had some driving gloves. I didn't mind using them.

The fourth key on Karger's ring released the lock. The door opened soundlessly. I stepped into the house. The closed windows had trapped the heat of the day and held it inside. Beneath the stuffiness there was a sharp chemical smell.

I closed the door behind me. Then I stood without moving as I listened and let my eyes adjust to the darkness. The house was silent until I heard a dry metallic snap, like a pistol dry-firing. The refrigerator compressor came on and my pulse dropped back toward normal. Finally, satisfied that the house was empty, I started to prowl.

The streetlight in front gave me plenty of light. The house was a conventional three-bedroom, two-story model, the kind that had been common back in the twenties and thirties. The place had been redone in furnishings that were painfully modern—leather, glass, chrome and white walls. Very San Francisco, right down to the colorful slashes of art popping off the walls.

There was a night-light in the bathroom. Karger had enough beauty aids in there for a Miss America contest. I found the bedroom by smell. Cologne, musky and flowery at the same time. The sheets must have been washed in the stuff.

The wall between the second and third bedrooms had been knocked down, converting the area into a single work space. It was on the street side of the house. I adjusted the slim venetian blinds to admit some light. One end of the big room was a makeshift lab complete with worktable. There was a stereo microscope and a batch of lab equipment—beakers and retorts and test tubes. The cabinets were filled with chemicals. I could smell alcohol, the kind that doesn't come in burgundy-shaped bottles. There was some other odor, too. Maybe ether.

The other end of the work space contained a conventional desk and library shelves filled with books and bound volumes of scholarly journals. A quick glance down the shelves turned up nothing surprising.

I opened the blinds another notch, enough to give me more light and a slantways view of the street at the same time. Then I went to work on the desk, keeping one eye on traffic at the same time.

The second car that went by was a white Ford sedan with a light bar on top and a big decal on the front door. It was a cheap thrill. No police car responding to a prowler call arrives with his headlights on. The Ford rolled past slowly without pausing, then disappeared down the street. I waited. It didn't reappear.

I sat down in Karger's high-backed chair and went back to work. Karger might have salted his test results, but he wasn't a sloppy sort of man. He was methodical to the point of being clinically interesting. Papers were stacked neatly in a wire basket with all edges squared. I flipped through the papers. There were Xeroxes of research articles, letters from clients and order blanks for scientific supplies.

The desk drawers were locked. That was hopeful. The key was on Karger's ring. The belly drawer opened, revealing neatly arranged letterhead and pens, mailing envelopes and paperclips each in separate compartments. The belly-drawer lock opened the three drawers down the left-hand side of the desk as well. The top drawer had an assortment of field gear—portable microscope, a set of calipers and a case of instruments that would have looked right at home in the Spanish Inquisition. The middle drawer had the makings for coffee and tea, including a hospital-clean mug that had been stored with a paper towel in it.

The bottom drawer had files filled with receipts recording the purchase of everything from gasoline to pencil leads. Karger had been incredibly methodical. Behind the carefully logged daily trivia was a drawer file full of manila folders. There were three years of tax returns which showed unremarkable income from an assistant professor's salary and a few consulting jobs. There were neatly filed health, auto and life insurance policies.

Then, at the back of the file, I found the folder marked "Personal."

The first thing I saw in the folder were letters. I opened the first and confirmed my earlier suspicion. It began "Dearest Eric . . ." and ended "Love, Guy." Karger had been Guy Rocheford's lover. The letter was more than a year old. The affair predated Karger's move to the valley. I wondered if they had met in one of San Francisco's gay bars or if it had been a faculty club affair.

The letters were pretty much of a piece. Both men regretted having to hide their affair, but both men had their reasons for doing so. Karger more so than Rocheford. What goes in San Francisco doesn't necessarily play in Napa Valley, particularly among some of the old-fashioned growers who were Karger's clients.

There was an envelope marked "Will," a birth certificate and a valid passport which showed a single trip the year before to France. There was also a locked, fireproof metal box. True to form, Karger had the key for it on his ring. The only thing inside the box was a sealed brown mailing envelope. There was no writing on the envelope, no neat label to reassure Karger that his life was safely categorized and filed away in perfect order.

My pocket knife slit the envelope cleanly. The contents were an odd assortment of pink and yellow cash receipts. I held them in the striped light from the blinds and tried to understand why Karger had felt it worthwhile to put these receipts in a sealed, unmarked envelope inside a locked box inside a locked drawer. The receipts were for a seemingly random variety of hardware and nursery stock, including a bill for $4,392.57 from a local construction company for erection of "one steel frame utility building." The address for the new building wasn't given, and there was nothing resembling that kind of construction in Karger's backyard.

I kept on going. There were several rental receipts from a local equipment yard and a plain paper envelope with a Healdsburg return address. Inside that envelope was a bill from Swede Swensen Trucking Company Unlimited. According to the bill, Swensen had hauled "one covered load one hundred and two miles" and had billed Eric Karger a total of $450. I checked the dates on the other bills. They were spread out over a three-month period ending thirty days ago.

I wanted to keep the receipts but didn't want to get in the way of the investigation that Fleming would be forced to make when the case against Sandra fell apart. I memorized Swensen's address, replaced the receipts and locked up again. A minute later I was back out in the darkness, just another honest citizen with driving gloves in one pocket and two sets of keys in the other.

20

Beltrán was waiting for me on the porch of Deep Purple, smoking a Marlboro in the darkness. When I turned on the light he looked remote and hard-edged. It was easy to imagine him as a cop in a country that had no love of law and order. He looked at me with the patient, cold eyes of a predator.

"Can you find Swensen's trucking on West Soda Rock Lane in Healdsburg?" I asked.

"*Sí.*"

"Let's go. You can tell me what you found out about the knives on the way."

Beltrán said nothing until we were headed north up Highway 29. Then he spoke quietly.

"There were four or five of the knives when we left here. No one remembers the number," he said. "We counted the knives tonight. There are now three." He shrugged. "What is missing may be at the house of Señor Traven. Or it may not. It is not possible to be sure. There were many chances to steal one, many people going to the kitchen for more wine or water or to find a *baño.*"

"So we can prove nothing in terms of access to the knives," I said.

He nodded, watching the night with dark, brooding eyes. Mexicans are preoccupied with death and honor; I got the impression Beltrán had been thinking a lot about both lately.

"How serious is Sandra's trouble?" Beltrán asked after a long silence.

"Fleming has his mind made up that she's guilty. His life is so much simpler that way."

"Can you not go to his *jefe?*"

"The sheriff? I will if I have to, but until I have something more to take to him than hints and hopes, it's a waste of time. Here in

California the sheriff is an elected politician. He leaves the cop work to civil service deputies like Fleming. Besides, the only finger I can point goes in Traven's direction. The sheriff would much rather convict Sandra."

"But such politicians need more than convictions, no?" Beltrán said softly.

"Like what?"

He ran his thumb over his fingertips, back and forth.

"Mordida?" I asked. "Around California we call it 'campaign contributions,' and sheriffs tend to be very careful about accepting them from accused felons."

Beltrán smiled ironically. "Then the police in California are very different from the police in Mexico."

"That's something Jake never learned," I said. Beltrán looked sideways at me. "My Uncle Jake," I said. "He died trying to get a load of marijuana out of Culiacán late in 1968. Somebody sold him out up here or he paid off the wrong cops down there."

For a moment Beltrán was very still. Then he reached into his pocket, pulled out the crushproof box of Marlboros and lit up with a paper match. A long stream of smoke spun out through the open window into the night.

"Then you know what the *narcotráfico* has done to my country," Beltrán said roughly. "You know that honor does not exist there anymore. It has all been purchased or killed."

"Or exiled."

Beltrán laughed bitterly. "Exile. There is honor in exile, but do you call it exile when you chase a dog away with stones?"

"There's no dishonor in withdrawing from an impossible position."

"There is no honor in it either," Beltrán said coldly.

His anger and pride were easy to read in the sudden, hard bursts of light from his cigarette. After a few moments he reached into his hip pocket, drew out three worn pieces of paper and spread them like cards in his hands. There was just enough light from the dash for me to see that the papers were checks—blank, signed checks.

"It is my—*¿cómo se dice la herencia?*"

"Inheritance," I said.

"Sí. My inheritance. Three checks, drawn on three different

Mexico City bank accounts, all three signed by different *narcotrafi-cantes*. The checks, they are blank. You understand? Blank!"

He drew hard on his cigarette before he continued. "When I first received them I called the banks. There is at least one hundred thousand American dollars in each of those accounts. It was mine if I wanted it. I looked at those checks for a very long time."

Smoke hissed out, and with it an epithet. *"Hijo la chingada!* The fuck-your-mother bastards wanted me to put my own price on my honor!"

"How long ago was that?"

"Five years," he said. "The checks can still be made into money. The accounts still exist and there is more American dollars in them than ever before. You understand? The *traficantes* have bought every cop in Sonora but me. It is important to them to purchase me as a lesson to all who oppose them. Or they must kill me. There is no difference to them." Beltrán grunted. "I can have no sympathy for your dead uncle. *Narcotraficantes* take the honor from my country."

"Jake wasn't much interested in sympathy. Adrenaline was his game. He loved Mexico for its wildness. He said more than once that it would probably kill him someday."

"He was right," Beltrán said.

At Calistoga I veered left and took Highway 128 out through the vineyards and the dry countryside. It was almost midnight. There was no traffic. The road twisted and climbed over a little pass before dipping down into a place called Knights Valley.

The late moon shone like frost on acre after acre of vineyards. This was new grape land, almost raw by comparison with Napa. This valley hadn't been overrun with boutique winery buildings and re-conditioned farmhouses. The ranches that were left were real, complete with dry-land pasture and the smell of cow shit.

Neither Beltrán nor I spoke as I drove down the tunnel of head-lights through the vineyards and pastures, into the Alexander Valley. Beneath the moon it looked like a familiar place, closer to Calistoga than to what Oakville and Rutherford had become. Sandra had told Fiora that the Alexander Valley was like going back in time to Napa before the Paris tasting. I could see what she meant.

"Is this good soil?" I asked Beltrán.

"Primo," he said. "Very good. Someday I will buy land here.

Maybe then I could live like a *gringo vinatero* instead of like an uneducated *indio* from the mountains."

I wondered if that was what kept Beltrán from being more to Sandra than a respected friend and majordomo. Not that Beltrán's lack of money would have bothered Sandra. His pride was another matter, however.

"With those checks in your pocket, you're a wealthy man," I pointed out.

"But I would be a poor man if I spent them," he said. "Turn right at the next crossing."

Beltrán guided me to the address on West Soda Rock Lane without a hitch. It was well after one o'clock. Moonlight made the Russian River shine like hammered steel where it ran through the low side of the valley.

Swede Swensen's trucking yard was a working farm as well as a shipping business. The smell of manure was strong, as was the smell of damp earth from some kind of irrigation. A dusty Kenworth truck tractor stood beside the driveway, a muddy set of logger's dual wheels stacked on its fifth-wheel platform. Beside it a gondola trailer stood on its wheels and support legs. Behind that a ten-wheel Mack dump truck was parked. All told, Swede Swensen ran a mustang operation, hauling whatever needed to be hauled. It was a hard way to make a living.

As I stopped the car in the yard I caught a glimpse of movement in the shadows between the vehicles. I shone my pocket flashlight through the open window. A German shepherd with rumpled ears moved quietly among the vehicles, then stopped when the beam picked him out. He didn't bark and he didn't wag his tail. His eyes were blue-green in the flashlight's glare.

"Don't suppose you're the friendly type," I said.

The dog didn't reply. He stood motionless, watching, waiting. He wasn't a bit intimidated.

I pulled ahead past the trucks and stopped just short of the front door of the run-down bungalow. The dog trotted along beside and leaped up on the porch. I turned out the headlights, left the parking lights on and tapped the horn three times. After a minute a lamp came on in the bedroom. I hit the horn again, lightly.

Finally the front door opened and a figure emerged. Potbellied, hairy and wearing only Levis, Swensen was as wide as the door and looked as mean as his junkyard dog. There was a double-barreled shotgun in his thick hands.

"You got a problem, mister?" he said loudly.

"I'm interested in some information," I said, fanning five twenties in my hand and shining the flashlight on them to demonstrate my good intentions.

"You a cop?"

"You know any cops who have a hundred to burn?" I retorted.

Swensen's laugh was as rumpled as his dog's ears. He broke the shotgun and laid it across his arm. He aimed a barefooted kick at the dog. "Go lay down, Bruno," he said quietly. The dog left as silently as he had come.

"You can git out."

I moved carefully. Swensen was the kind of guy who could put the shotgun back in operation with one flick of his wrist.

"You did some hauling for a man named Karger a month ago down in Napa," I said. "Remember him?"

Swensen grunted. "Hippie kinda fella? Long hair and bell-bottoms? Yeah, I remember him."

"Do you remember what you hauled for him?"

"Nope."

I added another twenty to the fan. "Did he pay you to keep the load quiet?"

"Nope, he just never told me, and he loaded and unloaded it himself. Even bought me a new tarp to cover the stuff."

"Could it have been building materials?"

Swensen yawned, stretched and shook his head. "Nope. You don't haul lumber in a gondola."

"A gondola?"

"Yep. That there trailer," he said, motioning with the muzzle of the shotgun toward the equipment yard where the dog lurked. "Hauled it over to a place down in Monterey County. Two days later I came back and he had it all loaded and covered over with canvas. I just hooked onto it and drove it back up to St. Helena and dropped it off again. A day later he called me and told me to come get it. It was empty then."

"A little strange, wouldn't you say?" I suggested.

"I got paid. Nothin' strange about that."

"This place where you dropped the trailer to be loaded," I said. "Was it a laboratory?"

"Nope," Swensen said. "It was a vineyard south of Salinas and up against the hills. New place but it looked like it was on the skids. Vines dying like they ain't been cared for."

I remembered the chits for a new utility building. It had to have been built somewhere.

"Was there a new building on the property?" I asked, adding another twenty to the fan.

"Nope."

"How about the place you hauled to up here?" I asked. "Was it a vineyard too? Maybe one with a new building on it?"

Swensen yawned again. "Yep," he said. "One of them Butler buildings. You 'bout finished? I got to be to Willits by first light. I'd like some sack time 'tween now and then."

"One more," I said, and matched the words with another twenty. "What was the address of the place with the new building?"

"Didn't have none," he said. "It was just at the end of a dirt road clear to hell out in the boondocks. Closest thing with a name was Langtry Road. Know it?"

I looked at Beltrán, who was leaning against the car, listening. He nodded.

"Give me the best directions you can and I'll make it an even two hundred," I said.

Swensen talked, Beltrán listened and we were on our way in two minutes flat.

It was quicker to take U.S. 101 south from Healdsburg. We cut inland on Highway 12, but before we got to the Valley of the Moon, Beltrán signaled a left onto a choppy little two-lane country highway called Calistoga Road. I recognized it after a mile or two. It followed the old stagecoach route over Spring Mountain and back down into Calistoga. A few miles up the flank of the mountain I took the right fork and a half hour later we popped up over the summit.

Napa Valley was laid out before us, with the lights of St. Helena itself at our feet. The air was cool and damp. The headlights picked up a few wisps of fog sliding among the madrona bushes and pines at the top of the divide, but the sky overhead was brilliantly clear and glistening with stars.

Langtry Road was a one-lane tar track that wound out through

Spring Mountain's rugged Chardonnay vineyards. A few miles up
the road the pavement gave way to a graded dirt surface. I was
driving without lights now, and the feel of the Detonics digging into
my spine was comforting rather than uncomfortable. The memory of
Karger face down in the fountain was very fresh.

I caught a flicker of movement as we rounded a bend. Disturbed
by our passage, a big owl dropped silently from a tree limb and
ghosted off down the mountain. Night hunters have an eerie silence
and grace that people seldom get to appreciate. The owl moved like a
living shadow.

Swensen had said it was seven miles from Spring Mountain
Road to Karger's building. When the odometer rolled up five I
started looking for a place to hide the car. I found a little dirt track
that led off uphill and ended in a thicket. I pulled past, backed in and
shut off the engine.

Suddenly it was so quiet that I could hear the ticking of the
quartz clock on the dashboard. The brilliance of the moon was veiled
behind clouds in the northwest, blurring the landscape into shades of
black. Way off in the east there was the faintest suggestion of dawn.

"You have a gun," I said, more statement than question.

"*Sí.*" Just that. No explanation, no apology.

"*Bueno.*"

I opened the door and stepped into the chill, clean air.

21

The lights in the big valley just below us were brilliant white pinpoints. Up where Beltrán and I were on the mountain there were no lights, no signs of other people, nothing but a sense that day was slowly gaining on night. The road itself was smooth rather than rutted, sandy rather than rocky. We jogged for most of the first mile. Then we walked quickly.

The subtle shifts that announce dawn began to show around us. Starlings in the meadows were chattering and chirping as they stirred and began to plan raids on the sweet grapes down below. Off in the trees a mockingbird sang his scales up and down, reassuring himself that he hadn't lost the touch overnight.

With every step we took the light strengthened. It became bright enough to distinguish a lone crow dipping its wings through the gray dawn like an oarsman in a skiff. The crow passed so close we could hear the whispering whistle of air through his feathers.

There was enough light now to see the three lightning-struck old redwoods on the ridgeline off to the left, just as Swensen had described them. The water in a small irrigation pond beside the road reflected the gray sky so seamlessly that the surface looked like mercury. An orderly zinfandel vineyard fell down the hillside into the crease below. Nothing moved among the grape-laden rows.

Swensen had said that the utility building had been constructed at the end of Langtry Road, on a pad in a little grove of blue oaks and digger pines. I couldn't see the building from the ridge where we were, but I could see the grove and the spot where the road unraveled into ruts.

After a short discussion Beltrán and I split up and dropped over the ridge on either side of the vineyard. I took to the brush, following a narrow game trail. Beltrán slipped between two rows of vines and disappeared. Halfway down the slope a covey of mountain quail scurried out of my path, racing for the safety of the tall grass. The little valley was silent except for the sounds of birds.

Beltrán and I reached the end of the vineyard at the same time. We were about seventy-five yards apart, motionless, listening. I could see the utility building now, a pale rectangle showing through the trees. Its steel sides glowed dully in the increasing light. A flicker of movement on the roof peak caught my eye. A Steller's jay was perched there, jeering the morning.

With a motion of my hand I sent Beltrán one way around the perimeter of the building. I circled in the opposite direction through the woods, walking quietly enough to startle the gray squirrels who had begun to rustle through the fallen leaves. Within two minutes Beltrán and I were in sight of one another again on the far side of the grove.

There were actually two buildings in the grove of trees. One was the shiny new Butler building on its concrete pad. The other was an old farm shed that was dissolving back into the evergreen needles and weeds.

Beltrán was fifty yards away, sheltered behind the smooth-barked trunk of a small redwood. I gave him an openhanded gesture, asking whether he had seen anything. He shook his head. I drew the Detonics and nodded toward the two buildings. Beltrán's hand moved and suddenly, as though by magic, he held a small, flat semi-automatic pistol. He handled the gun the same way he had handled the old Buck knife, with utter familiarity.

We moved in on the buildings one at a time. I covered while Beltrán slipped forward to the shelter of an oak. Then he covered while I moved to the corner of the old shed and listened very carefully. If there was anything inside, it could hold its breath longer than I could.

I risked a quick glance through a window whose glass had been broken out long ago. Several bags that had once contained argricultural chemicals were discarded in one corner, and a few farming tools lay on a sagging wooden bench just beneath the window. The most dangerous thing in the building appeared to be a hoe with a broken handle and a rusty blade.

The new building was as silent as the old shed had been. No sound but my own breathing, no movement but my own as I turned away from the closed door. I motioned Beltrán in. He took up a position on one corner that would allow him to watch both me and the road.

There were no windows to peer through. The building's double doors were secured with a big Schlage padlock. It was new, shiny and tough enough to discourage even heavy-duty bolt cutters. I pulled Karger's keys out of my pocket. I had to turn toward the morning sky to read the letters. There was only one Schlage. It opened the lock with a single smooth turn. I unhooked the padlock silently, eased back the hasp and waited for Beltrán to move into position. He nodded. I threw the door open, leaving him a clear field of fire.

Beltrán stared into the building, listening, watching. Nothing happened. After a minute he slowly lowered his pistol and turned to me with a baffled expression.

"Dirt," he said softly. "Why would a man put a lock on a building full of dirt?"

I stepped into the building. It contained a mound of earth fifteen feet long and maybe five feet high. The pile began a few steps inside the doorway. The air in the building was dank, jungle-humid, thick with the smell of damp earth and a hint of decay.

Despite the onset of dawn, the interior of the building was dark. I dug out the little Maglite I had used in Karger's house. The beam showed me twisted arms and straggling tendrils of uprooted grape-vines that stuck out of the dirt at odd angles. It was as though someone had bulldozed a vineyard, then scraped up the vines and a half foot of dirt and dumped them here in the windowless building.

I flashed the light around the interior. The building had been put up with great care. The steel joints were caulked with some kind of plastic or silicon compound. Beads of moisture glittered in the flashlight's beam. The floor was covered with the heavy-gauge black plastic sheeting Napa farmers use to line their irrigation ponds. It, too, sweated. I looked at it for a moment, wondering why Karger had bothered to keep the building watertight.

And then I was afraid that I knew.

"Get in here," I said to Beltrán. "Close the door."

He quickly pulled the door shut behind him.

"Karger wasn't trying to keep people out," I said. "He was trying to keep something *in.*"

I handed the light to Beltrán and holstered the Detonics. I went

down on one knee and probed gingerly through the dirt until I found
a vine that had been completely buried. A yank on the tough stem
pulled the vine free of the mound.

The flashlight caught the rusty brown of the dirt, the darker
tone of the vine wood itself and the veneer of sulphurous yellow that
suffused both. I looked more closely. The yellow veneer was writhing
like a mass of tiny maggots.

Beltrán leaned in over my shoulder. When he caught the suggestion of seething life he shrank back instinctively.

"Yeah," I said. "No wonder phylloxera got such a fast start in
Traven's vineyards. Karger had enough of the goddamn bugs to in-
fest the whole Napa Valley. And that's why Karger put up this her-
metic building. He knew that he had a biological time bomb here."

I pulled the light and walked around the dirt. Every vine I
pulled out told the same story. The mound of earth was laced with
phylloxera. The infestation was much heavier than I had seen in
Traven's vineyard. I wondered whether Karger had in effect discovered a way to culture the pest. It made sense. He had been a lab man,
accustomed to dealing with test tubes and scientific supply houses.
He would need a steady source of phylloxera for his experiments. If
none existed, he would have to create it.

When I got back to the front of the building Beltrán held his
hand out for the light.

"Por favor," he said quietly.

Beltrán trained the flashlight beam on the vine I had uprooted.
The hard white light went up and down the trunk several times as
though searching for something.

"This vine, it has no graft," he said, pointing to the spot where a
clump of roots turned into a slender trunk and then branched into
several vines.

"Does it matter?"

"The vines, they are old rootstock," Beltrán explained.
"Vinifera."

"You mean this particular type of vine isn't resistant to phylloxera?"

"Sí," he said emphatically. "Some growers tried this kind of
vine as an experiment in Paso Robles." He shook his head. "It was a
very serious mistake. The phylloxera, it could not be controlled."

I stood in the dank building and looked at the mound of silently

seething dirt. No wonder Karger had been silenced. The grape growers of Napa would have lynched anybody connected with this little
house of horrors. Karger had understood the potential risk of intro-
ducing phylloxera into the richest vineyards in the United States. He
had been the one to seal the building so tightly that no moisture
could escape.

Maybe Karger had been murdered because his conscience finally won out over his science. Or maybe it was greed rather than
conscience that had made Karger approach Sandra. Maybe he had
asked Traven for more money or less risk and Traven had turned
him down. Maybe Traven had decided to maximize his own gain and
minimize his exposure. Exit Dr. Karger, a research scientist who was
no better than he had to be. Enter Eric Karger, murder victim.

I sat on my heels and looked at the yellow-skinned vine writhing
in slow motion as parasites fed on it. The receipts sealed up in
Karger's desk, Swensen, the workmen who had been paid to put up
this building . . . I had more than enough to convict Karger.

And not one damned thing to convict Traven.

The building wasn't in his name. It wasn't on his land. There
wasn't one solid piece of evidence to tie Vern Traven to any crime
more serious than trying to turn a profit on an infected vineyard. In
ten seconds I could think of three explanations for the circumstantial
evidence that might raise a reasonable doubt in the minds of a jury.
A defense lawyer with time on his hands could probably dream up
twice as many. In the end, people might talk and whisper and specu-
late, but the worst that would happen to Traven would be that his
popularity around Napa Valley would take a dive. No problem. He'd
just bring in folks from the city to populate his own personal stage.

That wasn't good enough for me. I wanted to see the curtain go
down on Sandra's tormentor and never go up again. The only way to
do that was to prove that he had had a good and urgent reason to
want Karger dead.

That's the irony about legal cases. They don't really rely on
facts; they rely on *provable* facts. Some facts aren't amenable to
proof. Others get slippery in the retelling.

The only answer was more and better evidence. I had to demonstrate that Traven had what is known as "guilty knowledge" of this
shedful of phylloxera; in short, that he had a motive for seeing that
Karger ended up face down in the fountain. The best way to do that

was to get Traven to come to the shed . . . without giving any specific directions.

Tricky, but quite possible. I suspected that Traven was being pushed hard by circumstances. That's when mistakes are made. Lethal mistakes. Karger's death smacked of a very hurried operation, the kind done in the name of damage control. Perhaps he had had an attack of conscience and had gone to Sandra to confess all. More likely he wanted to see if she would pay him more than Traven. Either way, Karger was a dead man walking.

I doubted that Traven had wanted to unveil the phylloxera before he had a legal lock on Sandra's land, either. Fiora's running the numbers on Deep Purple and making them look good had forced his hand. If the bank refinanced, Deep Purple was out of reach, and so was the keystone of the Napa development scheme.

Enter phylloxera. A little early, but what the hell. Better early than never. If he lost a few million paying off Sandra, so what? There were a whole lot more millions waiting, thanks to a dead man and a shed seething with tiny yellow bugs. That evidence would have to be destroyed sooner or later.

My job was to see that it was sooner rather than later.

"You mind baby-sitting the bugs for a while?" I asked Beltrán, standing up and rubbing my hands hard on my jeans. "Just to make sure that nobody comes along and cleans house while I'm gone." I moved the light so that I could see his eyes. "And play it safe. One man has already died to keep this secret."

Beltrán nodded.

"I need an extra pair of eyes for a few hours," I continued. "If it all goes from sugar to shit before I get back, you just keep your head down and stay out of sight. *Claro?*"

"From sugar to shit? *Sí,* Fiddler. That is something I understand very well."

But his humorless smile said that he would do what he damn well pleased if the man who had framed Sandra came into sight. I didn't like it, but there was nothing I could do about it. I had two phone calls, a small bit of burglary and a trap to set up. I couldn't do that sitting here counting bugs.

We relocked the double doors of the storehouse and tried to obliterate the footprints we had left in the dust. Beltrán took up a station in the shed and I jogged back to the BMW.

The highway dumped me right back into St. Helena near Karger's house. Everything looked the same—except for the white Volkswagen parked in front. Apparently someone else was interested in what Karger might have left behind. I parked around the corner.

A man in a white shirt and necktie came out of a house two doors down and walked slowly across the lawn to his car, his coat thrown over his shoulder. A paper boy on his bike tossed San Francisco *Chronicle*s on driveways as he passed. Nobody had canceled Karger's subscription yet. The paper skipped across the rough concrete and slid beneath the Volkswagen.

I went in the back way. The kitchen door opened without a sound and shut behind me the same way while I held my breath and listened to the silence.

Only it wasn't silent, and the first breath I took told me someone had been burning paper.

I used the side of the stairs, where the wood was silent. The hallway was the same. I hugged the side, looking through the open doors. Nothing but furniture. Then I heard the sound of a chair being moved. It came from the office. I edged up to the open door, hoping to catch Traven here, now. Alone.

Guy Rocheford was standing at the desk, staring at the big mixing bowl he must have brought up from the kitchen. As I watched, he dropped in the colored receipt from Swensen trucking. It wasn't the first thing he had burned in that bowl. The smell of charred paper was very strong. A thin haze of smoke had spread through the room.

Rocheford had lost his willowy appeal. He looked as hard as one of Sandra's knives. The civilized veneer had been peeled away, revealing the essential coldness of the man beneath. Watching Rocheford, I doubted that grief had been among the emotions that had driven him to his dead lover's house to stir among the memories. In fact, if Rocheford had been six inches taller and twice as wide in the shoulders, I'd have wondered how he would look with a knife in his hand.

There was a brooding look about Rocheford, as though he were wondering if he had found all the love letters linking him to Karger and all the receipts linking Karger to a shed crawling with phylloxera. Rocheford was a man with a real problem, and he knew it. It shouldn't be hard to convince him that I knew enough to track down the shed but that I hadn't done it quite yet. He'd pass the word along real quick and Traven would come racing to destroy the shed—and run right into the trap that I would lay.

I held the Detonics down along my leg. When I stepped into the doorway Rocheford made a startled sound.

"You're a little late," I said, indicating the ashes in the mixing bowl. "I've got the names and addresses on those receipts that you're burning. I'm going to run down every one. Sooner or later I'll find out what was trucked, what was built, where it was built and why."

Rocheford was tougher than I'd expected. The only sign that he'd understood what I said was a sudden, fine sheen of sweat amid his stubble.

"I don't know what you're talking about."

I smiled. He didn't like it.

"Trying to frame Sandra was a mistake," I said. "By the time I'm through you'll wish you were as dead as Karger."

I left him standing there, sweating. I only had one call to make, now. Rocheford would take care of the other, the one to the man who had set Sandra up for murder.

All I had to do was get the trap in place before he came running.

22

I called Sandra's house from a public phone. There was no answer. I tried the guesthouse. Benny nailed it on the first ring.

"That you, mate?" he demanded.

"Yeah. You still have that linear CB in your van?"

"Bigger and better than ever."

"Then meet me in front of the hardware store on Main in St. Helena as quick as you can," I said.

He didn't ask one question. He just hung up and headed for the hardware store. I did the same.

The piece of equipment I wanted was in the automotive section at the back of the store, behind the farm tools and poisons that made your eyes water when you walked down the aisles. The remote location didn't surprise me; citizens-band radios aren't nearly the hot novelty they used to be. Nowadays nobody uses them except truckers and farmers—or people in a jam. There was a Radio Shack at the edge of town but it didn't open until nine, so I had to settle for one of the CBs that come as part of a roadside emergency kit. The radios are designed for occasional use. They have little power and less reception, but in a pinch they get the job done.

The CB that Benny installed in his van could be used to talk to the moon, if he had to. The rig is powered by a 150-watt linear amplifier that is technically illegal because you can light up your neighbor's microwave oven with it. Hitting a cheap receiver two miles away would be no problem for him.

I paid $39.95 plus tax for the roadside emergency kit, pulled the radio out and put the rest in the trash.

The problem of a weapon required more study, and a more expensive solution. Maybe I was thinking of what Fiora had said about the Detonics not being enough. Maybe I was thinking of how quickly Karger had died, and how easily. It's a lot harder to kill a man armed with a Remington Model 1100 shotgun.

The store only had one in stock, so I got a Winchester Model 94 carbine for Beltrán. Something about its frontiersman styling made me think Beltrán would like it. I just hoped the sights hadn't been beaten too far out of alignment because there wasn't going to be any time to test-fire it.

When I got out of the store Benny's van was nowhere in sight. I loaded the weapons and put them in the trunk of the BMW along with the boxes of ammunition that I had bought. The cheap CB went into the car with me. When my watch told me Benny should be about within range I hailed him on 21, the channel he normally monitors. After a few tries I raised him.

"You're five by five but real scratchy," he came back. "What are you using?"

"Two tin cans and a string. I'm waiting in front of the hardware store."

A few minutes later Benny pulled into the parking space beside me. Fiora was with him. The look on Benny's face told me it hadn't been his idea.

Fiora got out of the van wearing casual clothes and a tight-lipped expression. I thought it was anger until I saw her eyes. Then I wished to hell that Benny had cold-cocked her and left her behind. She was no more cut out for this kind of thing than I was cut out for the boardroom bloodletting.

"Why don't you call the police?" Fiora said by way of greeting. "Why do you have to be the one to—"

"There's no time to explain the concept and relevance of guilty knowledge to a deputy who would fuck up a wet dream," I said flatly, interrupting her. "There's no time at all, period. I don't want you here, Fiora."

"That makes two of us."

"Great. There's a cafe down the street. I'll pick you up after I'm through."

"No."

Just the one word. No negotiation, no whiff of compromise. Fiora was rarely like that, but when she was, nothing moved her, not God, not the Devil, and certainly not the man who loved her.

Benny was watching me with his dark, shrewd eyes, but there

was pain and compassion in them, as well as intelligence. He hated it when Fiora and I argued.

Without another word I turned to Benny and told him what I wanted from him. I wrapped it up by saying, "You're going to do two things for me. One, you'll give me warning when Traven or his hired gun is coming up Langtry Road. I'm hoping it will be Traven. If not, we'll just have to persuade whoever shows up to talk. Either way, you'll be a witness to the fact that Traven or his thug showed up. That will prove that he had knowledge of the building and its contents. Once we have that, even an elected politician will have to swallow hard and do his duty."

"I'll also be around to witness murder one if the bastard shows up with an army," Benny pointed out. "But stuck up on the mountainside the way you've described, there's bugger all I'll be able to do in the way of help."

"Beltrán will be in the little valley with me. He'll have a rifle. We'll do all right. Traven won't bring an army. The more people who know, the less chance he'll get away with it."

"It?" Fiora said coolly. "Murder is the word you're looking for, Fiddler. You're setting yourself up as a target for a man who has already proved that execution is his style."

Her tightly clipped words didn't tell me anything that I didn't already know. A look at my watch showed twenty-five minutes gone. I turned back to Benny.

"Follow me up the road. We'll be looking for a place where we can hide the van, see the Langtry Road turnoff and still be able to transmit down into that little valley where I'll be hiding."

"Down?" he asked.

"Probably," I admitted.

"Bloody hell," he muttered. "If it's not line of sight, you'd be better off with mirrors or rockets or whistles or smoke signals. You can fiddle a lot of things, boyo, but Mother Nature ain't one of them. Hills and valleys suck up radio signals the way a frog sucks up bugs. I can hit the top of a mountain if I can see it, but I can't pull a signal out of the bottom of a valley a mile away, not even with a base station."

"Don't worry, I'll hear you just fine."

He grunted. "But I won't be able to hear *you*. Not across several miles of hilly terrain with you using that piece of Taiwanese shit you bought. Christ, I won't even know if you get my transmission."

That was true, and unavoidable. I turned and climbed back into the BMW to avoid further arguments. Fiora climbed back into Benny's van without even giving me another look. We snaked up the mountain as fast as Benny's van could make the curves.

As Benny had feared, the only place we could find that was even half good for him to hide the van and still see the Langtry cutoff was too far away for my cheap CB to punch out a return message. Nobody argued the choice, though. As Benny had pointed out, fiddling Mother Nature just wasn't possible.

Two more miles down Langtry, I tucked the car out of sight, gathered up everything I needed and jogged off down the road toward the grove. I took the same game trail that I'd taken earlier, but this time I was carrying two long guns and a CB radio, had my pockets full of ammo, and the sunlight was like a hammer on my shoulders. By the time I dropped over the small, rumpled ridge into the valley, my clothes were dark with sweat and I was breathing hard.

The valley and grove were just as quiet as they had been when Beltrán and I had been there after dawn. There were no vehicles parked nearby, no new tire tracks in the dust. I hadn't expected any, but it was reassuring just the same. I hung back in the trees and gave a low whistle to warn Beltrán that I was on my way in. After a sleepless night, a man sitting alone in a crumbling shed waiting for a murderer can get jumpy; I didn't want to get shot by mistake.

From the corner of my eye I caught a motion. I dropped the guns and radio to reach for the Detonics, but it was too late. The stock of a short-barreled shotgun connected with my head like a wooden mallet. The ground came up and hit my knees. If I hadn't grabbed onto a tree trunk, I would have gone face first in the dirt. Somebody twisted the cold, hard muzzle of a sawed-off shotgun into the soft flesh behind my jaw as I tried to make the world stop turning around.

"You know," a voice said, "I should have just shot you that first night. Would have saved me all kinds of trouble."

The voice was not the one I had been expecting, but I didn't have to turn my head to recognize Fleming. No wonder the arsonist at Vintage Harvest had been so calm—he had known that when the cops were called he'd be the one to answer.

"Into the shed," Fleming said.

As I shoved off from the tree I tried to grab Fleming but my reflexes were a joke. He stepped back easily and kicked me in the side of the head. It felt like he was wearing steel-toed safety shoes instead of soft leather boots. This time I went all the way down and stayed.

Fleming wasn't very meaty, but he was strong. He got my head in the crook of his arm and levered me to my feet. I had just enough sense left to know that if I made a try for him before my vision cleared he would chop me up and leave me for the flies.

He was used to handling drunks and other cripples. He easily rolled me into the dark interior of the old shed. Beltrán was slumped against the rough wood wall, his hands pinned behind him. His face was covered with blood. There were several dark cuts where the shotgun butt had connected with flesh and bone. His eyes were open but I couldn't tell if they were focused on anything.

Fleming was too damned quick. I never saw the blow that sent me sprawling. When my head cleared again I heard the sound of handcuffs ratcheting down. After I rubbed the blood out of my eyes with my left hand I saw that my right hand was cuffed to a ringbolt about six feet off the ground. The bolt was sunk deep into a four-by-four redwood post. Judging from the rust on the iron eye, it had been there a long time. It was still strong, though. When my knees sagged, the ringbolt took my weight without a whimper.

Fleming dragged Beltrán over to the same ringbolt, pulled out another pair of handcuffs and fastened him in place. Despite his injuries, Beltrán struggled fiercely. Fleming took a half step back and whipped a blow across Beltrán's face. His head snapped back against the post with a thick sound. He slumped and didn't struggle anymore.

The blow opened up the skin on Beltrán's cheek right to the bone. Fleming was wearing sap gloves—leather gloves with a few ounces of lead in the fingers. Back-country cops use them in bar fights. They're supposed to be less lethal than a hickory baton, but you couldn't have proved it by Beltrán or me. I got the impression Fleming was half killing us now so that the rest of the job would be easier when he got around to it. He was the kind of sportsman who jacklighted deer.

As I fought my way back to my feet I wondered if Traven would be in on the kill or if he would stay back in the woodwork with the rest of the cockroaches.

Fleming stood watching me, his short-barreled riot gun in one hand and my Detonics in the other. He was mean and tricky, but he wasn't very bright. He had missed the sharp little shark's-tooth dagger that was disguised as part of my belt buckle. The holdout knife had saved my ass once before, but it wasn't worth a damn against a twelve-gauge at point-blank range—especially when I was forced to fight one-handed.

My sole, small consolation was that my left hand was the one that remained free. Fleming had gone with the odds and hooked my right hand to the ringbolt. It wasn't the first time that my being left-handed had given me an edge. I hoped it wouldn't be the last.

I didn't move until Fleming walked into the bright rectangle that was the doorway and was swallowed up in blindingly painful light.

"How badly are you hurt?" I asked Beltrán in a low voice.

For a moment I was afraid that he was unconscious rather than stunned. He was hanging from the steel restraint with most of his weight on his arm. He shook his head slowly like a club fighter trying to shake off a knockout punch. Then he spat blood.

"*El otro . . .*" he said, but the rest was lost in a jumble of sound that meant nothing.

"*No comprendo,*" I said.

Beltrán groaned and spat blood again. "*Lo siento. He came . . . fire . . . road.*"

"*No importa,*" I said, realizing that Beltrán was trying to explain how he had been taken, how we both had been surprised.

An emergency four-wheel-drive road leading from the valley floor up the side of Spring Mountain would get someone within striking range of this little side valley without ever showing a trace on Langtry Road. I could only hope that Traven wouldn't use the back entrance too.

Benny would get real restless if he saw Traven go in and then didn't see me walk out a few minutes later. But if Traven came in the back way Benny wouldn't be any wiser.

"Don't talk," I told Beltrán. "You'll need your strength when Fleming comes back."

Beltrán tried to speak, groaned and then was silent. I took my own advice about being quiet, because talking was like chewing on glass. The temporary anesthetic of shock had already worn off. My jaw was bruised or cracked and one of my molars was on fire. I tried to ignore it but the pain had one salutary effect. It told me that I was alive, like the blood running down my forehead into my eye. It's only when you quit hurting and bleeding that you really have to worry.

I wiped my face against my right sleeve and did a quick survey of the interior of the shed. There were a few potential weapons around—rusty harvest knives and two feet of heavy steel reinforcing rod that was a perfect length to bend around Fleming's head. But everything was beyond my reach. Carefully I stretched as far as I could in all directions. There were at least two yards between me and anything of value. I tried reaching out with my feet. Close, but not good enough.

That left the post and the ringbolt. I tried using the attached end of the handcuff as a lever or screwdriver to unseat the threaded bolt. The bolt was Excalibur; it had been frozen in place for years. It would take me hours to gnaw the bolt from the post with the short-bladed holdout knife. I knew that I didn't have that kind of time.

When I yanked hard on the handcuffs the nickel-plated metal chain joining the cuffs clashed and jangled but didn't give a bit. A close look at the cuffs showed the brand name—Bianchi Model 505 —stamped into the locking shield. They looked as though they had seen a lot of use, but they still got the job done.

Beneath the ringing in my ears a memory was trying to form. I shook my head to clear it. Dumb. Really dumb. The motion brought the kind of pain that didn't clear the mind. When I could breathe again I took hold of the handcuff that went through the ringbolt and tested it by throwing my weight against it. As I shifted, the chain links rattled harshly. The old memory stirred again.

Link. Something about handcuffs and the links that joined them.

"Hey! Settle down in there or I'll split your skull for you like I did the Mex!"

To make sure I obeyed, Fleming came and stood in the doorway for a while, letting his eyes adjust from sunlight to shadow. He carried the short shotgun in one hand, like a pistol. He still had the sap gloves on. He came into the shed a little more, looking at the handcuffs that held me.

I yanked hard again, trying to get Fleming anxious enough to come in closer. Most men forget that feet reach much farther than hands. If Fleming forgot, it would be the last mistake he made this side of hell. I shifted my weight slightly and got ready to put my heel through his head, but he stayed just beyond the range of my feet. Before I could curse his animal wariness, he turned and went out again, satisfied that the cuffs would hold me.

In frustration I yanked down. The chain rattled dryly. Fleming didn't pause or look back. Suddenly the memory that had been gnawing at me beneath the ringing in my ears came into focus. I studied the handcuffs that imprisoned me and felt a small stirring of hope.

By twisting and bending, I pulled the cuffs into the best light. One of the things I had learned during my short stint as a cop was that, with enough time and strength, a man can beat handcuffs. If you're wired on PCP, you don't even need time. I wasn't wired, so I'd have to do it the hard way.

The weakness lies in the case-hardened links of chain that join the two cuffs together. Usually the chain is nickel-plated and appears seamless. But there is always a joint concealed somewhere beneath the plating of the broad link that connects the two bracelets. Convicts and jailhouse regulars know about the hidden weak points. Fleming either figured that I didn't know or he expected to kill me soon enough that it didn't make any difference.

At first I couldn't find the joint. I wiped the blood and sweat out of my eyes and tried again. As I stared at the broad, open link I saw places where the nickel plating had been worn away. Then I found the seam midway between the two heavy steel swivels, one on each cuff.

The welded joint was close enough to center that it could be torqued and broken—given time.

Using the ringbolt as a stop on the other cuff, I carefully turned my wrist over a couple of times, taking up the slack between the two bracelets. By holding the cuff with my free hand, I could jam the swivels, turning the loose chain into what amounted to a bar. I took one more twist on the chain, jamming the swivels tight against the cuffs, and wrenched.

It was like trying to braid sand. The chain slipped in all directions and went loose. I gathered chain again. It got away again. Blood dripped onto the links. I throttled down on my urge to yell curses and yank futilely at the chain. The only answer was patience, inhuman patience, a steady, gradual buildup of pressure to keep the chain links lined up like a bar. You had to do it just right, a little bit at a time, until the chain got away from you and you had to start all over again . . . or until something solid was torqued beyond its tensile strength and it came apart and you were free. All it takes is patience and time.

Voices came from outside, telling me that I had run out of time. I lifted up the cuffs to try again and then froze as I heard the new man clearly. Not Traven.

Ramsey.

23

The realization hit me as hard as Fleming's sap gloves, stunning me. My breath hissed in, rushing over the broken molar like a metal probe. Pain stabbed in a vicious reminder that it didn't matter whether it was Traven or Ramsey out there. I was chained in here. Right now, that was all that was important.

"We got another problem," Fleming said.

"Now what?" Ramsey said, exasperated.

"Sandra's Mex and Fiddler are cuffed in the shed."

"What? How the hell did they find this place so fast?"

"Damned if I know. Want me to ask him?"

Ramsey must have decided to pass on the opportunity, because no shadows came to dim the bright rectangle of sunlight that was the door.

"God damn Karger to hell," Ramsey snarled. "And Traven with him! *Shit!* First Art keeps giving Sandra more time and then more, when any sane banker would have called in the loan six months ago. So I push the timetable up and plant the phylloxera. Art finally gets moving, but Traven sticks his oar in and bids twice what I can afford for Deep Purple—and then I find out he stands to make a fucking fortune on development! Shit! Who would have thought of it?"

Their voices were quite clear but I couldn't see either man when I looked over my shoulder. I guessed that they were standing out of the hot sun in the shade beside the shed.

"You still would have been okay if Karger hadn't gotten jelly-leg," Fleming said. "He sure did want to be the hero that wiped out phylloxera in Napa Valley."

If Ramsey answered, it was lost in the sound of metal twisting. I leaned hard on the cuffs but nothing happened. When I rested, I could hear voices clearly again. They were closer.

"Can they still walk?" Ramsey asked.

"Hell, yes," Fleming said in disgust. "You think I want to pack out something Fiddler's size on my back?"

I was still working on the cuffs. Left alone, a really smart con is supposed to be able to perform the Houdini bit in under ten minutes. With practice, some can even do it with their hands cuffed behind their backs. I had the advantage of the ringbolt, but the disadvantage of being a rank beginner.

"Then let's get it over with," Ramsey said.

"You sure we have to haul them all the way to that gully?" complained Fleming. "Why don't I just torch this mother like we planned, and them with it?"

Blood and sweat ran into my eyes but I didn't do anything about it. What I was doing right now was better done by feel than by sight.

"Don't be so damn lazy," Ramsey retorted. "We've hunted these mountains since we were six. No one ever goes back in that gully and you know it. There's no deer, no water and no birds. Nothing but brush and snakes. It's a lot more anonymous than fire."

"But—"

I lost track of the argument about then, because there was one fine point that the cons had forgotten to mention. Putting torque on the chain hurts like fiery hell because all the force has to be exerted right through the wrist into the cuff. The steel bands of the cuff are narrow, probably to discourage the very kind of leverage that I was applying.

A round of pain now or an open grave in a few minutes. Not a tough choice.

I leaned into it and twisted, gaining more leverage with my forearm as the links came tight and stayed that way. Tendons stood up and something creaked. I swiped my eyes across my shoulder, trying to clear out sweat and blood so that I could see. It took several passes before it worked. After a moment of squinting I saw that the nickel plating on the handcuffs had crinkled slightly around the seam.

I slammed more force into the chain. The cuff itself slipped away from the torque, greased by the blood welling up from my wrist. I picked up a full crop of redwood splinters when the back of my hand grated over the pole.

result was the same. I couldn't work a pump shotgun with one good hand.

The Detonics was still jammed into Fleming's belt. I grabbed the pistol and dove to the side of the door, wanting to be in place for an ambush when Ramsey rushed in to find out what had happened.

But Ramsey was smarter than that.

"Fleming?" called Ramsey. "What the hell's going on? You all right?"

"Fine," I grunted.

It didn't work. My voice was too deep. I heard the sound of footsteps running away.

I crawled back to Beltrán. His eyes were half open. They were dark, glazed, and the left pupil was more dilated than the right. It took a few seconds to find the keys where Fleming had dropped them. I opened the cuffs, eased Beltrán to the shed floor and checked him. None of the shotgun blast had caught him. His skin was clammy and his heartbeat was too fast, but he was breathing. His pupils seemed very slow to react. Nothing I could do for him in the next ten minutes would make a difference in his life one way or the other.

Bob Ramsey was a different matter.

I dove out the front door of the shed and rolled into the shade of a nearby tree. No shots came. I got into the open just in time to see Ramsey disappear into the brush. He was fifty yards away and gaining with every step. It didn't take a genius to figure out that he had transportation stashed somewhere nearby.

Running made my head swim but gritting down on the broken molar cleared that up. Nothing helped the pain as blood and shock waves pounded through my right wrist with every running stride I took. The pain was short of my blackout threshold, which was all I cared about.

There were ambush sites along the vague trail through the brush, but I didn't slow down to check each one. Ramsey was either unarmed or he was too scared to fight.

And if I were wrong about the ambush, at least the bastard would be close enough for me to shoot back.

The brush began to thin. I caught glimpses of Ramsey. The boots he wore were slowing him down, but I was working under a handicap too. Even so, I was closing in. He was still too far away for me to waste a bullet.

There was a flash of sunlight off glass up ahead. I squinted and saw the glare of a windshield through the thinning brush as I burst out onto the rough, rutted fire road. The windshield belonged to a dust-colored Jeep that was parked two hundred yards away in a stand of trees just off the emergency road.

I made up some more yards over the ruts and the rocks but it wasn't enough to ensure a decent shot at Ramsey. Fiora had been right; the Detonics wasn't going to get the job done.

Ramsey yanked open the Jeep's door and leaped beneath the canvas cover. Fleming must have left the keys in the ignition because the engine fired up instantly. Ramsey could have gotten away then, leaving me to fire futilely after him, but there was more in the Jeep than keys. He leaned out the window and pointed a long-barreled pistol in my direction.

Maybe he was just trying to make me duck by firing wildly, or else he was a piss-poor shot because he was too winded to take proper aim. The first three shots kicked up dust five feet in front of me. I ran harder, not bothering to zigzag because I knew I didn't have the strength or the balance for it. Things were getting a little dark around the edges.

On the fourth shot Ramsey got lucky. The bullet caught me in the upper thigh, spun me around and dumped me flat on the road. There was no shock of lead against bone, which meant that the bullet went on through. Even so, it took me several tries to get up. I was bleeding fast and hard, but the leg finally took enough weight that I could roll over and lever myself to my knees. Running wasn't possible. I couldn't even walk. Shock made me lightheaded. I knew it was only a matter of time before I would be face down in the dust again.

I brought the Detonics up and took aim. My first shot missed Ramsey, but it struck the steel window strut and the wind wing beside him. Glass exploded in his face. The bullet didn't hit him but it sure surprised him. He flinched and threw up his hands in a reflexive gesture meant to protect his eyes from glass and lead. The long-barreled gun banged against the steel window frame and went flying from his hand.

My next bullet missed him by two feet, taking out the windshield instead of the driver. I wiped blood and dirt out of my eyes and squeezed off a shot just as the Jeep's door opened. The third bullet went through the door and ricocheted off a rock beyond. Ramsey changed his mind about retrieving the gun he had dropped. The steel door slammed shut while I squinted over the Detonics, trying to make the target stop revolving in slow circles around me.

The Jeep's engine revved. The target got bigger with every second. Ramsey wanted to finish me with the Jeep. I put two more shots as close to the steering wheel as I could, as fast as I could. Between gasping for breath and dizziness and blood running into my eyes, I knew I'd be lucky to hit the Jeep, much less the driver.

Thirty feet away from me the engine revved wildly. The Jeep bucked over a rock and slewed sideways, slamming headlong into a dirt bank. The engine stalled out. A burst of dust expanded and spun away on the wind. Suddenly the whole mountainside was silent except for the ragged sounds of my own breathing and someone groaning off at a distance.

I had just figured out that the groans were mine when the driver's door squealed open. Ramsey came out of the Jeep and went to his knees in the same motion. His back was turned to me. I couldn't see if his hands were empty. Frankly, I didn't much care whether or not he had a weapon. It was taking everything I had just to keep the world from spinning away.

As Ramsey straightened I braced the Detonics and fired until the slide locked back on the empty magazine.

EPILOGUE

The first time I came to, it was in the middle of the night. All I really remembered of the recent past was having one of those horrible dreams where everything was in slow motion and my mind was screaming, *"Run or die!"* and I couldn't run so I was going to die. Then Fiora came and knelt in the dirt and cursed and cried and my blood was all over her and she told me she loved me and if I died she would turn into a witch and torment me until hell froze solid with both of us in it.

That must have done the trick. I was alive and I wasn't in hell. Hot or cold, hell doesn't smell like green soap and bedpans.

The second time I woke up I saw Benny just beyond the foot of my bed. He was reading a book with the kind of focus that made the rest of the world irrelevant. I turned my head a little more, looking for Fiora. A shaft of pain burned through my mind like lightning through midnight. The change in my breathing brought Benny's head out of his book. He wheeled up along the right side of the bed.

"I won't ask how you're feeling," he said.

It took me a few tries, but I finally got the word out. "Thanks."

"For what? Fiora was the one who saved your bloody hide. You hadn't been gone half an hour when she told me to drive to the building. I argued with her because we hadn't seen anyone go up Langtry. Know what she did?"

"What?" I whispered. Talking was easier the second time, but my mouth still felt and tasted like cardboard.

"She opened her purse and pulled out that little Beretta you gave her and told me to get my bleeding arse down that hill."

I was too shocked to say anything. Next to me and her dead twin, Fiora loves Benny as much as she has ever loved anyone.

Benny saw my reaction. He nodded. "Yeah, mate, I felt the same way. I probably could have taken the gun from her without hurting either of us but, Christ, if it meant that much to her

. . ." He shrugged. "So we went down that hill like hell on fire. When we got there she hit the ground running, went into the old shed and then ran out again before I could get my wheels lowered. She told me to call an ambulance and then she took off running in the opposite direction."

For a moment I prayed that my nightmare had been just that—a dream, not reality. I didn't want to know what I'd put Fiora through, and what would happen as a consequence.

"Beltrán?" I asked, my voice rasping in the silence.

"Next room over. Doing fine, after they pulled out the bone chips. Helluva headache but everything still works. They make 'em tough down in Mexico. Sandra's been sleeping on a couch in his room, keeping him company."

I smiled slightly. It sounded like Sandra had figured out that Beltrán might be much more to her than a quiet, proud majordomo.

"Fiora found you," Benny continued. "Eventually so did everyone else. It was like Can Tho and Khe Sanh all over again. Medivac choppers and cops with radios and young paramedics hanging IV bags from every limb. They had you and Beltrán trussed and strapped to stretchers and shipped out real quick." He paused and his dark eyes narrowed. "Know something, mate? They told me you would have bled dry if Fiora hadn't put her thumb in the dike until they got there."

I wanted to ask where Fiora was now but I didn't have the nerve, so I asked the easy questions first.

"Is there a cop outside the door?"

Benny's smile was quick and hard. "Oh, they wanted to arrest you. Cops surely do hate to bugger one of their own. But by the time Fiora and that San Francisco lawyer you hired for Sandra got through with the sheriff, and the lawfully anointed officers of Napa County marked all the shell casings and measured all the bodies and plotted all the angles and trajectories, the sheriff decided that Ramsey and Fleming were scurvy sods who got what was coming to them."

"Rocheford?"

"They're questioning Rocheford now." Benny shrugged. "He's a shrewd little sod. They'll make him sweat, but they won't be able to hold him for Karger's murder. Same for Cynthia. If she helped Ramsey sabotage Sandra's restaurant, there's no way of proving it now."

I tried to tell Benny that it didn't matter; Rocheford hadn't killed Karger, Fleming had. As for Cynthia, I doubt if she had been guilty of much more than soul-deep malice.

But the effort of explaining it all didn't seem worth it.

"Sandra?" I asked.

"All charges dropped and official apologies issued. And there's a bonus," Benny said enthusiastically. "The bloke from Davis took a look at her vineyard. Seems that Karger's special little bugs do better in a humid lab than they do in real Napa soil, especially around harvest time when the vineyards have been dry for weeks. They'll be able to pick grapes without a problem in all but a few acres. In fact they started this morning."

Benny paused and looked at me as though judging my mood or my strength. Whatever he saw must have satisfied him, because he kept on talking.

"Traven and the bank—and the newspaper—got together and decided that Sandra deserved another chance. Traven withdrew his offer to buy Deep Purple, the bank will roll over Sandra's note, and the Board of Supervisors have never heard of the word 'development.'"

Which left just one more question. The one I was afraid to ask. But I did, because in the long run it was the only answer that mattered.

"Where is Fiora?"

Silently Benny pulled a folded piece of paper from the pages of his book.

"She stayed with you until half an hour ago," he said. "Then she kissed you, told me to give you this and walked out. It was like she knew you would be all right."

I didn't want to open the paper, but I did. The splint on my wrist made things awkward. I didn't mind. I was in no hurry to read Fiora's good-bye.

Her handwriting was like her, slender and elegant and humming with fierce energy.

> *Other people must have lived our lives before. They left*
> *a legacy of words to prove it.*
> *Can't live with you, can't live without you. Easier said*

than done. A stitch in time saves nine. Stubborn as a mule. Independent as a hog on ice.

All the neat little phrases describing messy lives.

Blood is thicker than water.

There's a good one for you. Your blood certainly is. It's thick and bright and terrible. I could have bathed in it.

In my nightmare, there was a harvest. When the grapes were squeezed, blood ran out. Gatsby's harvest . . . violence and death.

I love you, but I can't live with you.

I closed my eyes and told myself that the last six words were only half of our legacy. The other half was *Can't live without you.* And somehow, someday, I had to prove it to her.

AFTERWORD

A great many people deserve thanks for extending the hospitality of their Napa Valley to A. E. Maxwell. Bernard and Belle Rhodes of Bella Oaks Vineyard were gracious host and hostess more than once. Pam Hunter opened a dozen doors. Bob and Harolyn Thompson were congenial conversationalists. Bob's authoritative book, *The Pocket Encyclopedia of California Wines,* is the best reference work in the field. Elaine Wellesley corrected several crucial misconceptions about wine making and wine tasting.

Naturally, the fictional world of *Gatsby's Vineyard* represents a very different reality than the Rhodeses, the Thompsons and Ms. Hunter and Ms. Wellesley enjoy.